MER-
CHARMER

WORLD OF ALUVIA, BOOK TWO

MER-
CHARMER

WORLD OF ALUVIA, BOOK TWO

AMY BEARCE

SECOND EDITION

Snowy
&Wings
PUBLISHING

MER-CHARMER
World of Aluvia, Book 2

Published by Snowy Wings Publishing
www.snowywingspublishing.com

Cover Art and interior art by **Amalia Chitulescu**
http://ameliethe.deviantart.com
Map by Ricky Gunawan
Licensed from Wampa LLC

The Library of Congress has cataloged the 2016 original editions as follows:
ISBN 978-1-62007-541-8 (ebook)
ISBN 978-1-62007-545-6 (paperback)

Second (Revised) Edition 2019
ISBN 978-1-948661-16-4 (ebook)
ISBN 978-1-948661-17-1 (paperback)

To Keira and Julia

The ocean never gave up. It just kept rolling in, no matter what else went on in the world. Phoebe Quinn liked to think she and the ocean shared that in common.

Today, Phoebe's chest still heaved from her run down to the shore. The gut-wrenching memories had slithered into her mind again, setting off the panic. When those recollections came calling, four years dissolved in a heartbeat, leaving her a terrified ten-year-old all over again.

But she wasn't ten anymore, she reminded herself, taking in a deep breath.

Phoebe perched on the edge of her favorite rock along her favorite coastline and tried to lose herself in the haunting call of the seabirds and the inevitability of the foaming waves. She knew she shouldn't have disobeyed her big sister by coming here, but she couldn't stay inside the house another minute. Besides, Sierra wouldn't be back until tomorrow. She'd never know.

The salty tang of the coastal air usually lifted Phoebe's spirits, but even the power of the ocean couldn't quell her anxiety today.

She bit her lip, fixing her gaze on the horizon. When she'd arrived back home four years ago, Phoebe hoped she could forget what she'd suffered. And at first it seemed like everything was fine. Life went on, after all.

But the horrors she'd experienced in Elder Bentwood's dungeon whispered in her mind more and more often. It didn't seem to matter that she'd only been locked up for days; those few days felt like years. The vivid memories clung like the stench of a dead thing, growing increasingly difficult to ignore. Especially lately.

The sun would set before too long, already a ball of fire painting the sea with shades of pink and red. The forest hung back from the coast here, leaving a thin ridge of sand and rocks between the shady pine trees and the shoreline. A natural jetty in the middle of the cove reached out into the deeper waters, the boulders uneven as if sent tumbling like dice from a giant's hand.

Her favorite was the last in the row, where water lapped right along the edge during low tide. She loved to daydream there, nearly surrounded by water yet sheltered from the worst of the waves by the outcroppings further into the ocean. On the far side of the jetty, an inlet held a delightfully deep pool. Yet on the other side, the sandy shore was shallow, easing into the sea with a gentle, lazy slope. The cove was a cozy place, and Phoebe could use a little cozy now.

Sea foam sprayed her legs as the wind blew, and she shifted her position. Her knee twinged as she leaned on it, the same spot that ached in the cold. She ruthlessly ignored a vision welling up from the past: her leg bruised and purple, swollen like a sausage. *That's not reality. This is now.* She closed her eyes and focused. The silence of the cove. The wind lifting her hair from her face. But she couldn't quite resist touching her knee in affirmation. Strong, straight, supple. They hadn't broken her. At least not her body.

She took a deep breath and craned her neck to watch a gull spiral over the coast. A glimpse of white poking out from behind a small boulder alongside the pool caught her eye. A quick smile lit her face, lifting her dark thoughts.

Nothing brought peace and joy like her merfolk friends. Even though she was fourteen now, within shouting distance of adulthood, she still loved getting little gifts from Tristan, gifts given for no other reason than him thinking about her. The fact that her best friend and his sister, Mina, were merfolk was icing on the cake. Phoebe often wondered how she could be so surrounded by magic but remain so utterly and frustratingly non-magical herself. If she had even a sliver of magic, she was sure she'd never feel afraid or alone again.

What would the gift be today? A giant sand dollar or conch shell? A smooth white stone from the depths of the ocean? She pondered the possibilities as she rose and picked her away across the slippery moss-covered rocks. It wasn't Tristan's usual place to leave a surprise, but, then again, he liked to keep her on her toes. She grinned with anticipation and then jumped around the boulder, hands spread, ready to grab whatever delight lay waiting.

A strange shape floated in the water, half-laying on the rocks. That wasn't a shell, no, and not a smooth stone, too many parts...

Phoebe's mind whirled as she tried to make sense of what she saw. White sticks of some kind, tangled together, with the green of seaweed.

Then everything came together in her mind with a snap. Those weren't sticks.

They were polished bones.

The bones swirled in ripples that rolled between the rocks. Bits of sinew and cartilage held the skeleton together, but barely. Her scream was short but intense.

Trembling, Phoebe swallowed hard and inched closer to the edge of the pool to get a better look, gagging a little with each step.

The half-submerged skull grinning grotesquely looked human in the water, but a tail fin made it impossible to doubt what kind of creature this had actually been. The merfolk remains must have gotten caught in the inlet during low tide. Tristan and Mina needed to know right away. Maybe they would know if someone was missing.

A wave crashed along the shore, and the skeleton bobbed and turned over, revealing a giant black handprint marring the back of the skull. Phoebe sucked in a deep breath at the sight, the print shocking against the bleached white of the bone. Worse, the skull itself was crushed at the tip of each fingerprint. Spider-webbed cracks branched out from each puncture as if strong claws had punched right through the bone.

This hadn't been an accident. Phoebe fought the roiling nausea, trying not to fall to her knees. *What could do something like this?*

Maybe her friends would come if she sang. They often did, along with the youngest of the merfolk, the little seawees. Shivering, Phoebe returned to the end of the jetty and lifted her voice, focusing on the way the sound skipped across the water. She chose a haunting melody, though she generally preferred cheerful songs. Right now, a soulful dirge best suited the situation. She let herself explore the dark nooks and crannies of her fears and the horror of the moment, her gaze creeping toward the corpse over and over before she yanked her focus back to the ocean. She scanned the water for the familiar tails, then paused, chewing on her lip. Why weren't they coming?

She hadn't seen Tristan or Mina in three whole days. In the past, they visited more often, especially when they knew her sister was traveling and Phoebe would be alone. But as they grew older, work took more of their time. Merfolk took responsibility to their community very seriously.

They were probably working in the deeper waters now. She should swim out past the rocks to better try to call her friends, but the thought of sharing the same water with the dead body was too much. Besides, a few months back, she promised Sierra not to swim in the ocean anymore. At the time, such an irrational request had infuriated Phoebe. Today, that promise gave her a handy excuse.

"Tristan! Mina!" she called with her hands cupped around her mouth, leaning forward into the cove. Her friends seemed to have a special knowing when she called them by name.

The water began churning, signaling the arrival of someone, but her best friends were nowhere to be found. Tiny fins of a dozen seawees broke the surface as the little ones arrived to frolic. Mischievous grins beamed up at her from under the water as they waved, long hair floating about their heads.

She waved back, pleased to see them but alarmed at

the possibility of them finding the skeleton. The little ones had come daily when Phoebe first returned from Bentwood's dungeon, but she hadn't seen them often these days, either.

Luckily, they stayed a bit out to sea, squealing in delight when she began an upbeat tune for them. Next to the little ones, a green tail slapped the water, larger than the others. A bronze flipper broke through the surface beside it. Tristan and Mina were here. Phoebe smiled with relief, but her grin faded. She dreaded giving them the bad news.

The space between her shoulder blades prickled. She glanced uneasily behind her. Was someone there? But then Tristan popped out of the water next to her, his dark green hair streaming over his shoulders. He waved at her and shook his head, sending his wet hair flying. Brisk droplets sprinkled Phoebe's homespun dress. He did that on purpose, no doubt. He chortled at her, but since he was out of the water he only produced a guttural coughing noise. The deep green scales covering his tail ended at his waistline. Once he became an adult in merfolk society, ink-black tattoos would decorate his torso and arms, but for now, his chest was starkly pale beneath the water.

He was thinner than in the past, his ribs outlined along his sides. His twin sister, Mina, arrived a half-second later, her black hair a shocking contrast to her pale skin gleaming like an opal, also missing the tattooed marks of adulthood. Her bronze scales ran up her body from her tail to directly under her arms. It reminded Phoebe of the fancy strapless evening gowns worn by wealthy ladies in the biggest port cities. Though Mina, too, appeared more tired than usual, they were both still beautiful. The gills of their necks were dark slashes across their pallor, but their green eyes twinkled. Phoebe hated the thought of stealing the light from their eyes.

The idea of touching the water made her skin crawl, but there was no other way for them to speak together. The cold sting lasted only a second as Phoebe lay on her belly atop the rock, leaned her head over the edge, and lowered her face below the water without hesitation, bubbles sliding over her cheeks.

Her friends' green eyes darkened to solid black as they used magic to allow her to breathe. Phoebe understood the magic they could lend to her far more than the first terrifying time Tristan held her thrashing under the water during her escape from Elder Bentwood's fortress.

"Greetings, my friends!" she said. "I'm afraid I have some terrible news. You should send the seawees away. This isn't anything they should hear."

Tristan's grin faded as he examined her face. Phoebe had a moment of discomfort as she met his gaze. He'd grown from a cute little seawee to a *very* cute young merman over the last four years.

Mina swam to the little seawees swirling like otters in the water. "Go on home, now. You know your parents don't like you to be gone for long! And you aren't supposed to come to shore anymore!"

This was news to Phoebe. Why not? Did it have something to do with the body? At least it explained the strange absence of seawees over the recent weeks.

The little ones looked at Phoebe, lips pouting, but obeyed, scurrying away with speed. With a small smile softening her demand, Mina shook her head at the little ones as they retreated. Her amusement slid away as she returned to her brother and Phoebe. It was odd for Phoebe to see such a somber expression on Mina instead of her usual jovial one.

"Phoebe, what's going on?" Tristan asked.

A lump sat heavy in Phoebe's stomach. "Something washed up near the shore today. Something upsetting."

The two merfolk exchanged anxious glances.

Tristan asked, "Are you okay?"

"I'm fine, but I found... a body. A merfolk's body. A skeleton, really. It washed up into the rock pool, and it clearly has a tail. I'm so sorry."

Their faces looked like she had struck them, eyes wide and faces paler than usual.

"There's more," Phoebe added, miserably.

"Worse?" Tristan asked, his voice hoarse. The reddish hue of the sunset turned his green hair a strange shade of brown, a sickly hue quite different than the usual vibrant color.

She nodded. "The death looks intentional. There are strange marks on its skull and, well, holes. Like claws punched through it, while gripping the head."

"Where?" Mina whispered, hands pressed to her cheeks.

"No, Mina, you don't need to look," Tristan said.

"Don't be a fool, brother. We're doing this together," she said, though she looked ill.

The two exchanged a knowing glance, and Phoebe felt a stab of envy. *Sierra will never treat me like an equal.*

Phoebe lifted herself from the water and gestured to the inlet, standing up to point them to the body. The twins skirted around the skeleton. Tristan hesitantly touched the arm bone with one hand and shivered. Both leaned over the skull, examining the ruined back. They exchanged another long look. What did that mean? They returned to Phoebe, and she dipped her head underwater again.

"This body looks old, being stripped so bare, but I admit I've never seen dark marks like that or the crushed parts of the bone," Tristan said.

"What could do such a thing?" Phoebe whispered.

"There are many predators in the deep that would leave just bones, but we know of nothing that could burn into a skull, if that's indeed what happened. It can't be anything good," Mina said.

Alarm raced through Phoebe. "So, you're in danger?"

Tristan offered a reassuring smile and shook his head. "Our village is protected. You don't need to worry for us. But the elders will need to know. This merfolk must have gone off on his or her own." His voice trailed off for a moment.

"And needs a proper ceremony to be put to rest," Mina said. They both bowed their heads, and Phoebe, feeling awkward and uncertain, followed suit. She'd been fascinated by the merfolk from the first moment she met Tristan, when he helped rescue her from Bentwood, but there was still so much she didn't understand about them.

"Come back tomorrow morning, please, and tell me what you learn," Phoebe begged. She'd never stop worrying without knowing if he—*they*—were safe from whatever caused the death of the poor merfolk.

"We must work from early in the morning, unfortunately. We could come at our noon break… but your sister is coming home tomorrow, is she not? She wouldn't be pleased to see you back here with us, especially with the sad remains you've found."

"I'll take care of Sierra. Don't worry."

Tristan quirked his eyebrows. "She is very fierce."

"Maybe I can be, too."

Mina laughed, and Phoebe flushed.

"Apologies, sweet friend," Mina said after Tristan gave her a scowl. She spread her hands wide. "I mean only that your nature is so kind and sweet, I find it hard to see you engaging in combat. With a heart like yours, to wound another is to wound yourself."

Feeling only slightly mollified, Phoebe said, "Sierra's got plenty to worry about already. What she doesn't know won't hurt her."

Tristan's eyes grew wide. The dark marks under them were lilac half-moons. "You surprise me, Phoebe. I thought you honored your sister."

She flushed. "I do—but you know how she overreacts."

"Much like our family," Mina said dryly.

"Are they still upset because of our friendship?" Phoebe frowned.

"It's not *you*," Mina replied. "They just can't forget how many generations of merfolk lived in slavery to humans. And then that poor seawee died recently in the fishing nets of humans who ignored our new treaty. Some of our people are angrier at humans more now than ever, but that has nothing to do with you. Those old barracudas wouldn't like you even if you were the most perfect person in all of Aluvia, which you are!"

"I'm sorry if our friendship has caused you grief—" Phoebe began, but Tristan cut her off.

"Please don't worry, Phoebe. We know how to manage our families as you do. But I do think Sierra would want to know your daily habits. She loves you." He smiled, softening the slight chiding.

Well, Sierra might *want* to know, but this was one time she didn't *need* to know.

"If you meet me at noon, I'll be back before she is. Her journeys have been running longer now that some people want to use nectar again. They're already forgetting how bad things were. I'm afraid she's hiding how serious the trouble is becoming. It seems even on short trips, she's always late these days, arriving at dinnertime at least. And when she's home, she spends most of her time in the forest with her fairies, anyway."

She tried to keep the hurt from her voice, but must not have succeeded. Tristan shook his head ruefully.

He said, "You know you are her world, Phoebe. She gave up everything for you, fought for you, saved you—"

"You saved me, too."

This time, Tristan's face flushed, bringing delicate rose to his pale cheeks. "I did only what was right and just. Anyone would have."

No, they wouldn't have, Phoebe knew. She studied his familiar face, remembering the hectic underwater flight from Bentwood's, the way her gaze had locked on Tristan's when they said goodbye, as if something bound them. The same tension built between them now.

Mina cleared her throat. "We must go take care of this sad situation, Phoebe," she said, "but we'll come back tomorrow when the sun is at its zenith."

"Promise?" Phoebe replied, looking over to include Mina.

"We would never lie to you," Tristan said, eyes serious.

Phoebe smiled at him, thankful that Tristan, at least, didn't see her as a frail tag-a-long little sister. She gazed into his eyes and felt a flutter that had become familiar over the last year. She briefly wondered if one day he might see her as more than a childhood friend. Of course, that was just a dream. They lived in different worlds, even if she was able to visit theirs now and again.

She nodded. "Thank you."

With worry shadowing their faces, the two merfolk pulled the skeletal remains along with them as they swam away. The rock pool was empty now, but Phoebe was sure she'd never forget the whiteness of bone among the seaweed, like unexpectedly jagged, sharp teeth in the mouth of an animal believed to be docile. The ocean was dangerous, she understood that. But today, she began to realize just how little she knew about those dangers.

CHAPTER TWO

*P*hoebe was sure slumber would elude her, but stress forced her to sleep deeper than she had in a long time. Usually, jumbled nightmares plagued her. Tonight, though, dreams dragged Phoebe back in time to the event she couldn't quite seem to escape, repeating it just as she had lived it then.

She was ten years old.

Huddled in the far corner of Elder Bentwood's prison. Traded in a business deal like a sack of grain by her own father. The name 'training room' was just a euphemism. This was where they broke new employees and impressed upon them the single-handed rule of the boss's will.

Why did he even want her as an elixir runner? She didn't have strength or magic. She was just plain Phoebe. But her father was Jack Quinn the infamous dark alchemist, and having power over her meant power over him, or so Bentwood had bragged when he visited.

"So, little girl, ready to run some Flight yet? You ought to be real familiar with how it works, knowing your father. He and I are going to stay real good buddies, now that you're here. Not that he could love you much, sending you away like he did."

She shook her head, mouth dry with fear and lack of water. She always knew her father was merciless. He sold dangerous, addictive elixirs like Flight—made from fairy nectar—that made people willing to spend every last coin for one more drop. It was no surprise he'd trade off his own daughter to a coworker. But Phoebe didn't want to work for Bentwood. Didn't want to leave her home. Not now, not ever.

"Sierra will come for me," she squeaked.

And he laughed.

"If your fairy keeper sister was coming, she would've already been back with those missing fairies. The deal is sealed. She gambled. You lost. Better prepare to live the rest of your life as my servant." He grinned, a grotesque smile that tugged on the red scar line across his cheek.

He was right.

Phoebe buried her face in her hands, barely able to pull her legs tight to her body. At least they had undone the manacles around her hands and feet. It was clear she couldn't run by herself if she wanted to. One of the men, Donovan was his name, had visited earlier. To persuade her to work peacefully with her new boss, he said. And when she stubbornly refused to cooperate, he smashed a club on her knee, leaving it grossly swollen, maybe even broken.

The pain sent agony flashing through her, screams pouring from her mouth. But nothing could match the fear taking root deep inside her. Fear of pain, yes. But more, fear of being all alone in life. And the worst of all: fear of being powerless. She never, ever wanted to suffer this way again. But she had a horrible awareness that even if she survived and escaped against all odds, she'd never forget these feelings. They were stitching themselves to her heart. The best she could do was make sure it kept on beating.

Phoebe awoke with a gasp, sweat lining her brow. *I'm safe,* she reminded herself. *I'm not that girl anymore.*

Returning to sleep took a long time, and so morning found her bleary-eyed and exhausted. This wasn't the first nightmare where she relived the worst of her time at Bentwood's, and it wouldn't be the last, she assumed. It made her even more thankful she'd see her friends in a short while.

Her morning was solitary and quiet. She pushed the nightmare from her mind and set about doing the daily work that a house required. Wash the dishes. Sweep the floor. It helped. A little. But she couldn't help but think those memories were coming so often because she needed something more exciting in life. Some sort of purpose. Certainly, all this time spent alone didn't help.

Sierra and her beau Micah frequently traveled throughout the ports to teach about the importance of keeping fairy magic abundant throughout Aluvia. Sierra's best friend and fellow fairy keeper, Corbin, and his partner Nell often joined them to help persuade the more reluctant of the villagers. Some might not listen to Sierra but would come to see Nell, now famous for her prophecies.

Phoebe used to travel with Sierra and their friends, part of the important work being done. But Sierra began leaving Phoebe 'safe at home' over two years ago, after some dark alchemists attempted to assassinate the team on the road. They failed, of course, but Sierra said she couldn't stand risking Phoebe's safety. Later, Sierra asked Phoebe to stay on the beach instead of swimming in the ocean. And this last trip, Sierra said, "Stay in or near the house this week, okay, Phoebe? For me?"

Phoebe scowled but agreed, unable to ignore the stress visible on her big sister's face. And now this happened.

Sierra and the others would arrive home later tonight, worn out, no doubt. They were one big family, and Phoebe missed their noisy teamwork when they were all gone.

She set up the beans to cook all day, enough for everyone. At least they'd be home before she had to sleep another night alone. Every time she closed her eyes, she saw that skeleton, bits of ligaments and cartilage dangling like old thread. What if the predator wasn't confined to the sea, like the great reptiles that lived both in water and sand in the east? The thought made her wish even more that she wasn't alone. Corbin's parents came by each day to check on her, but of course, today of all days they couldn't visit because of a complicated healing they had to administer. She reminded herself that Old Sam, their unicorn, guarded the house somewhere out in his nearby forest, but it didn't help. Her nerves were still stretched raw.

Phoebe paced the floor, heart racing. What had Tristan and Mina found out? If only Phoebe could communicate with the merfolk the way Sierra could share thoughts with her fairy queen. The closeness fairies shared with their keepers was the main reason Phoebe had always wished to be one. She never would be, of course. Unlike Sierra, Phoebe didn't have a fairy keeper mark. She wasn't destined for magic. But it would have been nice to share such close contact with her merfolk friends.

Phoebe couldn't wait any longer. She'd be a bit early to meet Tristan and Mina, but the extra time along the ocean's edge would only soothe her more. Phoebe banked the fire under the beans then took off. Along the path, she fed Old Sam and gave him a few carrots as an extra treat, enjoying the soft fuzz of the unicorn's white muzzle. How she loved that animal. Unicorns, fairies, fauns, and merfolk—magical creatures of all kinds made life worth living. She petted his nose, and he left damp whuffles in her hair, bringing a smile to her face. She continued on down the path to the shore.

No fairies gleamed in the trees today. Where Sierra went, Queenie went too, taking all of her wee fairies in a glowing cloud of sparkles on their journeys. Phoebe missed the tiny fairies' cheerful presence, the constant proof and celebration that magic was real.

While picking her way through the trees, a rabbit dashed across her path, running right across her foot. Startled, she tripped and fell to one knee. A sharp spike of pain shot through her bone. The bad knee. She gasped. Memories roared over, stealing her breath. A club coming down on her knee, crushing it against the dirty floor of the dungeon. She could *hear* the grating laughter of the guards, feel the sting of the cuts along her back. Worse yet, she remembered the belief that her sister must have died on her perilous journey, for why else hadn't she come?

It was as if she were living it all over again, especially after her nightmare. Sweat ran down her face. Right there in the familiar path through the woods, she crouched down and rocked, her arms wrapped around her middle as if she were trying to keep from flying apart. Minutes passed while Phoebe's mind tumbled through fear, unable even to form words through her terror. The panic came on her like that sometimes. She'd learned to suffer through. She didn't even tell anyone how often it still happened. It seemed silly. Four whole years had passed. Sierra and everyone else worried enough about her as it was.

As soon as Phoebe could stand, she raced down to the coast. She'd get past this. She always did. Her mer-friends would help her forget.

The sun shimmered high in the sky, reflecting like a beacon in the water. The sea reflected the deep blue of the noon sky. The sea was faithful that way. It always showed what was true. Her mer-friends were still working, but they'd arrive eventually.

Her favorite rock was submerged from the tide now, but she sat as far out as she could. The waves beyond the outcroppings were softer today, leaving the water at her feet almost like glass. She took a deep calming breath and let the waves in the distance lull her as they reached forward and fell back, over and over.

An hour passed, but still her friends did not arrive. She sang a song, an upbeat tune, thinking maybe it would draw at least one of them or perhaps the happy little seawees again, but no one came.

Disappointment nipped at her. Tristan and Mina would be harvesting clams today, as they did all summer, but surely the elders would have already seen the skeleton, provided an answer. Phoebe needed to make sure her friends were all right, after a night full of worry.

Sighing, she turned to leave the half-submerged rocky jetty, but froze at the sight of two men leaving the edge of the woods, a mere hundred footlengths away. She recognized one of them immediately: Donovan, from her time with Bentwood's crew.

Fear burst through her, leaving her nearly breathless in shock. She wanted to curl into a ball and shake, but her feet wouldn't move.

"Hello there, missy. Remember me, then, eh?" Donovan leered at her as he advanced slowly across the rocky shoreline. Three big boulders stood between Phoebe and the men.

Phoebe's breath returned with a vengeance, and she started hyperventilating. That face had haunted a thousand nightmares in the last four years.

The second man was unknown to her, but his squinty eyes roamed across her, as if studying a pig for purchase.

Move. You've got to move! Phoebe shrieked to her frozen body. She staggered the several steps along the rocks to reach the shore. She'd never escape running, not with wobbly knees like over-cooked custard. Their eyes followed her as they stood wide-legged on the path, pushing on each other's shoulders as if sharing the grandest joke. She stepped farther away from the slippery rocks, and sand squished beneath her toes when she reached the shallows.

The men stepped casually toward her, not even bothering with weapons. They obviously thought she'd be easy to take. After all, she had been once. She took a step backward, and frothy surf kissed her feet.

"Ah now, lass, don't be like that. We're just here to talk, you know? Maybe a nice chat with you before we visit your sister about sharing some fairy nectar. Just a spot, now, won't hurt the wee critters too much. Some folks still got a fierce need for Flight, you understand. She just won't listen to reason, not even with the dragons running amok in the mountains because of her meddling. Maybe you could help… convince her," Donovan said.

Tamping down her fear, Phoebe didn't reply but instead scanned the horizon, the forest, the ocean. She'd known someone else had taken over Bentwood's dark alchemy business after his death. Though they lost most of his stronghold in Port Iona, there was always someone wanting a little lift after a bad day, or a way to get rid of an enemy without notice. But nothing had ever reached the popularity—or profit—of Flight, made from now-forbidden fairy nectar.

She took another step back. Cold seawater swirled around her ankles. Jagged pebbles pierced the lining of her cloth slippers. She hadn't worn her boots today, of all days. Trying to run in these would hurt, but any pain would be preferable to what those men could do to her. But where to run?

Help! She silently screamed. They had her cornered. They had split up, ensuring that no matter which way she ran, one of them would get her.

"Might as well come easy, then, right?" the other man crooned. "We don't want to hurt you more than we've got to."

The words jolted Phoebe to action like spurs to a horse. They had her path to the forest cut off. That left just one option, one they'd never consider.

She turned and ran into the surf, wading straight out to sea. Cold water sloshed up over her shins, past her thighs. Her pants and the edge of her tunic clung to her legs as she pushed farther into the water. She glanced over her shoulder to see if they were following, but they were laughing, arms crossed over their chests.

Keep laughing. Her friends would hopefully be here soon. She only had to wait long enough for them to come and take her to safety. Waist-deep, she reached the edge of the sandbar and swam headlong into the deeper water beyond the rock outcroppings, feet no longer touching the bottom. Tristan and Mina had taught her excellent swimming skills.

Phoebe moved smoothly through the small waves. She tossed another glance over her shoulder.

The men were yelling. "Come back, stupid girl!"

"No point in drowning, now is there?" hollered

Donovan. He pulled his hat off and twisted it in his hand.

Phoebe smirked and turned back to the ocean. She would do anything—*anything*—to not go back with those men. She'd die first, but she didn't plan on dying today.

She treaded water for a moment, despite knowing that it was a quick way to get tired. When the men began wading into the water, she yelped and kept swimming. She'd have to lose them. Obviously, they'd follow her. Maybe even think long enough for one of them to go grab a rowboat from port while the other kept her pinned here. She had to get away now.

Phoebe held her breath, hoped for the best, and dove deep. She swam as far down as she could, eyes open despite the sting, looking for her friends.

Come to me! She mentally begged them. *Come save me!* They always seemed to know when she wanted them. She prayed for today to be the same.

With her mer-friends, she could stay under the water all day. But if they didn't show up, she'd run out of air or energy sooner or later. Probably sooner.

With the sun high in the sky, she was surprised at how quickly the sunlight faded as she descended. Murky green swirls of water swooshed by, along with schools of vibrant fish and an occasional jelly. She steered clear of their dangling stinging tentacles. Hopefully no sharks would be nearby.

Her lungs were too tight. She needed oxygen. She kicked toward the surface, bubbles slipping out of her mouth.

Then something grabbed her ankle and pulled her down. Down, deeper into the dark waters.

CHAPTER THREE

*P*hoebe's leg felt as if it were sheathed in ice. She couldn't wrap her mind around the creature below her. It was at least twice her size. It had a long pointed black tail, more snakelike than fish, but its face was that of a beautiful woman, marble-statue-perfect. Glowing red eyes stared out from the center of that stunning beauty like twin flames. This was no mermaid.

Then the thing snarled, and large, sharp teeth pointed out in all directions. Phoebe screamed, her mouth full of water, and frantically kicked her legs, but it had an iron grip on her right ankle. Its hand covered half her lower leg.

Phoebe plowed her arms through the water over and over again, but the dull light overhead dwindled. She would die soon. Her lungs would pull in the salty water, and it would sink her to the sandy floor now coming into view. She had no hope that this growling, angry creature had any interest in helping her breathe.

Tristan! Her mind called out. Panic beat at her. Things were getting fuzzy now. Her mind felt lighter than a fluff of dandelion. The unyielding pressure made her ankle burn, then tingle into numbness. Her arms stilled. She fought to keep holding her breath. Her hair swirled around her as if alive, the only part of her left with any movement.

Her eyelids drifted shut, and an image appeared in her mind: a stirring shadow of some giant beast that glowed a sullen red. She somehow knew it was asleep, this terrifying thing. But it was rumbling, it was moving, it was waking...

The vision faded, and just before things went completely black, a bright light flashed, visible even through her closed eyes. She barely managed to crack an eyelid. Cool blue light shimmered in the water around her like a sapphire in the sun, but it disappeared as quickly as it came.

So pretty. Like sparkling jewels...

As she drifted into unconsciousness, a ragged voice called to her.

"Phoebe, stay with me," it begged.

Phoebe was perplexed by the pain she heard in the voice but was too far gone to look. It was a deep voice, a familiar voice that made her want to smile, but her lips wouldn't cooperate. She was a heavy anchor, stuck on the bottom of the ocean.

Something shook her, and a stubborn spark of life made her take a deep breath, before she remembered she was under the water.

Her eyes flew open when the cold water swirled inside her without harm, filling her body with energy. She gasped, grabbing at her ankle, but it was freed. No terrifying monster glared below her. Instead, Tristan held her in his arms. They had risen from the depths, the water now full of light all around them.

"Breathe," he urged, gazing at her face, black eyes tracking every inch of her, as if looking for wounds. "Have you lost your senses? Why did you come this far out to sea alone?"

"Something grabbed me!" she said, dazed.

"A *mer*?"

"Th-Th-This wasn't a mer," Phoebe stuttered.

Mina swam into view, her dark eyes wide. "What on Aluvia was it, then?"

Tristan's brow drew to a dark V. "Tell us," he commanded, pulling Phoebe toward the shore.

"Wait!" she cried, laying her hands on his shoulders. "The men. Bentwood's old enforcers, Donovan, and another. They came for me! They were up there!"

Tristan cursed, a low trill of sound in the merfolk's ancient language she'd rarely heard before. Mina darted above them and peeked her head above the surface for a moment before returning.

"Two men seem to be fighting on shore," she reported. "The ugly one just hit the short one."

"They're both ugly," Phoebe muttered.

Mina laughed, but then stopped short. "Are these the men, then? The ones you escaped when my brother rescued you from that prison?"

Phoebe nodded and shuddered, the reality of the moment sinking in. "Donovan was the one who beat me when I was trapped at Bentwood's. It sounded like they wanted to use me to force Sierra to collect nectar for the dark alchemists again."

She drifted a bit in the current, and Tristan pulled her to him, holding her steady. She blinked rapidly, both at the shocking events and at Tristan's sudden nearness. It had been at least half a year since Sierra had last allowed Phoebe under the waves like this. Even that short period of time had made a surprisingly big difference in Tristan's appearance. His jaw was squarer. The child-like roundness to his cheeks was completely gone. His ribs might be more prominent than they used to be, but muscles clearly lined his torso and arms. It was one thing to see him through the water, quite another to be pulled snug to his chest.

The merfolk had both come straight from work. Mina wore a bulging knapsack, and Tristan's work belt was cinched around his waist where his scales met the skin of his torso. A tiny knife was tucked in the belt, and a net dangled from the side, half full of clams. His eyes, so green above the water, had bled to solid black as he used his magic to allow her to survive. They were dark and shining as obsidian, and as beautiful.

"They're trying to control your sister?" he asked.

Alarm flared through Phoebe.

"I have to go home. What if Sierra gets home and they're waiting for her?" she announced, kicking her legs as if she would return to the shore immediately, but Tristan held her steady.

"Think, Phoebe. They're waiting for *you*! I can't let you do that."

Phoebe glared at him. "You think you can stop me?"

He and Mina laughed, and Phoebe glared harder.

Tristan smothered his grin and replied, "Well, yes, honestly, I do. But think, little songbird. They want to use you to blackmail your sister. If they don't have you, they can't manipulate her, can they? They didn't try to take *her*. But if you go storming out of the water, they'd take you for sure. And then what?"

Then what, indeed? He had a point. She chewed her lip. Sierra would be out of her mind with worry if she returned early to an empty house. Phoebe hadn't actually expected to still be gone when Sierra returned. But it would be foolish to leave the water now.

Phoebe groaned. "You're right, you're right. But I don't want to wait around here for that creature to come back, either. Can we hide somewhere safe just long enough for those men to give up? Like the sunken ship you took me to once? Then I could hopefully still make it home before Sierra does."

The twins exchanged another glance. Mina said, "This would be wise. Don't you think, brother?"

Tristan looked conflicted, but he finally shrugged. "Well, the sunken ship is too exposed, but I suppose we could take her to our secret place. It would definitely be safe there. Whatever attacked Phoebe could still be around here, but it would never find us in our hidden spot."

Phoebe shivered, tightening her grip on Tristan's arms. He whispered in Phoebe's ear, so softly that Mina could not hear, "No matter what attacked you, no matter what danger comes, know that I'll keep you safe, always."

His smile gleamed, charming despite the intensity of his black eyes. He tipped his head sideways, a habit of his from childhood. How many times had she seen that smile, that head tilt? She had missed it so much. Missed him.

Then his words sunk in.

"Wait a minute," she blurted. "You rescued me. Didn't you see what had me?"

He shook his head, face heavy with concern. "No, you were sinking, alone, when I arrived. I made it just in time. What had you captive?"

Phoebe's mind hurt. Where had the blue light come from, then? She'd assumed it was some sort of mer-magic she hadn't known about. And had she really seen a shadow moving in the darkness? No, that had to have been her mind playing tricks on her. Lack of air could do that.

"I was grabbed by some horrible creature I'd never seen before, with red eyes and too many teeth!"

"Hmm. There are many predators in the sea. There are creatures in the depths so strange and cruel-looking that they would shock land walkers, but such deep dwellers rarely come to shallow waters during the day. We'll need to talk more of this," he murmured.

Phoebe took a deep breath, always amazed by the miracle of breathing underwater. Her spinning mind slowed. Her friends' concern was a bandage, wrapping up a bleeding wound. "But won't this get you in trouble? You're not supposed to take me beyond the shoreline, you said. Your own people forbid it."

"Well, as you say, what they don't know won't hurt them!" Mina chirped.

Tristan scowled at Mina, but then relented with an exasperated smile. "We're not really breaking any laws, Phoebe. You're here already, almost terribly harmed by a creature of the sea. We wouldn't be doing our duty to our people if we didn't learn all we could about it and keep you in a safe, hidden spot until we can deliver you safely to shore."

"Exactly!" Mina said.

"No one could argue with these facts," Tristan added, almost as if convincing himself.

Phoebe didn't need much convincing. She would love to stay with them. A chance like this was something she might never have again, not if the relations between merfolk and humans continued to worsen.

"Well, if you think it won't cause you any trouble…"

Tristan reassured her. "It'll be fine. You can tell us about the creature that attacked, and we can share our news of the skeleton. It is good news, of a sort, as much as anything of that kind could be. But trust me when I say you are safe with us. We'll tell you more, but first, let us go farther from the shore."

Mina squealed and clapped her hands. "Oh, please say yes, Phoebe!"

Phoebe nodded. She couldn't face the shore. Not now, even knowing that horrendous creature was still sharing the ocean with them. But Tristan's touch radiated warmth that thawed the terrified frozen place inside her.

"Come," he said softly.

He held one of her hands; Mina held the other. And they pulled her deeper into the sea, where she'd always longed to go, no matter how many told her she couldn't.

CHAPTER FOUR

They swam in silence, Phoebe surrounded by her two best friends. She wished they could always be like this. She scanned everything, locking away memories deep into her heart for the day when she was back in an empty house, making yet another boring pot of beans. Unlike life at home, there was nothing remotely boring about a pod of dolphins speeding by, clicking and whirring at them, or magenta fish darting between the three friends like it was a game.

Despite the gruesome reason for being here, Phoebe gloried in being in the sea once again. It had been six long months since Sierra had forbidden swimming in the ocean at all for unexplained "safety" reasons. And longer than that since Phoebe could swim beyond the cove.

But here she was now. Finally.

As they swam deeper into the sea, Tristan and Mina seemed to glow. In fact, they didn't *seem* to glow—they *did* glow. A soft luminescence spread from every inch of their skin down to where scales covered their flesh. The soft brilliance of silver light made Tristan even more handsome than usual. Phoebe blushed.

"Amazing," she said breathily.

Mina laughed and lifted one arm for examination. "What, our moonglow? I forget you haven't seen it. We have no need of it along the shore. But now we're going a little deeper."

"You're both incredible," Phoebe said, awed.

The two merfolk just smiled back.

"We're almost there. I'll check to make sure the area is clear of predators." Tristan sped ahead then shot straight up into a tangled vine of seaweed and disappeared.

Phoebe gasped.

Mina laughed. "Oh, don't worry, sweetie. Our secret spot is well-hidden on purpose. This little side trip isn't just for you, you know. It's for his own good. That mer will never do what he wants. There was a time he would have done what his heart told him and toss the consequence, but not anymore. The old Tristan's got to be in there somewhere. We need the Tristan I know and love."

"We do?"

Mina glanced at her, then ahead to where Tristan was already returning, a broad smile on his face.

"The merfolk do," Mina whispered and then put her finger over her lips as her brother grew closer.

Tristan announced, "It's safe."

Mina pulled on Phoebe's hand, and Phoebe promised herself she'd ask her friend more about that mysterious comment later. They followed Tristan to the dangling column of seaweed and plunged into the darkness. Even the merfolk's moonglow was all but eclipsed by the plants. Slick seaweed tickled Phoebe's skin, and her stomach plummeted as they rose rapidly. They took a sudden sharp turn to the side and swam beyond the seaweed into an open area that made Phoebe's eyes pop wide in wonder.

Sunlight beamed down through clear water. The light bounced off pale yellow seaweed behind them. A rocky cliff rose in front of them, while reefs curved around the rest of the way like a bowl, making this spot quiet, serene, and beautiful. Orange sea anemones swayed back and forth in the currents. Vivid purple starfish dotted the reef like handprints left by an artist. Schools of red fish no bigger than Phoebe's finger darted among deep blue water plants, and transparent tiny squids drifted like balloons through the currents, their delicate membranes outlined in lacy white.

Phoebe floated in silence, jaw dropped with awe. Mina watched her, triumph in every line of her body.

Tristan began to speak, but the words on his lips died as his gaze focused on Phoebe, too. The twins gave her a long moment to just observe and absorb the beauty.

Tristan said, "This is where we come to relax and think. It's Mina's and my secret spot."

A thrill raced through Phoebe at being in on their secret.

"No human has ever seen this place," Mina whispered.

Phoebe turned to face her friends. Their own luminescence had mostly faded with so much natural sunlight present, but they were no less stunning.

"Thank you," she said reverently.

In this space, it was easy to forget that the sea could be as dangerous as it was beautiful.

"Now," Tristan said. "Remembering you are safe here, tell us about what attacked you, please."

"There's not much more to say," Phoebe said, still caught up in the scene around her, no doubt as Tristan had planned. Fear was distant in a place as magical as this. She went on to describe the experience. The red eyes made her shudder during her retelling. They asked a few questions, but it had all happened so fast, there wasn't much more she could add.

"I don't know what it could be," Mina said, frowning thoughtfully. She was reclining against a bed of sea flowers, spinning one bloom lazily in her hand.

"Me either," said Tristan, "but I suspect it was just a

wandering deep sea creature too far from home. I don't think we need to fear it any longer. It swam away, in any case."

True. Okay, so the sea had some mysterious dangers in it she hadn't known about. But her mer-friends had not yet explained about *their* safety. "What did you learn about the poor merfolk who died?"

Mina sat up and swam to them. Tristan's face grew serious again. Phoebe hated to cast a shadow on the moment, but she needed to know.

"The elders say this skeleton was a merman from many moons ago, a hermit who lived outside of our community after we were set free. He could have been dead for some time. The body must have gotten dislodged from wherever it had been... trapped." He gulped slightly and then continued, "The elders don't know what did the damage that obviously killed him. They think maybe he got caught in a riptide and was dashed against the rocks, breaking the parts of the skull, and the black mark might just be a birth mark of some kind, or even part of his mer-tattoo. They swore it meant nothing."

"But Mother told us differently."

Tristan shoved Mina's shoulder, but she held her chin high as Phoebe asked, "Your mother knew something?"

A thin red eel slid by, but Phoebe didn't even flinch. Her focus was on Tristan and Mina.

"She's the historian of our people, a mermaid of great learning," Mina explained, weaving her fingers through her long hair and pushing it out of the way. "She studies ancient myths and the golden age of the merfolk. She knows things others have forgotten and says there was once a creature that could have done it, but no one has seen or heard from such a thing in centuries. The others scoffed at her for even bringing it up."

"The elders scoff at everything not under their noses, but this time, I can't blame them." Tristan shook his head.

"What did she say?" Phoebe asked.

Mina explained, "She said there was an ancient sea beast called Baleros that lived in the deepest part of the ocean, in the midnight realm."

Tristan added, rolling his eyes, "Baleros is the story that parents tell naughty little seawees who disobey, Phoebe. He's the embodiment of evil, a very powerful, very greedy sea monster, often known as just 'the beast.' He's supposedly the reason our ancient civilization collapsed. They say he could steal the magic from within a merfolk, through touch. He physically burned the magic out of them, leaving them nothing but a husk."

It didn't sound like a myth to Phoebe. It sounded far too much like the skeleton. "Oh no! It sounds like you *are* in danger!"

"You don't have to be concerned for us," Tristan assured her. "Baleros has nothing to do with it. He's just a myth. And our limited magic is hardly something Baleros would crave anyway. Mother often makes a whale out of a minnow. She tends to be dramatic."

The two merfolk quirked their lips at each other.

"But—"

"Don't worry. We won't be going off alone anywhere, and our village is safe. We will be careful, we promise." Tristan tipped his head to one side as he watched her reaction.

Phoebe smiled uncertainly and nodded, though fear thrummed inside her like the surf pounding on the shore. Tristan obviously wanted her to drop it. So she would. For now. They had been so good to her, bringing her to such a wonderful place to distract her from her fears.

"Now, it's been long enough that I suspect the men are gone. Phoebe should probably return home if she wishes to arrive before her sister."

Mina pouted. "No fun. No fun."

"Life is not always fun, sister. It's full of problems for everyone," he replied with a sigh.

His voice was tinged with unexpected depths of sadness that made Phoebe pause. "Tristan, are you sure you're okay?"

"I'm fine. I'm just glad we were able to show you this place. It's more than I ever hoped for."

Phoebe flushed. What did he mean by that? She wished she could see his expression more clearly, but the water was growing darker and his glow had faded to nothing.

Regardless, Tristan was right. She should go. Time was so hard to determine underwater. An hour could feel like a day and vice versa. But she didn't move. She didn't want to cross the dark forest to her house or spend any time alone. Not today. The panic would be sure to come upon her. But Tristan was right. She had to go. The twins exchanged a worried look.

She took a deep breath, savoring the magic that allowed her to do so, and forced a smile.

"Thank you both for saving me. I don't think I said so yet, but you've saved my life again. And thank you for sharing this place with me, for thinking of me. It was the most wonderful thing I've ever experienced," Phoebe said. Her hair floated in front of her face.

Tristan reached out and gently pushed the wild red locks out of the way. Phoebe's cheeks burned. They were probably as pink as a sunset.

"We always think of you," he said.

His touch chased away her concerns over strange myths and mysterious handprints. She smiled at him, willing it to be a natural, friendly smile. She wasn't ready for him to suspect that she had sort of been… daydreaming about him.

She stared at Tristan, forgetting everything for a moment.

Mina hummed briefly, and then said, "I'll head home

now and distract Mother from noticing your lateness. See you later, Phoebe."

She winked at them both and zipped away, leaving Tristan and Phoebe alone.

Totally alone in the most beautiful spot on Aluvia, still holding hands.

CHAPTER FIVE

The moment was perfect, as if from a dream. Everything seemed surreal, a magical painting Phoebe had wandered into. Her heart felt so full, like a thousand songs were playing inside it. She almost couldn't stand it.

"Thank you, Tristan. You've always been so kind to me. You'll never know how much you mean to me," Phoebe said.

She looked up at him, hoping her face showed the feelings she was too afraid to say. She knew that he would one day choose a bondmate from among the mermaids of his village. As a human, she couldn't be more than a friend. He could never leave the water, nor could she live in the water as a proper bondmate.

Her mind knew all this. But her heart couldn't help

but thump erratically when his eyes closed briefly, as if overcome with emotion.

He whispered something she couldn't quite hear. But it sounded a lot like, "I wish you could stay."

"What?" Phoebe asked, throat tightening as she locked down the stirring hope.

A dark shadow slid across them. A quick glance showed it belonged to an illegal fishing boat, breaking the human-merfolk treaty by fishing too far into the ocean, in the merfolk's territory. Again. Tristan frowned and cursed in ancient mer. These fishermen were brazen to break the treaty even in the daylight.

Reality shattered their crystalline moment as Tristan pulled back, removing his hand from hers.

Her cheeks flamed. Had he guessed how she felt? The impossible future she often dreamed of?

"Phoebe, I must get you back to shore quickly. I will have to leave at once to report the boat, but don't worry. I'll keep you safe."

The return trip was a blur, her mind reliving every detail of their moment alone. Had she heard him right? Had he wished their lives could be more entwined? He certainly couldn't seem to deliver her to shore fast enough now. Sullenness pulled Phoebe's lips into a frown. Well, it was for the best. Better just to forget about the odd moment than get into some embarrassing discussion about it. She was glad, really. They were best friends, and nothing should ruin that. She would be grateful for what caring they could share.

As they neared the coastline, her mind raced ahead to the trip back to the house, to the explanation she might possibly give her sister if she'd come home.

Tristan sped through the water without any of his usual acrobatic flips and reached the cove in record time. They paused as close to the shoreline as Tristan could comfortably reach. From here, Phoebe would have to walk onto land on her own two feet.

This close to the surface, Phoebe could tell the sun touched the horizon, but plenty of light still filled the sky. Her journey underwater had felt like days, but had only been merely a short afternoon. The sea was magical and made time seem to stretch forever.

He checked and reported back, "They appear to be gone, but, Phoebe, I can't follow you on land to be sure. What if they're waiting in the forest? What if something happens to you? I don't think I could stand that."

His eyes were still dark with magic and perhaps something else, some sort of emotion? *Could* he feel about her the same way she had started to secretly feel about him?

She gazed into the blackness of his eyes, wishing she could fall right into them, but Sierra needed her. For once, Phoebe could actually help. If Sierra wasn't on guard when she got home, those men could hurt her. *They could take her.*

Panic zipped through Phoebe, and this time, it was she who pulled her hand from Tristan's. "I'm sorry. I've got to go."

He bowed his head and said, "I understand. Take care of yourself, and come back to us when you can."

Though fear still coursed through her, Phoebe's smile was brilliant in response to his obvious caring. "Always."

She walked onto the shore, her clothing dragging at her waist and legs, the water leaving goosebumps along her skin in the warm air. She turned and waved, and he lifted one hand in farewell. One in water. One on land. Just like their first goodbye. Déjà vu rushed over her, but she forced herself to walk away. She checked over her shoulder as she trudged across the beach and he remained, bobbing patiently in the cove. When she reached the forest's dark edge, she took one last look. He was gone.

She was all alone.

Sierra will be late, Sierra will be late, Phoebe chanted as she ran back to their house in Tuathail.

It was probably true. Her sister's journeys had been harder of late. As Donovan had said, some people wanted nectar again, despite the turmoil it caused before. Fairy nectar, made by the little fairies, held the very essence of magic. For years, it was collected—no, *hoarded and exploited*—for potions and elixirs, dropping the amount of magic in the world to dangerous levels. What people didn't know was that without the supportive net of magic spread throughout the land, their world was dying, earthquakes tearing it apart. After the littlest fairies had perished, starved of magic, the queens fled to the mountains to replenish themselves at the heart of magic, a hidden well-spring of power. Sierra practically saved the world by finding the queens again while also saving Phoebe. The queens' return and the rebirth of the little fairies was a joyous thing indeed.

Phoebe never begrudged anyone such happiness. She just wished she could be as useful and magical as her sister was. A moment of jealousy pinched at her, but she squashed it. It wasn't Sierra's fault that she had gotten all the magic in the family.

Ducking among the branches, Phoebe stayed on the lookout for Donovan. The shadows of the trees blocked much of the dwindling sunlight, but at least she was better hidden, even with her bright red hair. Oh please, let her beat Sierra home.

Phoebe reached the clearing where their house sat. Small, squat, and grey, their home was hardly anything to brag about. The corners still needed patching from the earthquakes that had rocked the packed mud and stone building for years, but it was theirs. With their dangerous father dead, killed during Phoebe's rescue, the sisters had more freedom and peace than they'd ever had.

Soft golden lamplight shone from the kitchen window in preparation for dusk. Phoebe hadn't left any lamps glowing when she left. Dread swelled in her. There would be no way to hide where she'd been. Water sluiced down her pants and tunic. She'd have to confess.

Let's see… dead merfolk, terrifying sea creature, and Donovan back to get her. She couldn't hit Sierra with all of those at once. Phoebe would start with the most important. Only one of those things was a danger to them now.

She twisted her hair to get rid of the worst of the water and squared her shoulders. Time to pay the piper.

Through the open kitchen window, Phoebe spotted Sierra setting the table, her long braid hanging over her shoulder. Her ornate fairy mark gently shone like a jewel on the back of her neck. No one else appeared to be home yet.

Phoebe stepped inside, and the heat of the cooking fire rushed over her cold, wet skin. The scent of baked bread filled the air.

"Where have you been?" Sierra cried.

She ran over and pulled Phoebe into a tight hug, surrounding her with the cinnamon honey fragrance of a fairy keeper. "I've been so worried! Where were you? I told you to stay by the house while I was gone this time!"

She patted down Phoebe's arms, as if checking for wounds. When Sierra's hands came away wet, her eyes narrowed, red dots of anger blooming on her cheeks. "Bug, tell me you weren't in the ocean."

Anger lit inside Phoebe, a fuse that might just explode. As much as she loved her special nickname, it had become a symbol of her childhood. And by all the stars, she wasn't ten anymore. Yes, she'd run into danger in the ocean. But she'd survived, hadn't she? Which was more credit than her sister had ever given her. She'd survived a lot in life, in fact.

"Sierra, I'm not a child! I'm not your little *'Bug'* anymore. And yes, I was in the ocean, but it's not what you think. And by the way, welcome home."

Queenie, Sierra's glowing fairy queen, peeked out from behind Sierra's braid, a wide smile on the fairy's tiny golden face. Queenie shook a little finger at Sierra and zipped over to Phoebe to caress her cheek before flying off through the window to join the little fairies dancing in the trees.

Sierra sighed and resumed setting the table, most likely biting back words of frustration. "Fine. Queenie's right. I apologize for snapping. You'll still need to tell me what happened, and we *will* discuss this breach of the rules, but first, you need to eat. You're too thin, Bug—I mean, Phoebe. And go put on your nightgown. At least you'll be dry."

Phoebe ground her teeth. She hadn't even decided how to break the news about Donovan, but, as usual, Sierra got to decide when and how Phoebe did everything. By all the magic in Aluvia, she was tired of being treated like a baby. She changed quickly, yanking on the first nightdress she found. But she couldn't eat now. Any food she choked down would most likely come right back up.

She padded barefoot back into the kitchen, reminding herself to stay calm. "Sierra, I need to talk to you about what happened today. It's serious—Donovan came here, with another man. I had to dive into the ocean to escape them."

The plates Sierra was holding clattered to the table. "What! Are you hurt?"

Sierra rushed over again. Her eyes were wide, eyebrows tilted up in worry, reminding Phoebe again of why it was she put up with such over-protectiveness. Sierra really did love her. She just had a hard time admitting her little sister was growing up, especially after almost losing her four years ago.

Phoebe thought about what she told Tristan. Could she really keep the secret of the mer-skeleton and the scary sea creature from Sierra? There had been a time when the two of them shared everything; it was Sierra and Phoebe against the world. She really missed that.

She missed the big sister who used to make up silly rhymes and sew stuffed animals for her. Where had *that* Sierra gone?

She'd gone on a quest to save Phoebe, that's where, and the fairy keeper who'd come back was a different person. Happier, but with a new mission—a mission bigger than the needs of one little sister.

Then Sierra grabbed Phoebe's shoulders and hugged her tight again, and Phoebe couldn't hang on to her irritation. Guilt pricked her conscience.

"I'm okay. But the men were here earlier and could still be around."

Sierra blanched. "What? What happened?"

"I was down at the coast again this afternoon—"

Sierra cut her off, her hand making a slicing motion as she lost her tenuous hold on her infamous temper. "Argh! You and that ocean! So you *did* leave the house! I swear one of these days you're going to grow scales from all the time you spend at that smelly place! If you had stayed home like I asked you, you wouldn't have had to deal with those men. Old Sam would have warned you if anyone was nearby, and our locks are made with the finest steel money can buy. You can bet I made sure of that before I left this time."

Phoebe gasped in sudden understanding. Rage boiled, at sudden flashpoint. She pointed a shaking finger at her sister.

"You *knew*. You knew we were in danger and didn't

warn me." She turned on her heel and stormed to her room, throwing herself onto her pallet in the little space that had once been *theirs*.

Phoebe held her pillow and waited for the tears to come. But today, her tears remained trapped inside. They clawed at her stomach like wild animals but couldn't push past the sense of betrayal.

The knock a few minutes later was not unexpected. But Sierra's relative calm was.

"You want to talk about what happened? We assume you went with Tristan and Mina, given that you're soaked," Sierra said.

Corbin peeked around the edge of the door. The others must have arrived for dinner. Perfect timing. Now she could tell *everyone* what she'd been up to in their absence.

The gentle fairy keeper's dark brown eyes were soft with some emotion. Pity? Sympathy? Knowing Corbin, it was both. "Hey, kiddo. We need to know what happened. Are you okay?"

Phoebe dragged herself into a sitting position. "You have some time?"

"For you?" Corbin said, putting his hand on Sierra's shoulder when she scowled and opened her mouth. "Of course."

Sierra pursed her lips, though her anger was evident by the two bright red spots remaining on her cheeks. Anger was always her first response to fear—so she must have been really worried.

Phoebe pushed aside the sting of guilt. "You can stop glaring at me like that, Sierra. If you'd told me Donovan and his men were coming after me, you can bet all your fairies I wouldn't have left the safety of the house."

Sierra paled. "They came for *you*? Micah, get in here!"

Micah glided in from the back room. He looked completely comfortable in the human form he wore so often these days. He was always handsome, but Phoebe privately thought he was more handsome in his natural state, in the glorious magical form of a faun. Who would choose to be human when they could walk around bursting with magic? Although, transforming into a human allowed Micah to better live in Sierra's world as her beloved. Phoebe's heart still warmed at their devotion to each other.

"Good evening, little sister. It's good to see you." Micah paused, furrowing his brow for a moment. He inhaled deeply, and his expression cleared. Then he bowed to Phoebe, as he often did in greeting. The four of them were crowded in the little room, but no one complained.

Sierra commanded, "Okay, now tell us. Clearly. Donovan came for you?"

"Him and some other man I didn't know. While I was at the water." Her hands twisted in her old quilt made by their mother years ago. The loose threads looked like lace. "I went down to finish a conversation with Tristan and Mina, but they weren't there."

Phoebe went on to explain how the men trapped her and why she ran into the water.

"You're sure it was Donovan? And that they were supposed to take *you?*" Sierra asked, biting her lip, exchanging a glance with Micah.

"I'd never forget that face."

Sierra sat down and looped an arm around Phoebe. "Go on, then."

"I knew Tristan and Mina were coming, so I swam out far into the sea, hoping the men wouldn't come after me."

"You're lucky the merfolk came in time," Micah said, solemnly. Phoebe considered mentioning the reason the merfolk had been meeting her, the discussion about the skeleton, but then Corbin interrupted.

"What's that mark on your ankle?"

Everyone stared. Huge reddened fingerprints marred the pale skin on her right leg. Phoebe hadn't noticed the mark until now. She hastily covered her bare legs and feet with a blanket, but it was too late.

"And what. Is. That?" Sierra chewed out the words.

Phoebe sighed. She was going to have to tell them after all. This wasn't going to be pleasant.

CHAPTER SIX

*P*hoebe told them the truth about the sea creature that grabbed her. She didn't tell them of the terror she'd felt, but she described the creature in detail.

"Wait, wait," Corbin gasped, waving his hands to stop Phoebe. "A *water wraith?*"

"A what?" Sierra stood, hands on her hips, ready for a fight.

Corbin gulped, staring at Phoebe. "It had... red eyes and sharp teeth?"

Sierra's eyes popped, and her gaze pinned Phoebe to the wall. "Yes, Phoebe, do tell. Did this thing have red eyes and *sharp teeth*, when you were under the water *where you weren't supposed to be?*"

Phoebe flinched, but she spit out, "What, you'd rather Donovan caught me?"

Sierra took a deep breath as if about to argue, but Micah hushed her with a finger against her lips. She complied with his silent request when she'd never listen to anyone else like that. He winked at Phoebe.

Corbin said, "The water wraiths are an old myth. I've only read about them in a few rare scrolls from countless years ago. The old tales say they are the servants of a giant, ancient sea creature called Baleros, and both preyed on the merfolk, stealing their magic."

Phoebe stifled a gasp at hearing that unusual name mentioned again.

"So, if one servant of a powerful, awful sea beast is awake again, doesn't that mean more wraiths could be around? Aren't the merfolk in terrible danger? Maybe even from this beast itself?" Phoebe asked.

She thought of the skeleton, of its crushed skull, of the faint image of the stirring shadow she sensed as the wraith had held her. Dread was an icy pit in her stomach. Maybe the horrifying shadow creature she saw when she was dying had been a warning, a vision of the thing that destroyed that poor merman. Maybe the elders were wrong, and Tristan's mother was right.

The others exchanged glances, but Sierra just said, "We don't know that for sure yet. Let's talk about that in a moment. First, though, what happened after this thing, whatever it was, grabbed you?"

Phoebe took a deep breath and continued. She briefly touched on the strange shadow she had seen as she lost consciousness, which distressed the others, but by the time she finished explaining what happened with the blue light, everyone's jaws reached the floor.

Sierra, for once, seemed at a loss for words.

Micah asked a question no one else had yet. "You said there was a *blue* light, when the water wraith held you, and then it let go?"

Phoebe nodded. "The light was bright blue, like sapphires. It pulsed once and was gone. I thought Tristan had done it, but he said he saw nothing near me when he arrived."

Micah was silent, though Sierra was eyeing him with suspicion. They were keeping secrets! That was most definitely a keeping-things-from-Phoebe-again face.

"What do you know that you're not telling me?" Phoebe demanded. She stood up on the pallet, feeling the need to be taller and more grown up than sprawling on her bed. "Why didn't anyone tell me there'd been new threats against us?"

Here the other three had the grace to look abashed. "I didn't want you to worry, Phoeb'," Sierra whispered. "I know I shouldn't keep things from you, and I really am sorry, but you were so frail after we got you back and you still, well, you still get upset sometimes. You know how you get?"

Phoebe hung her head. She'd tried to keep the worst of the panic from Sierra but apparently had failed.

"You don't see your old friends. You don't go

anywhere except to the ocean. What if I had told you my worries and made your… episodes… worse?"

Sierra's eyes watered, and Phoebe teared up in response. For once, she wished she wasn't so quick to cry with others. She wanted to impassively stare down at her sister, but impassive was never a word anyone would use to describe Phoebe Quinn.

"You've been really depressed, Phoebe," Corbin added, patting her hand. His kindness made tears press harder against her eyelids.

"I'm sorry," Sierra said, "I am, but I'm supposed to protect you, got it?" She hugged Phoebe like she'd never let go.

Part of Phoebe wanted to stay wrapped in those arms forever. Sierra had protected her from their father before he died. Since their mother had died birthing Phoebe, Sierra had taken the place of mother and father both.

But the other part of Phoebe, a newer part, knew those protective arms were an illusion. Something had changed inside her. Clearly, no one could keep her safe forever. And in the meantime, her dear friends were in danger.

"We've got to help the merfolk!" Phoebe said. "I've got to at least warn them! They won't know a water wraith has risen again, if that's what I saw. They had no idea what it was when I described it. Tristan dismissed it as a rare strange creature accidentally floundering from the depths. What if the evil sea beast is back, too? What if that was the dark shadow I sensed before I fainted?"

"That's a giant leap to make. We don't even know that what you saw is definitely this wraith thing." Sierra's jaw was clenched.

Corbin looked at the floor.

"You know." Phoebe's voice was soft. "You know, and you don't want to admit it."

"That's not true," Sierra snapped.

"But you won't let me go warn them tonight, will you?"

"Tomorrow is soon enough. I'll go myself, but they won't be expecting anyone tonight. You don't need to go back to the sea at all. You're at risk there!"

Phoebe groaned with frustration. "Sierra! These are *my* friends. And tomorrow, they could be dead, attacked by the wraith or maybe even the sea beast itself."

"Or maybe Tristan was right. It could be nothing."

"Then why won't you let me go?"

"Because I love you too much to lose you again."

Silence. Not even Micah broke the heavy tension.

This wasn't working. Knowing her sister's deep need for justice, Phoebe tried a new tack.

"When the merfolk were set free, where was repayment for the ship hulls they had fixed? For the fish they had caught during their slavery? They got nothing, except a promise that the oceans beyond the shore would be theirs alone to care for. But now more humans are violating the treaty, not even bothering to try to work with the merfolk. Just taking what they want. Some humans are even deep-sea fishing again. I was told a little seawee died in their nets, and we saw a boat today sneaking around past the coastline. It's so wrong! And Tristan saved my life, Sierra. Without him, we'd never have even gotten away from Bentwood's. You know that. I owe him my *life*! Twice. He saved me again today. Don't you even care?"

"First of all, we did help his people. We arranged for the treaty, even though the merfolk elders didn't even want to work with us. And of course I'm thankful for him for today, yes, but if you go to them, you'll be in great danger, trust me. I don't believe his actions are worth the possible sacrifice of your own life."

Phoebe did.

When she was taken to Bentwood's, Sierra had come to take her sister back, but to reach the dungeon, Sierra needed help. Tristan was the one who brought her across the waters. He was the one who brought them both back to shore. Phoebe would never forget that.

She'd spent long hours with the twins underwater during those first days and weeks after her rescue, letting the beauty of the sea wash away the anguish of the dungeon. During her captivity, the air had been thick with the stench of sweat and blood and death, but the ocean held the healing scents of rich minerals and tangy green growing plants. Even the whiff of decay along the ocean floor held the seeds of life inside it.

In the dungeon, the helpless sobs of the other new recruits slid into her brain like earworms as she tried to sleep and failed. But in the ocean, her ears were filled with the laughter of her friends and the powerful roar of the surf that boomed along the coast even below the water's surface.

Nothing could ever replace what the merfolk had done for her. She owed them her sanity, if not her very life.

Sierra wrapped her arms around her sister, and buried her face in Phoebe's hair. Phoebe's heart melted.

Voice subdued, Sierra said, "I don't get why you go down there, anyway. Why do you love the ocean so much? It smells like dead fish and is full of slimy seaweed."

Phoebe shrugged, pretending annoyance she no longer really felt. "Why do you like the forest so much? It's full of noisy screeching birds, biting insects, and it covers up the sky with all the jabby tree limbs."

Micah and Corbin laughed.

Leaning back to look at Phoebe, Sierra finally relaxed enough to smile. Tension ran out of her arms like water. Maybe they'd get through this okay.

Sierra thought for a moment. "I guess I like the smells, the freedom, the beauty. It just feels… right when I'm there."

"It's the same for me and the sea. I don't know... it just feels peaceful there. And now it's in danger. Don't you see?"

"No, I don't see," Sierra muttered. "I don't see why you have to risk your life for what could be nothing. I won't allow it!"

Sierra was asking Phoebe to abandon her closest friends. She struggled out of Sierra's arms.

"The merfolk *are* in danger!" Phoebe insisted. At her sister's continued silence, frustration pushed aside caution. There was one way to prove her point. She'd have to tell them about the skeleton. So much for keeping things from her sister. Her pathetic attempt at hiding the truth was like a giant rope coming completely unwoven, each strand blowing loose and open in the wind for all to see. Sierra would want to lock Phoebe in her room forever. But some things mattered more than her own happiness. The protection of the merfolk was one of them.

CHAPTER SEVEN

*P*hoebe took a deep breath. "Look, I found a merfolk's skeleton yesterday. It washed up on shore. It had a strange black handprint on the skull and five holes punctured right through the bone."

She ignored their gasps and hurriedly pressed on. "The elders said it was just an old skeleton that got crushed along the rocks. But what if this wraith grabbed it and sucked it clean? Or worse, what if it was that beast, Baleros? The merfolk have the same stories about him nearly destroying their people centuries ago. Don't you see? *They need to know.* You helped set the merfolk free, but we've done nothing for them all this time. I can't help them, but you can. You've got the magic in the family. Use it to help them. Please!"

Her voice was sharper than intended. Corbin's

eyebrows lifted to his hairline at her tone. Sierra paled. Only Micah looked on serenely, as he usually did.

"You found a *skeleton*? A merfolk that had died violently?"

"Last night."

"And you didn't tell me right away. Why?" The softness with which the words were spoken did not reduce the audible fury a single bit.

"Why do you think?" Phoebe clenched her fists and took a step closer, glaring at her big sister.

Sierra growled, but Corbin stepped between them. "Let's all settle down. Have some supper. Then afterward, when we're calmer, maybe we can focus on the water wraith. Let's deal with the, uh, other thing later."

So the group of four sat at the table, an uncomfortable silence filling the air between the clanking of spoons and clunking of mugs. Corbin tried to make conversation. He explained to everyone that Nell, his partner, would be back later tonight after visiting her family on the way home. Others chatted a bit about their trip, but it was a slow and painfully awkward conversation. Phoebe didn't think she could force anything into her stomach, but the yeasty bread melted in her mouth, and the beans offered sustenance she knew she'd need.

Sierra and Micah finished and left the room to unpack (and probably to talk about how to handle

Phoebe.) That was fine. It was easier to eat without Sierra's worried glare beating down on Phoebe like the noonday sun.

Corbin said, "You know she's only like this because she loves you so much."

"I know," she said shortly. "But love can't smother people, Corbin. It can't control them."

"Give her time."

"The merfolk might not have any time."

He had nothing to say to that. She knew he agreed with her. Corbin's love of magical creatures was as strong as hers.

A few minutes later, Sierra and Micah returned. Sierra looked sullen, Micah ever-peaceful.

"Now," Corbin said, building the fire up. "Let's discuss this reasonably. Phoebe wants us to tell the merfolk about this danger, and it sounds like she also wishes to somehow help the merfolk in greater measure, beyond setting up the treaties we arranged."

"You mean the treaties humans are beginning to ignore?" Phoebe said sweetly.

"Well, yes, uh…" Corbin stumbled.

"The merfolk aren't my calling," Sierra said between clenched teeth.

"But—" Phoebe began.

"No, I don't have a connection to them. I just don't. And if *you* go to them, *you'll* be in danger! What if *you're* the next one who gets their head crushed by some giant claw?"

Corbin let out a soft sigh. "Sierra…"

"No, let's do this. You want to have this talk? Fine. Micah, tell her about her smell."

Smell? Phoebe, ready to argue, lost her train of thought. Her sister thought she was smelly?

Micah chuckled. "Oh, if only you could see how much like your sister you look like at this moment, young Phoebe! I once told Sierra she had a scent, and she looked as mortified as you. However, this is not a bad thing. Let me explain.

"Every magical creature leaves behind a scent, a magical signature if you will. Humans have their own scent. When I met your sister, she smelled human, but the scent of magic was heavy upon her as well. I knew she was no ordinary human, or even a typical fairy keeper. Her magical scent was far too strong. After I met you, four years ago, I told her you had a similar scent, though unique to you. She smells of the cinnamon honey magic of her charges. You smell of the sea."

Sierra spoke up. "We didn't tell you, because I was afraid of getting your hopes up about becoming a keeper. I know you've always wanted that, but I didn't think it would happen. Not without the mark."

Micah picked up the thread of the conversation smoothly. "Such a thing seemed unlikely to me as well.

You showed no signs of magical power. So she kept this from you, in love, to protect you from heartbreak if this magic always remained dormant. Magic does run in you, too, Phoebe. We just don't know how it might reveal itself. I wasn't sure it ever would. We agreed to keep silent. It didn't matter in the long run, if nothing happened."

"M-m-magic?" Phoebe stammered. She couldn't quite wrap her mind around what was just said. She had... *magic*? And Sierra had kept that fact from her, despite knowing it was Phoebe's deepest wish? No. Sierra remained quiet because she didn't think Phoebe really had magic, not the kind she could use.

Surely Micah must be wrong about her scent. That was all. Phoebe had never done anything remotely magical that she could remember. Or had she? She thought of the way her singing always drew the little seawees to her. Tingles ran down her spine.

"But today there's more," Micah said.

Sierra scowled at the floor, but the worry in her eyes stood out starkly.

Phoebe had no words.

Micah continued. "The fragrance has changed since I last saw you. It's gotten far stronger, as if it's been activated the same way your sister's was from her fairy sting. I doubt that many magical creatures would have sensed you before, but there's no doubt now that there is something awakening inside you, Phoebe. I believe your magic has now been triggered and will grow even stronger."

"I have *magic*?" she said again, stunned. It felt like she was trying to find her way through a darkened room and could bash herself in the shins at any point.

Sierra's eyebrows were drawn heavily above her eyes. Phoebe didn't understand why. Sure, Sierra's relationship with Queenie started out rough, but look at how happy they were now!

Micah asked, "Did the water wraith break your skin? Bite or scratch you?"

She looked down at her leg, surprised again to see the mark left by the grasp of the water wraith. "No, it never bit me. It half-drowned me, but it didn't leave a scratch. The red mark doesn't even hurt."

"Well, whatever happened, I suspect it is this event that triggered a change in you. *You* actually could be the one to help the merfolk fight this wraith. To recognize the dark shadow for whatever threat it poses. You would not be the first in your family to have strange visions related to your charges." He gave a pointed look at Sierra, softening it with a smile, referencing the strange flickering visions Sierra had experienced when her fairy queen called to her.

She crossed her arms and huffed, looking away.

He continued. "At any rate, you will need to experiment to see what you can do. Magic is something that will take control of you, if you don't take control of it."

Sierra glared at him, but he shrugged. "It is the truth, and you know it."

"No, I don't. And if it is true, how can she even serve the merfolk while living on land? With us, where she belongs?" Sierra snapped.

Phoebe barely noticed the tense debate. Hope fluttered in her chest. The world coalesced around her, a jumbled grouping of shapes that suddenly snapped into a recognizable image. "So you're saying I could have a relationship with magical creatures like a keeper, only different? Like with the merfolk, maybe, tying me to the ocean and them to me?"

"Yes, that's what I mean."

"Because you said I smell like the sea. But maybe you're just smelling salt water on me?"

Micah laughed, an open, joyful sound. "No, little sister, I assure you, it's not that simple. To me, you smell of the sweetness of the sun breaking over the waves for the first time in the morning, of the wildness of the pounding surf upon the cliff walls, of the freshness of the salty air of the coast. I believe you have a magic that binds you to the sea or to something in the sea. It is a part of you."

He shrugged again. "It is just my poor guess, but I challenge anyone to think of something more logical. Scents do not lie."

Though she longed to believe him, doubt crawled through her. Images popped in her mind, of the way she cried in the dungeon, the way she waited helplessly to be rescued. And again today, her friends had to save her from drowning, hide her from Donovan. Could she really be strong enough to help anyone else? Could she really be *magical*? Like her sister? After a lifetime of thinking of herself as ordinary, this new possibility made her head spin.

Phoebe longed to race to the ocean's edge where she could best think, but she couldn't do that right now. Instead, she took a deep breath and imagined she was at her favorite spot, on her favorite rock, on her favorite shore. At the thought, it was as though the ocean itself roared through her. She could almost smell the salty air, hear the crashing waves. Something in her settled, deep inside, like a bone snapping into joint. As incredible as Micah's explanation sounded, maybe he was right. Certainly a faun understood magic better than any human.

She turned over the concept in her mind and tried it on, like putting on a new coat. What if she *was* special, unique? She could have a special tie to the merfolk and a connection to Tristan, the first merfolk she had ever cared for, loved as a dear and lifelong friend, maybe more. Joy trembled inside her, a newly turned leaf in spring.

Maybe her dreams were possible.

In that moment, she made up her mind: she'd never be just plain Phoebe again. The merfolk deserved help. Her friends needed her.

Her sister had taken her fate by the shoulders and pushed back. Phoebe could do just as much. Sierra wanted her to be safe, she understood that. And she loved her sister for it. But staying at this house forever would smother her. Phoebe wanted to be strong.

Her sister always swore real magic involved a choice: embrace your calling to fulfill it, or refuse and turn the other way. So Phoebe would choose to believe she had some kind of magic. And she was going to use it to help the merfolk.

CHAPTER EIGHT

*P*hoebe waited until evening to set her plan in motion, hoping Corbin might go home after dinner. One less person to sneak past would be good. But instead, after dishes were washed and put away, Nell finally arrived at the house, adding to the crowd.

At only nineteen, the blonde girl wore her sword with the easy comfort of someone who had made her living with it for years. She was still tall and lean like a hawk but smiled much more now than during the days she worked as an enforcer for Phoebe and Sierra's father. Ever since fairy queens stung Nell four years ago, she'd never been the same. Now she was prone to speak prophecies about healing the world, which brought her violent career as an enforcer to a sudden end. Her love for peaceful Corbin helped direct that decision, too, Phoebe was sure. Nell frequently traveled with Sierra, Micah, and Corbin, often acting as the voice for whatever mysterious power sought to persuade people to leave the fairies alone and let magic in Aluvia grow.

Nell was used to being the medium for delivering the messages, but that didn't mean she liked it. She intended to apprentice with Corbin's parents as a healer, but her travels with the others kept her too busy for the time being. She kept swearing it was a temporary situation. Four years seemed a little more than temporary, but Phoebe held her tongue, knowing Nell's sore spot about the topic.

Wiping the road dust from her face and neck with a towel, Nell stayed silent during Corbin's retelling of the day's events. At the end, she just shook her head and said, "It's always something. Can't anyone be normal around here?"

Nell wasn't one to make conjectures about things she didn't understand, so the topic moved on to her trip and how big her siblings had grown. As the others talked, Phoebe watched the shadows along the walls as the fireplace flames lowered. She went to her room early, picked out swim clothes for her journey, and crawled beneath her bedcovers.

Waiting until the main room grew silent, she was almost ready to slip into her swim clothes when someone tapped on the door. She jumped back into the bed and pulled the covers up, shoving the incriminating clothing under the pallet.

"Phoebe?" The voice at the door was soft, tentative. Sierra's. The door cracked open.

"Come in," Phoebe said, chewing on her bottom lip. She really didn't have time for another argument.

Her eyes widened when Sierra stepped through the door with a shy, non-Sierra-like-smile. She had on the bright blue socks Phoebe knit years before, along with a silly hat in pinks and greens. They clashed terribly. Phoebe snorted, trying to hide her laughter, no doubt as Sierra had intended.

"I found this hat in my trunk, and I remembered when you made it for me. Do you?" Sierra asked.

Phoebe swallowed. "That was the first thing I made you after I got back. From Bentwood's."

Tears shimmered in Sierra's eyes, reflecting the light of the little oil lamp in the corner. "It was the first time I believed you were going to be okay. You had gotten through all the chaos of the fortress crumbling from the quake, and then sort of fell apart yourself when we got home."

"I remember." Phoebe kept her head down, voice low.

She didn't like remembering those days. It was as if she had been a stained glass window, sturdy against the wind and rain. But someone had thrown a rock through the carefully designed images that glowed in the sunlight, and afterward, there had been only shards of darkened glass all over the floor. But she'd put them back together, over time. The artwork looked slightly different now, with some new scenes present, and other familiar ones crooked, but light shone through brilliantly just the same. At least on most days.

Sierra explained, "I love this hat, as silly as it is, because it reminds me of the hope I had for you then. I know I've been hard on you lately. I just don't want to see you so hurt again if the worst happens. It would destroy me. I'm the one who's weak here. It's not you."

But I could be, Phoebe thought. If she sat quietly by and allowed her friends to suffer, that would be weak. Cowardly. And she'd hate herself for it. She accepted she still suffered moments of unbearable panic from her past experiences. She couldn't help that. But she had a choice now about her future.

"I love you no matter what," was all she could say to Sierra without lying. And Phoebe didn't want to lie. Didn't want to pretend. But she would go ahead with her plans to help the merfolk, despite the risks, because she knew Sierra wouldn't budge. Her sister was loving, but stubbornness itself could take lessons from that girl.

Sierra gave another hug, squeezing hard. Phoebe had a moment of misgiving, even guilt about her plans, but she just buried her face against her sister's neck and tried to show her love through the embrace of her arms.

After Sierra slipped back to her room, Phoebe wiped

her eyes and waited until the crack under her door went totally dark, indicating the fire was out in the front room. She listened against her door until only silence floated in the air, then she quickly changed clothes, slipped on her boots, and crept out.

She yelped at the sight of Nell sitting near the front door, tipped back with her feet kicked up on the table. Phoebe glanced around, but no one else came running.

"Going somewhere, little songbird?"

Nell probably used Tristan's nickname for her on purpose.

Phoebe gulped. Words deserted her. She should have guessed there'd be a sentry posted. Sierra was too cautious to leave Phoebe's safety in her own hands.

"Looks like you're after a midnight stroll. Perhaps to the beach, hmm?" Nell smirked at her, eyeing the smoothly fitted top and tight leggings Phoebe always wore into the water.

Nell stood up, brushing off her canvas pants. "I get it. I want to help the merfolk, too. But I can't let you go off by yourself. Look what happened yesterday and today already! Not to mention your sister would kill me."

"She wouldn't have to know," Phoebe whispered.

Nell snorted. "Right. Because your sister would believe that I just fell asleep on duty. Please."

Nell would never do that, Phoebe knew. Her heart fell. She had to think of a way to get to the water. She'd go crazy if she stayed here, when maybe she had a real chance to help Tristan. What if they could figure out how to use this power she had, whatever it was, to fight the water wraith if it attacked the merfolk? She needed to at least warn them that Tristan's mother was right—Baleros was probably returning, and his water wraiths were back, at least one of them. That was Phoebe's only plan, as far as it went.

"Nell, you and Sierra were my age exactly when you went seeking the wild fairies, don't you remember?"

"And we nearly died."

"But you didn't. She won't even let me journey with you anymore. It's been two years. I'm tired of sitting here and cooking and cleaning. I want to make a difference."

Nell wrinkled her brow in sympathy but shook her head.

Phoebe tried one last thing. She padded over to the tall warrior who had become a friend and laid a palm on her arm. "Please, Nell. This is something I need to do. I know it in my heart."

Nell said, "I'm sorry, I—" She stiffened, and her words gurgled and cut off as her eyes turned black as night.

Phoebe shivered.

The gravelly voice that had spoken warnings and prophecies over the last four years poured out of Nell's mouth like honey, softer than usual, almost a whisper.

"So willing to serve. So eager to sacrifice. You can

indeed serve the merfolk well. But be wary, young one. Though the sea-dwellers need you, if you accept the gift you are given, the sea will claim you. Now go if you so choose."

With those last words, Nell's eyes closed, and she sank to the floor, as if the forces that worked through her were conspiring to set Phoebe free. Nell hardly ever fainted after a spell anymore.

"I'm sorry," Phoebe whispered then ran out of the house. She dodged through the woods, trying to keep a low profile in case Donovan and his partner were still around. Her pulse thundered in her ears—*tha-thump, tha-thump, tha-thump*—as she raced unerringly toward her favorite spot.

She called to Tristan and Mina in her heart as she ran, trying hard to believe in this magic she supposedly had, but it was easier to hold onto hope in her living room than running alone in the dark.

She didn't have much time before Sierra came to get her. Phoebe called Tristan and Mina in her mind. *Come to me! I need you!* She sensed no response. Feeling foolish, she just focused on reaching the beach.

Branches tugged in her hair as she ran. She lacked the grace and strength of her sister or Nell. But that didn't mean she couldn't help. Anger surged through her, adding speed to her steps. Her mind churned through all the possibilities for her future.

During their battle with Bentwood's people, her

sister used her link with the fairies to guide them to her. She bonded so deeply to Queenie, they had shared magic and saved each other's lives. If Phoebe could use her magic the same way, maybe she could actually protect the merfolk from a creature like the wraith, either giving them warning or sending them her magic and strength when they needed it.

And if that happened, maybe Sierra would finally offer Phoebe true respect along with her love.

Phoebe ducked through the field where the old fairy hatch had been. She could smell the briny purity of the sea. *Close.* Her mind kept returning to one odd thing the voice said, though, that bit about the sea claiming her. She wasn't sure what it would mean to accept the gift from the sea, but having the sea claim her didn't sound like things would end well.

Her breath shuddered in her lungs, and her lips were numb from fear. But she wouldn't give up. Sierra had been willing to die for her fairy queen. Phoebe felt the same about the merfolk. She didn't understand why no one else cared, but she was determined to help them now.

The woods ended and opened all at once, like a split water bag, pouring Phoebe out into the rocky sand. Hopefully her friends had heard her call through whatever magic she supposedly possessed. She couldn't get far on her journey without a merfolk to help her, and there was no time to waste. She berated herself for not describing the wraith in better detail to Tristan, even for not being more observant during the attack.

The cove was beautiful but empty. The silvery moonlight picked out every crevice, every rock, but no merfolk popped up to greet her. Not even a bird called out. She stumbled over to her favorite rock. It seemed long ago she had last sat here, singing, trying to forget her past. Was that just yesterday?

She slapped her hands into the water and called for her mer-friends as loudly as she dared, uneasy at the way her voice amplified over the water. Surely Donovan had given up, though, and left hours ago.

"Tristan! Mina! Come on, I need you!" She hoped perhaps her supposed magical draw would pull them forth, out of love for her. She even tried calling under the water to them but felt certain the gurgles she made traveled no further than the jetty.

No one appeared. Phoebe lowered her head onto her legs, wet hair sticking to her cheeks. What if the water wraith got to the merfolk before she did? What if Tristan or Mina died because she had run home? She should have gone with Tristan to see the elders and told them what she'd seen. They might have known what it was and taken precautions.

She stared miserably at the sea, scanning the horizon. Her vision blurred. No one else made her giddy and all coiled up inside like Tristan did. No one else made her so happy. She should have told him how she cared for him, more than just hints. And Mina was a best friend, too, and Phoebe might never see her again. Her shoulders wracked with sobs.

Her hand brushed against an odd shape on the rock beside her. It had been sitting there, but at first she thought it was just a clump of seaweed. As she blinked tears out of her eyes, she realized it was seaweed, but it was wrapped around something, like a package. It was one of Tristan's gifts!

She snatched up the small object, which nestled easily into her palm, and tugged on the sea fronds looped around it. They were squishy against her fingertips. The cold seaweed unfurled, leaving a single glowing pearl in the middle of her hand, the size of a berry, hanging from a thin silver chain. Soft white light swirled inside the sphere. This was no ordinary pearl.

This had to be a merfolk tear. She'd heard stories about them. Who hadn't? Stories by the fire, stories for little children, but her mer-friends said simply that merfolk generally had no need for tears, or even the ability to shed them except in cases of extreme grief. Tears from merfolk were so rare that it was said they coalesced into glowing pearls that, when given freely, granted the owner one wish.

Her friends had never confirmed that part, laughing when she'd asked. But maybe the myth was true? A normal pearl wouldn't glow like that. Phoebe threw away the seaweed and gripped the pearl in her hand, the slightly gritty surface reassuringly solid in her hand. The chain dangled between her fingers. Nothing would crush this pearl. It felt like iron.

Her pulse raced like a merfolk's tail. What could have made one of the merfolk cry? Had Tristan's tears formed this pearl? She blanched at the thought of him crying over anything.

But what to do with it?

She took a deep breath, taking strength from the rich scents of the beach. She tried to relax, so the answer could come to her. She let her ears fill with the soft rumble of the waves rolling in farther down the shore. Here, the surf was almost always gentle and quiet. She let the quietness spread through her. She reached for the unexpected peace that had risen inside when she thought she would die beneath the waters. There was a blue light then. Maybe Nell's prophecy had something to do with that.

Phoebe stood up, took off her boots, and crossed over to the shallow end of the shore. She didn't feel bold enough to slide into the dark waters by the pool. The water in the shallows was so clear she could see the bottom along here in the moonlight. It was probably safe. The chilly water lapped at her ankles. She shivered and waded forward a few more steps until the water reached her hips. Had the sun been up, this would have been refreshing. Now, her feet ached from the chill. The sharp edges of crushed shells pressed against her skin. She walked until the water touched her chattering chin.

She examined the pearl. It glowed brighter, or perhaps that was just her imagination. *Concentrate, Phoebe!* Things must be dire for Tristan to have actually cried.

She kept her palm open, staring at the pearl. "Please," she said, not knowing to whom she spoke and feeling foolish for it. "I need to help them. But no one's coming. I need to reach them. Just let me breathe."

She put on the necklace. Slowly, so slowly, she sank below the water. Her swimming shirt stuck tightly around her, but she was used to the sensation. She kept her eyes open despite the burn. The pearl flared even brighter under the water. She understood then. It would have to be a matter of trust.

She opened her mouth, letting the cold water fill it.

I can do this, she thought.

Please.

She took a deep breath of sea water.

CHAPTER NINE

A splitting pain knifed through Phoebe's body. Icy cold spread along her skin, racing from her toes to the back of her neck. She tried to scream but could only gurgle as her throat felt like it burst into flames under the water. She forced another breath.

Water swirled into her lungs—and sent oxygen through her. Her body relaxed, took another breath without resisting. *Yes.* The pearl was working. She could breathe and see clearly underwater. Her hands flew to her neck, but her skin was as smooth as ever. No gills, unlike the merfolk. Her stomach did a slow roll. Breathing underwater magically with her friends was one thing. Being deep underwater alone, depending on an inanimate object she didn't understand, was another.

She looked down at the necklace resting on her chest. Clearly, the magic was coming from it. But she'd better move fast, just in case there was a time limit on how long the magic lasted.

The water slid against her skin like satin, not chilly at all now. She wrapped her hand around the pearl and whispered a word of thanks. Then she summoned all her courage and swam into the dark waters as Tristan taught her long ago. Mina and Tristan needed her. And nothing would stop her. Not Sierra, not the ocean itself.

The thought of Sierra made Phoebe hesitate, just for one heartbeat. Her sister was going to lose her mind. Well, Sierra would just have to understand. It was done now, anyway.

Electric yellow fish darted away from Phoebe's reaching hands as she pulled herself forward through the water. A sea turtle stared at her in what might have been surprise, but she kept going, smiling a little. Beneath her, a forest of tube worms fanned out, waving in the dim light, feathery red petals of gills slurping suddenly into their tubes as she passed by.

The sea floor dropped away as she swam farther, and the light grew dimmer. She wished it were daytime. If only she could glow as her mer-friends did. Their steady light would be comforting about now. At least spots of light floated in the increasing darkness. The pale bluish lights around her looked like a carnival as glowing sea creatures rose from the twilight depths of the sea to seek food in the shallows under the cover of darkness. The sea was full of magic.

Also full of danger, she could almost hear Sierra say. A jolt ran through Phoebe. Pulling her attention from the surrounding beauty, she swam faster toward where she thought the merfolk lived. Fewer creatures lit the gloomy waters here, and a shiver of fear threaded through her. She was without her friends... and the water wraith might still be out there.

She gulped and kept a close eye out for jellyfish and sharks. Kicking her legs faster, she picked up the pace, looking over her shoulders into the growing blackness behind her, watching the pinwheeling dots of lights spin. It was other-worldly, completely different than the ocean she knew along the coast. She felt incredibly alone.

When Phoebe was scared, one thing she always did was sing. She hadn't really ever sung underwater much before, but now she found herself singing softly as she went, the melody of a plucky, happy tune pushing past her stiff lips. The notes chimed like bells.

For a moment her breath froze in her chest as a large shadow moved along the floor below her. When it turned out to be a giant school of sleek black fish, she almost sobbed with relief.

Mina's stories about the kraken octopuses crept through Phoebe's mind. They were rare in these waters, she reminded herself. *But not unheard of.* Even regular octopuses were dangerous. The loathsome, many-armed, baggy-headed creatures made her want to curl into a ball and hide ever since one grabbed her when she was first learning to swim in the ocean with Tristan. It took days for the sucker marks to fade from her leg. Luckily, Sierra had been gone on another trip, or that would have ended Phoebe's visits to the ocean right then.

As fear rose, so did her voice, but just for a moment. Perhaps singing as she swam wasn't the best way to stay hidden. She stopped, just as a hand wrapped around her wrist and yanked her into a forest of seaweed. Another hand clamped over her mouth.

"By the great shell, what on Aluvia are you doing, Phoebe? Trying to kill yourself?"

Relief flooded her, leaving her weak-kneed like soggy kelp. She spun in Tristan's arms to face him, her hair tangling around her neck and shoulders. Luminescence lit his skin all over. It wasn't bright, but it was enough to see the green of his eyes, the first time she had ever seen their natural shade underwater. Those eyes grew rounder than sand dollars as his gaze traveled over her. He looked around and must have realized she was alone, as his mouth dropped open in shock. His lips moved in some sort of prayer or curse, and his gaze snapped back to hers, eyes still wide.

"How did you get down here? Did Mina bring you?"

"No... no... no one brought me," she stammered. She thought he might be pleased to see her initiative, happy to see that she came to him, of all people. But maybe not.

"Then how did this happen?!"

Was he angry? He didn't sound happy. Phoebe recoiled, her stomach twisting. But urgency pressed her past hurt. He needed to listen.

"I had to warn you. The thing I saw—Tristan, I found out it's a water wraith, and your mother could be right about Baleros. It's possible that merman skeleton wasn't as old as we thought—the marks on it could be from that thing. You're in danger!" She paused, then added, a little awkwardly, "Your people are at risk!"

He raised his eyebrows. "The water wraiths are just a myth, Phoebe."

She shook her head and grabbed his arms. His muscles bunched under her hands. "So were dragons on land, Tristan. And they're out there now, setting fire to whole sections of the mountains, causing all kinds of trouble not even the fauns can stop. We need to tell the elders!"

"You're serious," he whispered to himself. Then looked again at Phoebe more closely. "By the shell! A mer-tear!" he gasped. "So that's how you got down here?"

She froze. "You didn't leave it for me?"

He shook his head, his dark green hair swinging wildly in the current.

"It was left where you usually give me presents. If you didn't send this to me, who did?"

As white as she'd ever seen him—which was a feat, considering his pale skin—he pursed his lips and said, "I don't know. We'll need to tell my people. We're forbidden to share mer-tears with humans. Whoever did it will be in serious trouble, but that's not your concern. And you can share what you experienced. Maybe the elders will know what creature attacked you. Let's go. But don't sing. You called me straight to you. Who knows what else you might have called? Don't forget sound travels far under the water."

Mute with surprise, she nodded.

Then he smiled a little half-smile at her. Softer now, he said, "When this is all done, though, I hope you will sing to me again. I do love to hear your voice, Phoebe Quinn."

Phoebe looked down at her body, surprised she wasn't glowing from pleased embarrassment. Fine, she could keep from singing out loud. What he didn't understand is that the music rarely went truly silent inside her. Sometimes it was just a quiet tune harmonizing in the background. Other times it took the lead in her thoughts as she daydreamed. Right now, the music in her mind picked up its pace into a happy jig.

Before she could reply, though, Tristan said, "I'll have to take you to the village. You'll need to see the elders."

Phoebe gaped at him. "*The* village?"

"Yes. To Morgance, the home of the merfolk."

Her heart tripped in her chest. These days, humans were not permitted in Morgance at all. Mina might have broken the rules and secretly shown her the village, but never Tristan. He said Phoebe couldn't understand the importance of cooperation among his people. If he defied the elders, he could be cast out. She definitely didn't understand. Sierra had defied their father and came out on top, but Tristan insisted the merfolk were different. Community was like the ocean itself for them, impossible to live without.

This was her chance to see the merfolk's village, which was built along the line of the shallows and the twilight realm of the sea. Forget her exhaustion. Forget Sierra. For a moment, she even forgot about the water wraith.

Tristan's eyes were so close, she could see herself reflected in them, wild red hair swaying all around her like chaotic seaweed, eyes wide and round.

"Let's go, then," she replied.

"The elders won't like it. Are you prepared for that?"

She lifted her chin. "I'm ready for anything."

"Let's find Mina, first," he said. "If anyone can talk their way out of trouble, it's that girl."

Phoebe laughed. He took her hand and led her into the dark waters.

With Tristan pulling her, they sped through the water faster than the quickest shark of the sea. The deeper they went, the more he glowed, his skin letting off an even brighter silver radiance that shimmered, illuminating the fish and sea plants as they passed. If Phoebe was still breathing air, he would have taken her breath away.

"During the day, this area is full of sea creatures you'd recognize, but at night, completely different fish and animals swim from the depths to enjoy the feeding," he explained.

Rainbow lights glittered on a rising squid and reflected against the coral.

"Those are night hunters," he commented. "They eat fish and crabs. We're not their prey, don't worry. You're fortunate to be here at night, to see the display. We often douse our own light when traveling, but this area is safe for us and quite beautiful. You'll be able to see better if I show the way."

Phoebe's body relaxed as she let him pull her along. She was safe now. She was with Tristan.

They didn't have to look long for Mina. She found them before they swam far. Merfolk slept only briefly, so they were often looking for ways to pass the time. Mina in particular was frequently out looking for fun and adventure.

"Tristan!" a sharp voice called, lined with both shock and mischievous pleasure. "What are you doing with Phoebe? You finally decided to take my advice?"

Mina spun into sight from behind a wide column of

coral, her eyes flashing like a cat's as they reflected Tristan's light and her own. Her smile was wide and demanded a smile in return, as always, and she winked at them.

"It's serious, Mina. She has a great deal to report to the elders."

"Why can't you tell whatever it is to the elders yourself?" Mina smirked at him. "You know you're just glad to have a reason to finally show off our home to her."

Tristan looked flustered. Phoebe hid a smile. He had wanted to bring her to his home? Warmth filled her, bubbling like fizzy apple cider.

"You know why I haven't," he muttered, neck and back stiff.

"Oh relax, Tristan! You're going to get everyone's tail in a twist, and I, frankly, cannot wait to see it!"

"Phoebe's message is serious business," he chided.

Mina whistled, a strange warbling under the water. "So you're going to take a human to *all* the elders? In our home? Ha! The chance to see you finally stand up to those old barracudas makes all the tragedy almost worthwhile."

He rolled his eyes. "We'll see what happens. But I cannot allow things to go on as they have."

Mina kissed his cheek. "It's about time."

CHAPTER TEN

"Will you really show me your village?" she whispered to Tristan as Mina swam alongside them. It was one place in the sea he had never shared before.

He nodded and gulped at the same time. She almost regretted asking.

"I don't want to cause any problems for you," Phoebe said as they glided through the water.

Mina laughed and teased, "Too late for that, little *songbird.*" She emphasized the nickname.

"Mina!" Tristan groaned, but Mina was unrepentant.

Phoebe looked back and forth between them, pinned as she was between their bodies. The ocean floor flashed past at a dizzying speed. "Tristan?"

He growled in frustration but glanced at her before looking away. "What my sister means is whether or not our family approves of our friendship, it's a choice we've already made, and we wouldn't make a different one."

"That bad, huh?" Phoebe said, unhappiness lodging in her belly.

Mina answered when Tristan did not. "Let's just say that when Tristan helped rescue you, our mother and father were unhappy that he didn't ask permission first."

He glared at his sister, who glared right back.

Phoebe looked back and forth between them, eyebrows arched high. "That was four years ago. They're still holding that against you?"

Tristan said, "It doesn't matter—"

"It does," Phoebe interrupted. "You never told me you got in trouble for helping me."

Sighing he said, "Our people value cooperation above all things, you know this, along with respect for our elders and tradition."

Phoebe nodded. "So?"

"So, by aiding in the conflict against Bentwood, I not only violated our peaceful way of living, I didn't ask the elders before involving the merfolk."

"But because of your actions, Bentwood could be destroyed. Don't they appreciate that? Without you, they'd be in slavery still."

The two merfolk were silent for a moment. Then Tristan said, "Not everyone sees things in this light."

"Then they're fools," Phoebe snapped.

A horrible thought occurred to her. She whispered, "Did they hurt you?"

"They punished me—but not physically. They told me to stop seeing you. They told both of us to avoid you, four years ago. They couldn't stop the little seawees from coming to your singing but said we were old enough to know better. Obviously, we ignored them, though it has been harder and harder to sneak away to visit."

"Tristan! You've been sneaking? What about honoring your elders and all that?" She could hardly believe it. He was always so cautious about following the rules. She must mean *something* to him, to risk such behavior!

He looked uncomfortable. "They were being unreasonable, and our friendship hurts nothing. But when we told them of the skeleton, it came out that we've still been in contact with you. They were... displeased. And with humans breaking the treaty so often these days, it has only added water to the flood. They wanted to reduce your influence in my life from the very beginning."

Horrified, she stared at him with her mouth open.

He closed it with a light finger under her jaw. "Obviously, they've failed."

Bright pink stained her cheeks, she knew from the burn, that tattletale blush, the bane of redheads. She wanted to say something, but no words would come. Absolutely nothing. Great.

Mina nudged her shoulder. "We both chose you, Phoebe. *We'd* be the fools if we didn't. You're our best friend. Never forget it. No matter what they say when we get to the village."

And with those words, Phoebe felt she could conquer anything. Her friends loved her. She mattered. They'd never leave her. And no one could take that away from her.

The waters were darker on the far edge of the shallows, but a glow along the ocean floor was clear on the horizon, growing larger and larger. *The village.* A sudden flurry of nerves shouldered aside her moment of exhilaration, and she gripped Tristan's hand tighter as he pulled ahead of her. He smiled at her over his shoulder as they came around a bend, and waved his free hand at the cliff that dropped below them.

"Welcome to Morgance," he said, with a wry twist of his lips. "It's not what it used to be, but it's home."

She understood his tone as she gazed down at the village, which grew almost organically from the cliff's wall, like wild mushrooms popping up among the forest floor. The village was smaller than she had imagined. Village seemed to be the wrong word, actually. It was more like a sketchy version of a tiny port city: crowded, basic, falling apart.

The trio swam lower along the cliff face, and Phoebe was surprised to see merfolk-sized holes in the rock, clearly dwelling places. They were like the many dwellings in taller buildings of the ports, but no building on land ever reached so high. Nets of lantern fish hung along the craggy wall, where the living, glowing fish provided a low illumination matched by the soft glow of the merfolk's skin. A silver bubble of light condensed below where a large crowd of merfolk congregated.

Phoebe, Mina, and Tristan followed the cliff down toward the sea bottom. As they zoomed past the cave openings, Phoebe noticed most had swaying curtains of sea grasses covering the entryway like a door. Within the open caves, many of the merfolk were too young to have their tattoos yet. Some strummed musical instruments, creating a waving, sonorous melody rippling through the water. Others reclined on cushions eating and chatting with each other.

A crowd of merfolk gathered at the base of the cliff. The silver glow here pulsed with their agitation. White crabs scurried from their light, and flattened fish flopped and buried themselves in the sand. Screeches and wails clashed as the merfolk argued below. Bubbles flew past Phoebe's face at the rapid pace of her friends' swimming. The light from Tristan and Mina's skin dimmed as they approached the brilliance of the gathered merfolk.

"Uh, Tristan? Mina?" she said, voice wavering, and not just from the water speeding by her lips.

"Shh!" Tristan said, pulling her behind him as he all but skidded to a stop behind the crowd. "Something's happened. Something else," he whispered to Mina.

The two exchanged a glance, and then Mina slipped from their side and slid into the crowd with the ease of an eel.

Phoebe was practically hidden behind Tristan's broader frame. She peeked out around him. Most of the merfolk were facing away from them, toward a group in the middle of what had to be their elders. Long braids floated above the shoulders of the seven mermen and mermaids in the middle of the circle, each wearing a necklace of clam shells. All of the adult merfolk had black tattoos decorating their arms and shoulders. The mermen's bare torsos were embellished as well.

These tattoos appeared magically on every merfolk upon reaching adulthood, at some mysterious ceremony her friends said they could not talk about. Naturally, it always drove Phoebe wild with curiosity.

She only knew that each tattoo pattern held deep personal meaning. The dark lines of their tattoos stood out against the glowing luminescence of their skin, leaving a breathtaking design across their bodies.

Despite their wild beauty, most of the merfolk did

not look well, appearing even thinner than Mina and Tristan. The lines on their faces were too sharp; their collarbones jutted out, all points and angles. Some of their scales were dull and even cracked.

They were speaking. Phoebe could understand most of what they were saying in trade speech, as most merfolk rarely spoke their native language anymore. Tristan and Mina had explained to Phoebe that the constant use of trade speech required during their years of slavery to humans had left its mark on their culture. Just one more reason for merfolk to resent humans. All seawees still learned the merfolk language, of course, but only the most staunchly conservative elders spoke it regularly.

"I've seen one, I tell you!" a seawee was saying, face red. He couldn't have been more than eight or nine, and his skin shone like diamonds. He did not cry, but if he did, surely a fountain of tears would leave an avalanche of pearls to wish upon. His anguish made Phoebe want to comfort him.

An elder made a noise, but the seawee refused to acknowledge it.

"Liam," the elder tried to sooth him again.

"You think I'm crazy, but I'm not! I saw a water wraith! It looked just like every story I'd ever heard, and it looked at me and hissed! It was huge." He shuddered.

An agitated murmur rolled through the crowd.

Phoebe stiffened, and Tristan reached back to put a restraining hand on her arm.

"We all know things have been hard for you since the disappearance of your father last month," continued the elder mermaid, whose arms were covered with tiny dolphins and whale tattoos. "Perhaps your grief has led to some confusion?" The old mermaid raised one eyebrow, as if to suggest that, obviously, this was the explanation.

The little seawee glared at the elder, causing a number of matronly-looking merfolk to shake their heads at the youth.

"This is not our way," the elder admonished. "You must control yourself, Liam."

Several seawees floated closer and closer to Tristan, tiny frowns on their faces. One craned her neck past Tristan and met Phoebe's eyes. The little one's eyes lit up. The seawee grabbed the arm of her friend and pointed over at Tristan. Any moment now, Phoebe was going to be exposed, she just knew it.

"Are you going to tell them what I saw?" Phoebe whispered to Tristan.

He spoke low over his shoulder. "Wait. Let Mina see if she can find out anything. She knows Liam. His father often disappeared for days at a time, and she always kept a special eye on Liam."

Mina's face was ashen from Liam's intense distress.

Even the little seawees who had spied Phoebe paused in their pursuit, staring over at Liam.

"Those eyes! You'll never forget them once you've seen them. And if we don't do something, you will see them! You'll all see those blood red-eyes—and you'll die! They'll steal your life, strip you bare!" The boy was raving. His voice rose shrilly.

The chill of the water reached Phoebe for the first time since Tristan saved her. A number of mermen gathered the seawee up in a hurry and carried him off while he jabbered about the end of the world. Mina stared after them.

Phoebe couldn't stand it anymore. She pulled herself from behind Tristan and announced loudly, "I saw it, too. A water wraith tried to kill me."

A groan and a quiet curse came from behind, and then Tristan took her hand and swam forward with her.

CHAPTER ELEVEN

Uproar ensued as the merfolk caught sight of Phoebe, holding hands with Tristan.

"*Human!*" one of the merfolk shrieked, while an elder made a piercing squawking sound from the old language.

Phoebe winced at the high-pitched screech.

Tristan pushed her back behind him and said, "No, please, listen! She has news you need! She also has seen this creature that Liam speaks of! We are in danger!"

Silence filled the water except for the nearby lantern fish nets creaking as they swayed in the currents. Phoebe swam sideways out from behind Tristan. She wouldn't hide again today. The merfolk had to believe that seawee.

They gazed at her with shock. Mina peeked out from behind a taller merman, and her own eyes were wide. A dozen seawees swarmed Phoebe, cooing and patting her arms and hair. Their hands tickled like starfish, and their giggling was a loud babble of sparkling noise.

"Enough!" called one of the elders with ominous-looking shark tattoos lining his arms and chest. Wrinkles creased his face, but he had a dart pipe attached to his hip belt, along with a pouch full of stinger fish, which were no easy prey. The little seawees darted away like startled minnows.

The elder approached her with a thunderous expression. "Who are you? And why do I feel like I know you?" Each word seemed as if it were pulled from his lips against his will. Fear, tinged with righteous anger, blossomed in Phoebe.

She drew herself to her full height as best she could in the water. "I'm Phoebe Quinn, sister to Sierra, fairy keeper. My sister and I were involved in the fall of Port Iona four years ago." She forced the words out though shyness wrapped itself around her throat and squeezed.

The merfolk erupted in cries of surprise and recognition.

"The singer? The one who always draws our little ones away from their chores with her songs?" said one, wrapping her arm around a little seawee.

"The human Tristan helped," one whispered to another.

Hmm. Looked like Phoebe was famous among the merfolk. Well. Infamous, maybe, based on the glares from many of the adults. The young ones, though, beamed at her like a long-lost friend.

"Quiet!" shouted a merman with ships tattooed along his shoulders and arms. The clamor ceased. The silence was almost more frightening.

"We have a few questions for you, Phoebe Quinn, Singer, sister of the fairy keeper."

Phoebe gulped and gathered her courage around her like a shield. Too bad the shield was full of holes. She leaned against Tristan and took comfort in the curl of his fingers against hers. At least they were together. For now.

"Describe what you saw today."

Phoebe glanced at Tristan, who nodded and whispered, "Elder Maher is fair."

Drawing a breath, she reminded herself to be as clear as possible.

"And why should we trust you, a human?" the merman with the shark tattoos interjected before she could speak. Her heart seized at his expression. So much fury. But she'd never done anything to harm him. She wished he wasn't armed with a dart pipe. Surely he wouldn't use it. The merfolk were pacifists.

"Elder Seamus!" one mermaid objected.

"I've always been a friend to the merfolk!" Phoebe said.

"No human is our friend," snarled the brown-eyed merman, the one called Elder Seamus.

A flurry of voices broke out at his angry words.

Tristan straightened his shoulders and lifted his chin. His voice was deep and strong, carrying like the deepest note of a cello through the hubbub. "She's been a true friend to my sister and me all these years."

"Yes, and we will address your disobedience later, Tristan," a striking mermaid with deep black and silver hair said, scowling.

"Those who disobey the elders repeatedly are not likely candidates for leadership, wouldn't you say, fellow elders? Especially when the disobedience involves cavorting with *humans?*" Elder Seamus said, his voice dripping with disdain.

Phoebe flinched. So did Tristan. He lowered his head for a moment.

Seeing him hurt lit the fuse of her own anger. She might deserve their scorn, but Tristan most certainly did not.

"I think you're missing the point, with all due respect," Phoebe interrupted, amazing herself and shocking the elders into silence. She could almost guess their thoughts: A human daring to speak against an elder?

Mina's lips twitched suspiciously.

Phoebe continued before she lost her nerve. "Tristan brought me here knowing he would be punished. But his concern for his people's safety overrode his concern for his own comfort and security. I think he holds the very essence of a leader. He's willing to admit there's a problem. And that problem is what brings me here now." She pulled her pant leg up to show the red hand print still vivid on her skin. "The problem that did *this* to me."

"Anything could have made that mark. It means nothing." Elder Seamus dismissed her leg with a wave.

"We will discuss your claims," Elder Maher sighed, sending a quelling glance at Elder Seamus. "But it would be helpful if we had this message from any other creature. I'm sorry to say so, Mistress Quinn, but your species has not comported itself in a trustworthy manner as of late. Nor in the past, for that matter."

Phoebe nodded. "I do not deny it. It shames me greatly. But I'd like to show you I am sincere. How can I do that?"

"There is one option, but it is a novel one. All elders must be in agreement, and it cannot be discussed in front of you. For now, young lady, go with Mina. We'll call for you when we decide."

Tristan turned to leave with Phoebe, but the mermaid with black and silver hair called sharply, "Not you, Tristan. You need to stay."

Phoebe gulped and met his eyes. *I'm sorry,* she mouthed.

He offered a ghost of his usual smile and mouthed back, *Don't be.*

"Come on," Mina said, taking Phoebe by the hand.

As she moved through the village with Mina, she caught numerous merfolk staring as if trying to place where they'd seen her before, their faces alive with curiosity. But she was sure she'd never met them—other than some of the seawees, who swam alongside her with welcoming grins. Some of the adults even glared at her like Elder Seamus had.

A few minutes later, Phoebe slumped wearily in a shadowy cave empty except for a few small boulders dotting the sandy floor. When she'd imagined swimming to the rescue of the merfolk and warning them of a dangerous threat, a group of angry, disbelieving elders hadn't been in her plans. It made her doubly glad she'd never confessed her true feelings for Tristan. He'd never be permitted to be bondmates with a human, even if he wanted to. That much was painfully clear.

At least neither he nor Phoebe had mentioned that Mina had been a part of Phoebe's journey to the village. They'd severely underestimated how badly the merfolk would take Phoebe's arrival. None of the elders understood that what she had to say was more important than breaking the rules about humans in the village.

With Tristan gone, Mina sat with her instead, the mermaid's skin producing only the faintest shimmer. The silence of the cave was a relief after the commotion below. Phoebe asked Mina, "What's happening? What does all of this mean?"

The maid crossed her arms and simply said, "You should rest while you can. You're only human, and it's been a long day for you."

That was a very unsatisfactory answer. Phoebe wanted to argue, but she was so exhausted that she actually drifted off to sleep sitting up, lulled by the soft currents. When she jerked awake—who knew how long it had been?—she found nothing had changed. They were still waiting for Tristan to return.

"Okay. I've rested. Now please tell me what's going on," Phoebe begged. "Your village looks, well, a little rundown. There seems to be an lot of strife for such a peaceful people. And everyone looks almost ill. It worries me."

Mina sighed. Her next words were reluctant, barely audible. "Things have been difficult the last few years."

Phoebe gaped at her. "What? What does 'difficult' mean?"

"As magic has increased, old magical sea creatures, unseen for years, have been reappearing out of the midnight and twilight realms. Dangerous creatures. We thought they were just myths, but they must have come out of some type of magical hibernation."

"Well, that makes Liam's story even more believable!"

"The elders are slow to accept change, Phoebe, even

when the facts are undeniable. It's one thing to fight off some sea dragons. It took the elders *years* to finally accept those were real. But it's quite another to discuss our most ancient of enemies, especially when our own powers have remained low as they ever have. The old ones had powers that let them build magical barriers around their city and fight off large predators when foraging. They could live without fear. Now we have neither the magic nor the skill. We don't know why. It's become rather... dangerous for us to gather our food and trade goods, so we've been doing with less, especially as humans keep fishing in our waters."

"Dangerous! That's an understatement! You've never said anything about hard times!"

"We weren't supposed to." Mina fidgeted with a bracelet, avoiding Phoebe's gaze.

Realization dawned. "So you were keeping things from me?" Hurt bloomed in Phoebe's chest. "Lying to me?"

She had told Mina and Tristan more than anyone about the traumatic time with Bentwood's people. She had shared her heart with her two friends. Her bottom lip quivered, but she bit it before it showed. Ice flowed through her veins. Her most trusted friends had been treating her as a weak child, just as Sierra did.

Mina darted over, her glow dimming and fluctuating wildly. "No! No, it wasn't like that! It didn't involve humans, and your sister told us—"

Her words cut off suddenly, her eyes widening.

"*Sierra* said something to you? As in, Sierra, my big sister?" Phoebe gritted her teeth so hard she was surprised sparks didn't fly even under the water.

"Well, she was worried about you," Mina said, twisting her hands together. "And then she was so angry when we took you deeper into the sea, like we might break you. When she learned that we were having problems with sea dragons and so on, she asked us to sort-of-not-mention-it-to-you." The words came out in a rush.

"She *asked* you to not tell me? What, did she ask you nicely?"

"Maybe more like told us." Mina dipped her head. "She said if we told you, you'd worry more and make yourself sick, and she'd forbid you coming to us at all."

Yes, that was more like Sierra. She didn't ask. She told. She pushed. She *demanded.*

Mina *should* be ashamed. She should have told Phoebe anyway. And Sierra should be ashamed, too, though she wouldn't be. This was even worse than not telling Phoebe she had some unknown kind of magic.

She scowled, spinning a bit in her haste to rise. She had always said she would do anything for her mer-friends, and here they'd been suffering, and she'd not known. Because her *big sister* didn't think she could handle it.

Fury swept through her, colder than the cave waters. Her spine stiffened. Something shifted inside her, something deep down without a name. It stirred, like a wave growing, crashing powerfully against her heart.

"Well. Sierra's not here, and I am. Tell me now." Her voice vibrated with a new strength. The trembling thing in Phoebe's chest solidified, settling there like a firebird sinking into its nest, ready to scorch anyone who threatened her charges.

Mina's face crumpled, and Phoebe's anger softened a little. She took her friend's hands. "Please. Mina. I need to know what's happening. I love you."

Mina sniffed. "Tristan will kill me."

"I'll kill him, and we'll be even." Phoebe's voice was grim.

"The sea dragons are staying in the deeper waters for now, but they are interfering with our gathering and fishing. We're afraid they'll start invading our village. The elders really did say that the merfolk you found must have died by accident a long time ago, but now they're reconsidering. And more merfolk have gone missing. Just gone out to collect food or supplies and never come back. We don't think it's humans taking them, either."

Phoebe blinked at the flood of information. "How many are missing?"

"Enough that the little ones have been forbidden to leave the village as of this morning. The rest of us can't venture into the twilight realm at all. The midnight realm is completely forbidden, and has been for years beyond counting. As you know, humans have been intruding in our waters, stealing from our dwindling supplies of deep sea fish. And now you've said you've seen a water wraith, and with that skeleton found, with those marks on it, like the stories of Baleros—Phoebe, they might make us all migrate to the other side of the sea. I imagine that's what they're discussing right now."

The bottom dropped out of Phoebe's stomach.

"No," she whispered.

Lose her best friends? Tristan?

Mina shook her head miserably. "I wanted to tell you. I know Tristan did, too. He'd never hurt you on purpose; you don't know how much he risked to help you in the first place. In our culture, you simply don't make decisions without the elders. And you certainly don't risk war with the humans by helping one of their prisoners escape. Bentwood had some of our people locked up in a pen under his fortress; Tristan risked the deaths of those merfolk by aiding you."

"We've got to convince the elders the wraith is real, and the beast might be rising. They have to fight!" The answer was clear to Phoebe.

Mina gave a soft laugh, one devoid of humor.

Then Tristan's voice cut through the cave.

CHAPTER TWELVE

"The elders would never be that reasonable." Tristan's voice was rough. Phoebe couldn't see him yet, but just the sound of him sent adrenaline sparking through her. His tail fin moved so slowly that he simply drifted into view, rather than swam.

"Why didn't you tell me?" Phoebe cried, swimming over to her friend. He had no glow left shimmering from his skin at all. She couldn't stay angry, not at him.

"I made a sacred promise to your sister. It was the only way she'd permit us to keep seeing you. I'm sorry to have kept our troubles from you, Phoebe. More than you know." He sagged to the cave floor.

Mina cried in dismay, grasping her brother by the shoulders. "What did they do?"

"They asked many questions in their fury and made ugly accusations. Especially Elder Seamus." He paused and raised an eyebrow. "He used to wrestle sharks, you know."

"I feel sorry for the sharks. Well, what do we do now?" Phoebe asked.

"The elders want to speak to you, but they won't do it in the village. They worry that a land walker isn't to be trusted and want to question you in a way that they will know you're telling the truth." He rubbed the back of his neck and gave a deep sigh.

They thought she was lying? Phoebe's heart sank like a battered ship. She'd told them everything she knew, hadn't she? Didn't spare a single detail. Telling them should have been enough to goad them into action. She'd even showed them the huge handprint on her leg. And they still weren't doing anything. She'd done her best and failed.

But what if the water wraith came at Tristan and Mina? Or someone from their family? She'd have to keep trying to convince them, even if they looked at her like she was a sea slug. And if she proved she was right, maybe then they'd stop being furious at Tristan for bringing her.

Then a thought occurred to her. "Don't they believe Liam? He's a merfolk."

"Unfortunately, Liam isn't known for his truth-telling. His father drank jellyfish liquor too often, wandering off and telling crazy stories. Though it's unfair, they think of the boy as untrustworthy too."

Mina scowled. "Liam would never lie about something like this. He's a good pup. He tells tales just like all seawees do at times, but it's obvious when he's doing it. He was petrified today."

Phoebe agreed. The shrill terror in his voice had rung with sincerity.

"They don't want to believe wraiths are real at all, Phoebe, much less that you've seen one. They'll cling to any possibility that allows them to stay buried in the sand like a sea frog, even if it means calling you and Liam liars. If we must fight against these wraiths, our whole culture would be forced to change. If Baleros *has* risen, which even I find hard to believe, don't expect the merfolk to react well," he warned.

She could understand that. The merfolk's response was much like the way she usually reacted, compared to Nell or Sierra. Phoebe had never wanted to fight. Until now.

"Okay, what do the elders want me to do to prove myself?" she replied.

"They wish to take you to an old place," he answered. His gaze swept over to Mina as he said, "We're going to the ancient city. To Lyr."

Mina gasped, hand rising to her throat.

"I don't understand. Why does Mina look like that?" Phoebe said

They didn't respond for a long moment. "Tristan? Mina? Talk to me!"

Tristan explained. "Lyr is a mystical place for our people, the original home of the merfolk, in the deepest part of the twilight realm. Our time there was one of prosperity for us, until Baleros and his wraiths supposedly destroyed our civilization. With little magic left, our people moved to the shallows and soon became slaves to humans."

Phoebe looked out of the cave opening. Tristan and Mina joined her, the three of them looking out at the merfolk's village. The crowd below seethed, screeching and hollering. The elders swam off, waving at them imperiously to follow. Time to go.

Phoebe turned quickly to Tristan. "But what about Baleros? What happened to him?"

"No one knows. The beast faded into myth, though it has remained forbidden for most merfolk to return to the ancient city, except on two occasions."

"And what are those?" Phoebe asked.

"One is the coming-of-age ceremony when we receive our tattoos from the sea and dedicate ourselves to its service. They take us to the sacred temple, the same one where you will go."

The elders were already distant specks. Mina tugged on Phoebe's hand. They had to leave, but she had to know. "And the second time?"

"After our death. Last rites are performed at the sacred temple, where our bodies are returned to the sea."

"So neither of you have ever seen this place," Phoebe murmured.

Mina said, "We've got to go. Come on!"

Tristan ignored her. He gazed steadily at Phoebe as if they were alone. "No, we've never been there, but our mother is the historian for our people. We've grown up with maps and stories that most merfolk don't. No human has *ever* been there. Mina and I are only permitted because we brought you here. We're to translate the ceremony for you."

"Okaaay." He wouldn't meet her eyes. *Hmm.* "And why would they let you do that? And don't try to lie. I can tell you're hiding something."

"It's nothing."

Mina said, "Tell us, Tristan. Quickly—we need to know what we're up against."

"Fine. I negotiated with the elders. They wanted to take Phoebe alone to the temple. I insisted we would join her, or there would be no interview. I know she will be returned to shore if we are there. I fear not all the elders would be so careful." His expression hardened.

Phoebe's mouth dropped.

Mina nodded in agreement. "Good for you, brother," she said. "The elders couldn't have been happy, but I'm proud of you."

"Well. It had to be done." He coughed a bit and brought the conversation back to the ceremony. "At any rate, the rituals truly are still in the old tongue. The elders cannot make the magic work when they change the words to the invocations."

"But why are they taking me there? I'm not mer-anything. Can we do something else? I mean, I'd love to see the ancient city, but not if it puts you two at risk."

Mina rolled her eyes in exasperation. "The only danger we'll be in is if we make the elders wait for us any longer!"

"Since when do you worry about what the elders say?" Tristan asked.

"Since you took the fall for me just now. They would have done worse to me, and don't think I don't know it. I'm drowning in guilt. Help a maid out, and let's go, okay?"

Tristan gave his sister a swift hug then turned to Phoebe, who was wringing her hands. "We'll be fine. The elders use the remaining magic of the temple for key rituals, but they realized long ago that the power of the temple could also be used to force someone to tell the truth. They don't even understand how it works or why."

He laughed, but it was a bitter one.

Mina added, "It was made with old magic, and they won't use it on children because they're not sure what it would do to them. Liam can't go."

Then the choice had to be Phoebe. So be it.

Tristan said, "It's farther than I'd like you to go. Your sister will be most displeased."

Phoebe snorted. That was the biggest understatement of the year.

"If you don't wish to go, I'll take you home right now."

"And what would happen to you?" Phoebe whispered.

"Nothing that would pose a true problem."

Mina's face suggested otherwise. Phoebe was sure he was lying, to keep her from feeling responsible. She understood better now why he was so cautious about breaking the rules. Yet he was offering to do just that, for her.

"No, we'd better just get this done. Sierra probably already knows I'm missing. At least if I help you, it'll help make up for the fact that I probably won't be able to leave the house for ages after this," she said, voice glum.

Mina and Tristan both reached for her hands.

"I fear that might be the least of our worries," Tristan muttered.

Phoebe wondered exactly what terrible things had occurred down beneath the peaceful-looking waves that always soothed and charmed her. She promised herself to find out as soon as possible.

Then they were off, with Phoebe between the twins, speeding faster than a porpoise, leaving her questions behind. All she could think was how glorious the water felt. It glided like silk along her skin. With the magic of the merfolk, her skin didn't wrinkle like raisins, as it did when she played in the surf too long on land. Her legs didn't have to kick to keep up, not with two young merfolk pulling her along between them. Her hair streamed out like a banner behind her.

The water was still and quiet, the animal life sparse. The difference between here and the busy life of the shallows was obvious even to a land walker, but the ocean around them was not empty even now. Phoebe's keen eyes spied crabs, lobsters, even tiny creepy crawlies for which she had no name, all zipping along. A few big-eyed fish swam lazily, mouths agape as if waiting for their prey to swim inside.

The three friends dodged through lace vines of seaweed. The plants looked all the more surreal for appearing suddenly in the merfolk's light before melting back into darkness as they passed. Iridescent jellyfish cast strange shadows as they floated like cloud puffs.

Phoebe's heart thudded. She, Phoebe Quinn, would be the first human to ever see the merfolk's sacred ancient temple and original city. The joy of sharing such an experience with her mer-friends clashed against a heavy dread of the upcoming experience, surrounded by many who loathed her.

Behemoths of some kind swam far above, like dark ships sailing through the clear waters. Here and there, sparkling lights glittered through the forests of kelp and tangled vines.

Tristan and Mina had no eyes for such wonder. Their lips were pinched, their expressions tense. Phoebe's excitement dimmed as their skin did when they approached a circle of glowing merfolk, the same elders from before. Behind them lay an underwater city in ruins, gloriously spread out like the cloak of an ancient queen.

Dome-shaped roofs, pyramids, obelisks, and columns dotted the landscape, along with moss-covered statues of majestic-looking merfolk bearing scepters, still overlooking the city they once guarded. Small sandstone cottages with clever rooftop entrances lined the curving pathways. Sparkling glass roofs arched above buildings that Tristan identified as centers of government and grand theatres.

"They created the glass in the depths, using a special sand in the incredible heat of the thermal vents. We've lost that skill as well," he said with a sigh.

From their position, it was easy to see that the city spread out like a spiral, with a tall, arched building made of delicate coral in the middle. Phoebe had imagined a small village, maybe something similar to their mer-village tucked along the cliff. The city of Lyr was at least as large as Port Ostara, but only wild plants and fish lived here now.

Such a sad loss, Phoebe thought. She'd had no idea that mer-society ever reached this level of splendor and wealth. Why were they determined not to fight for themselves? Didn't they want to live like this again one day?

The elders floated above the center of the city, faces all set in identical frowns. Once the trio came within reach, the elders swam down toward the tall center building.

"That's the sacred temple," whispered Mina into Phoebe's ear.

Something about the architecture invoked awe and respect. The temple sat on a small rise overlooking all of Lyr. Delicate coral columns gleamed in the low light, yellow seaweed winding up their lengths. This building had no walls or true ceiling. The columns were the gateway to the interior, where a circular marble platform waited in the center of the structure. Four stone arches ran from the columns to unite above the dais, topped by a white, glittering crystal. Such a structure would have been impossible on land but was a perfect fit for this magical underwater city.

The seven elders waited together by the temple, Elder Seamus still visibly seething.

An old mermaid with wrinkles surrounding her eyes and mouth approached them. Her arms were decorated in intricate tattoos of sea fronds, curling gracefully around her muscles. She said something in the trilling and rasping sound of the merfolk language.

"The human must approach the dais alone. One of

you may stay near enough to speak our words to her," translated Mina.

Tristan immediately said, "I will go."

Looking disappointed but not surprised, Mina stayed back, still visible yet outside the columns of the temple. She gave a quick wink to Phoebe, timed so no one else would see it.

The elders entered first and formed a circle around the raised, brilliant white-rock dais. The interior was easily seen from outside the columns, but Phoebe suddenly didn't want to go in. The place was powerful; anyone could surely sense that. What if the sacred place of the merfolk reacted badly to a human trespassing? Certainly the elders didn't like her. Maybe the ancient magic here wouldn't either.

She was about to find out.

CHAPTER THIRTEEN

*P*hoebe felt clumsy, never more aware of the inefficiency of her human legs slicing through the water. Mina's tail fin was a golden bronze that Phoebe always admired. Tristan's was a deep green. Phoebe would have taken any sort of tail fin at this moment. Leaving Tristan's side, she swam forward, working hard to stroke her arms just the way he'd taught her.

As she approached the dais, she mentally rehearsed her story. *Keep it simple. Just tell the truth.* She had to be convincing.

She floated into the center of the circle of elders, toes just touching the raised white rock. The sun might be directly overhead by now, but they were too deep to even make out the shape of the disk in the sky. Only a low glow from above showed its existence. A heavy pressure beat at her skin. She furrowed her brow. What was that?

The pressure along her body grew heavier. For a moment, blue scales appeared on her feet and ankles, startling her. She blinked and then was staring down at her regular legs, her plain pale feet. She shook her head at her own foolishness. Her wild imagination wouldn't help her here.

The merfolk elders looked toward the crystal at the center of the temple, all speaking the same words in their ancient language, words that meant nothing to Phoebe. Then they directed their gazes at her.

The elders spoke in unison, a chord of shrieks and a low rumble that raised goosebumps along her skin. She knew what they said, somehow, though, more in feeling than in words, before Tristan drew nearer and spoke for them: "Tell us what you witnessed, nothing more, nothing less."

A silver light curled up like smoke from the stone below her feet, frightening her for a moment. The light rose, spinning and swirling, and reached into the crystal above her. She squinted until her eyes adjusted. Now she could see more of the ancient structure. Intricate carvings with organic shapes and geometric designs were inscribed along the columns. The clear crystal reflected the light from the stone dais back down to her, so she stood in a sheath of light, flowing silver around her.

Tristan's eyes were huge. Even from this distance, Mina's beautiful face was tight with what looked like fear. The elders murmured among themselves for a moment.

Tristan whispered, "They aren't sure what's happening. The color of the light should be blue, they are saying. It has always been blue."

Phoebe wondered what Tristan thought of all this, his first exposure to such potent magic, with his human friend in the middle of it all.

Then the elders subsided into silence and waited, drawing her attention back to the moment. The light was cool in color but warm to the touch. It danced along Phoebe's skin like a balmy breeze. The words came easily to her as she basked in the unexpected warmth.

"I was hiding from my sister's enemies, the men who used to enslave you. I swam into the ocean to escape them, but they kept waiting for me. I knew they wouldn't leave. Then they entered the water. I dove deep, hoping Tristan and Mina would find me." Her voice was monotone, as if she were under the influence of the elusive truth-telling elixir her father had always hoped, but failed, to create. She didn't mind the sensation, though. It took less effort this way.

The elders watched her with impassive expressions on their faces. She found she couldn't turn to look for

Tristan or Mina. Phoebe continued, "I was running out of air and began kicking to the surface, but as I did so, something grabbed my ankle. Hard."

Her breath caught at the memory. No, she couldn't panic. She wanted to tell this clearly. Needed to. The light pulsed through her, calming her, and she rushed to continue. "It was a big creature, twice as big as any of us. It had a long pointed tail, but it wasn't like you at all. The tail was more snake-like, black and smooth, ending in a single point like an eel instead of a fin. Its top half looked human, except…"

She couldn't think how to capture the cruel savagery of that face. She paused, struggling to find the right description, and the pressure increased. It slipped right inside her skin and pushed the words out.

"Its face was pale and beautiful, like marble. But its mouth was full of wicked teeth, and its eyes were shining red. It pulled me down, and I nearly drowned. I saw a vision—" Here, Phoebe paused in surprise because she had never really thought of what she saw as a vision. More of a hallucination. But the magic chose her words, so it must be the truth.

Her words began again, without her own volition. "While the wraith gripped my leg, I saw a vision of a dark shadow stirring, of immeasurable evil, and I knew, I just knew, the shadow was a dangerous force waking. Then a blue light flashed, and the creature must have let go. The next thing I remember is Tristan telling me to breathe."

The elders whispered to each other. Tristan quickly translated the chaotic jumble of voices.

"It must be," said one.

"Like the sea dragons, the water wraiths are returning from the deep... and that shadow, could it be the beast?"

Elder Seamus spoke in trade speech, impatiently bringing their heated comments to a sudden stop. "Nonsense. She is tricking our minds with magic. Can't you feel it? She's a liar, like all humans."

Elder Maher swam close to Phoebe, so close she could count the number of clamshells on his necklace. He had many, a sign of long years serving as elder. His eyes were still black from the invocation of the magic. She saw herself reflected in them, tiny and alone inside the column of light.

"But the light—" he began to argue, as if on her side, before he was cut off by Elder Seamus.

"The light is the wrong color. It's been manipulated by her and is obviously not forcing her to tell the truth."

"Maybe the light is silver because she's a human," another elder murmured, but the angry merman sliced his hand downward like an ax.

Tristan stirred beside Phoebe but remained silent, though his hands were in fists.

"No! Can't you see?" Elder Seamus snarled. "She is

trying to deceive us all. The temple light has never shone silver, not once in the years since our historians began keeping track. So, even the temple's light cannot force her to answer honestly, because she is using her own magic. I can feel it." He turned to her. "Phoebe Quinn, what magic are you using against us?"

Phoebe stared at him, mouth open. Was he crazy?

"Tell us. Clearly, you have some sort of magic that calls to us. I can feel your presence even now, suggesting that I trust you, like you, befriend you. *Charming* me. What is this? I trust no human, but I sense an urge to accept you even now, to be your friend! What evil is this?" His teeth snapped together.

Tristan stiffened, the last remains of color draining from his face. Bubbles furiously burst from his gills as he exhaled a great gust of breath, looking between the angry merman and Phoebe.

Phoebe shrank away from the elder. The warmth of the light couldn't protect her from this hatred. Tristan swam up to her and tried to block her from the merman's angry gaze, but she refused to hide anymore. She hadn't done anything wrong. Mina tried to join them, but was held back by a mermaid with striking white braids.

"I'm not doing anything!" Phoebe protested. "Yes, my sister's betrothed, a faun, did tell me I had some new kind of magic that smelled of the sea. He said it reminded him of my sister's powers in a way. Maybe you sense that, though I didn't believe him fully myself."

"Your sister, the fairy keeper?" asked Elder Maher.

Phoebe nodded. "The fairies are drawn to her, but she has a keeper mark. I don't. I've always just been plain Phoebe."

The black and silver-haired mermaid kept her distance, but said, "Trust us, young Phoebe. There's nothing plain about you. You may not be doing anything on purpose, but you are doing something, something we do not understand. That makes you a risk. If Elder Seamus is correct, you could enslave us with this magic, as I, too, am drawn to you in a way I have never felt drawn to a human before. If you attract even the most powerful of us, what would you do to our young ones? Now that I've met you, I can see why they were always abandoning their obligations to hear you sing. I'm sorry, but you must leave immediately. Do not return to our waters unless we send for you. We will discuss your story; however, we must admit that Elder Seamus could have a point. We have no way of trusting you, not as a human, not with the irregularity in the temple's light."

"You can't—" exploded Tristan, but the mermaid cut him off with a pointed look. She raised her hand in a sign that clearly meant for him to wait. Not a word was shared between them, but their unspoken argument filled the silence.

Never return to the quiet, serene beauty of the ocean? The thought was a kick to Phoebe's stomach, all the more painful for coming without preparation.

She'd only just returned to the sea. And now she'd have to leave it forever. She pressed a hand to her aching heart. "Why? But that creature! The shadow! I could help you—"

"Even if the wraith is real—and maybe it is—a mere human will be no help against a water wraith or anything else, I am afraid. You would only get in the way," murmured Elder Maher.

Elder Seamus added with a sneer, "But you are not telling the truth. Humans only take and take. You perhaps have even charmed the mind of poor Liam, making him believe he witnessed a wraith. The skeleton you found means nothing. Anything could have killed our brethren. And unless my eyes are very much mistaken, you have a mer-tear, which is forbidden to give to a human. Who did you steal it from? What is your purpose? Need we any more evidence that you come only to rob from us?"

"I didn't steal it!" she shouted. The elders gasped at her temerity. She was past caring and had nothing left to lose anyway.

That merman might hate her, but she'd done nothing to deserve this kind of suspicion. She jerked her chin high and wrapped her hand around the pearl.

"Then who gave it to you?"

There was no answer for that. They wouldn't like

that Tristan had left presents for her, but she truly didn't know where the pearl had come from.

And she couldn't convince someone full of anger. She knew that from watching her sister speak to others about saving the fairies.

"Someone left the pearl for me, but I don't know who. I didn't ask for it. I thought it was a sign that I should come to you."

"It wasn't. That necklace was a mistake on someone's part, but we will deal with that individual later. Once you return to land, the pearl will be empty of its magic. Tristan will send you home but will not accompany you. Never return, young human. We are finally free of slavery from humans, despite their attempts to overtake us once again. We won't fall for another kind of servitude, especially some kind of emotional trickery."

Phoebe was speechless. No matter what Micah had said, she knew she didn't have the kind of power that this merman accused her of. Unfortunately, they also weren't listening to her.

The angry elder continued, "And neither of these two young merfolk will come to you ever again. You've clearly already wrapped them around your finger. You are too dangerous."

Sobs pushed at Phoebe's throat. *No.* Surely the elder was exaggerating. She turned to find Tristan's face stricken with horror. Mina looked stunned.

How could she be dangerous to her friends? Was she

somehow magically forcing them to care for her? Phoebe groaned, covering her eyes with her hands. The water went dark as the elders swam away. She floated above the rock, her feet barely grazing its surface, unable to move. But not from magic.

From grief.

CHAPTER FOURTEEN

Tristan tugged Phoebe's hand and whispered, "Come, we must go."

He darted into the waters. The gorgeous surroundings could not distract her this time. She supposed she should drink them in, as this might be her last time to ever see the underwater world, but she was too miserable. Mina swam beside them. No one spoke as the city dwindled behind them.

"I can't stand it," Mina burst out. She grabbed Phoebe in a tight embrace.

"You're like the sister I never had," the mermaid whispered.

Tears finally stung Phoebe's eyes then mingled with the seawater. Tristan kept swimming for a moment before he noticed the two girls had stopped. He turned and sped toward them.

"I'll miss you," Phoebe told her, pulling back far enough to look into Mina's dark eyes. "Take care of yourself, okay? And… take care of your brother for me."

Mina's face crumpled.

"He's never going to get over this," she whispered in Phoebe's ear, making her blush.

She didn't know what to say, so she was relieved when Tristan reached them. "Mina, she's got to leave. You need to let go of her."

"You're going to let her go to shore by herself, then? Knowing that a wraith is in the water somewhere? Or something worse?"

"You think so little of me, sister?"

Mina's smile curved into a smirk. "Quite the opposite, brother of mine. But the elders will be looking for us to make sure we've obeyed."

"And I'm sure you can assure them that we have and that I'm off sulking somewhere."

Mina's laugh chimed for a moment before her face grew somber again. "You impress me, twin. There's hope for you yet, no matter what the elders do. I'll cover for you. Look out for Phoebe. The ocean's a dangerous place for a human."

"It's dangerous for anyone, it looks like," Phoebe pointed out. "So just watch yourself, okay?"

The mermaid gave Phoebe one final hug and darted off toward the village without looking back. Phoebe raised one hand in goodbye anyway.

"Come," Tristan muttered. "It's time."

They swam a few furlongs before Phoebe's frustration ate too far into her patience. "Tristan, you've got to believe I'm telling the truth. What I saw is real. You can't ignore the danger, can you?"

"Shh. Just wait." He gripped her hand and pulled her into a thick tangle of seaweed.

He reached an empty hole in the weeds and spun to face her, hands wide, imploring. "I know you saw it. But I don't know what to do! They're just making excuses. They'd rather not risk anything or change our ways, even if it means our death!"

He cursed again in the trilling language of the merfolk. "Let me think. If I can find the lair where this thing lives, maybe I can be a witness. They can't use the temple's magic on Liam because he's too young, but I'm no longer a seawee. I'm of age, just as you are. They can test me using the magic they used on you. It should work, and they would have no more excuses. In the natural order of things, I would be traveling to the temple very soon to commit myself to serving the sea as an adult merfolk anyway."

"Would they really believe you?"

"I don't see how they could deny my testimony if I were questioned within the blue light. You are human. I am merfolk."

The stark summary pinched her heart for a minute, but she shook off the reminder of their basic incompatibility. "Okay. So you need to see this wraith with your own eyes so you can testify. But, Tristan, the ocean is huge!"

He nodded, leaning forward, his eyes shining with hope. "True. But my mother told us Baleros lived in the abyss of the midnight realm, which begins on the other side of the ancient city. I imagine this wraith could be somewhere around there, maybe near the old city itself. Maybe it would be drawn to the old power there, especially after the display of magic from the ritual today."

"That sounds risky. How will you know if the wraith is really there?"

"I have no idea." He rubbed his brow.

Phoebe chewed her lip for a moment, studying him. The elders' insistence that she drew merfolk to her was plainly ludicrous and yet... she'd feel better if she heard him deny it himself. It felt like poor timing to ask now, but there was no easy time to ask it and at least they were alone. "Tristan... can you sense this magical draw the elders spoke of? Does something about me, um, compel you to be my friend?"

She didn't really believe the ugly accusation of Elder Seamus, but she had to check.

Tristan sighed. His mouth twisted before he said, "It's true that I have always felt drawn to you, Phoebe, but not in any dangerous way. They're old fools, so afraid of the future that they refuse to see what's staring them in the face."

Phoebe raised her hand. "Wait. You said... you *do* feel something from me? And always have?"

No. *No.* Was Tristan only her friend because she had somehow *forced* him to be? The thought left ashes in her mouth. All those times of laughter and fun shared with her mer-friends twisted into something entirely different. Something unnatural. Something terrible.

He grabbed her hands. "Phoebe, listen to me. The day your sister rescued you, do you remember? You called to me, to help you. I didn't know it was you, but I knew I had to get back to where I left the fairy keeper. It was you, though. I've thought about it many times but knew you had no inkling of the situation. It doesn't matter. It's not why I... it's not why we're friends."

When she said nothing, he rushed on, "Please understand. After our first meeting, I had to meet with you to see if you were okay. I couldn't get you out of mind, the way you looked... so wounded, standing in the surf, watching me with eyes as deep as the sea itself. And after that, well, I simply enjoyed your company. It was nothing shameful or bad. You've done nothing wrong."

"Has it been just you that feels this thing? Does Mina? The elders complained about it, but I don't feel like I'm doing anything, and you never said anything about it!"

He had the grace to look ashamed. "I didn't know others would feel it. I assumed it was my own—" he flushed, an amazing shade of rose flooding his pale skin—"Mina and I never even discussed it. Phoebe, I have cared for you for many moons now. Surely you know this?"

Her heart was breaking. The elders were right. Tristan was finally trying to tell her what she'd dreamed about hearing all year, but it turned out she had tricked him somehow. He was saying she hadn't, but how could they know for sure? Irony. She had magic but couldn't use it to get what she wanted. What she *had* wanted was for him to desire to be with her. But now, she wanted him to feel that way without magic forcing him. And maybe that was impossible.

It wasn't like they had a future anyway. He would always live in the sea, and she was nothing but a temporary visitor here, forbidden to return.

She trembled. "It's probably better that I have to go, then. I wouldn't want to spellbind anyone into being my friend."

"Nonsense, I'm stronger than that. What do you take me for, some impressionable guppy? And your magic hasn't always been this noticeable—not since yesterday. Not even you could make me fall… make me care for you if you weren't so…"

He tripped over his own words, bringing a sad smile to her face. So maybe he did care as she did. But things

140

had changed. "Tristan, can you honestly say it doesn't bother you, not even the tiniest bit? That what you feel might be manipulated by my magic? Even a little? That our friendship might be based on a compulsion? Be truthful."

His eyes flashed. "I'm always truthful."

"Not always," she reminded him.

"Withholding information is not the same as lying." He jutted his chin forward, reminding her of when they first met and argued over which was the most magical creature in Aluvia. She said fairies; he said merfolk. It hadn't taken Phoebe long to be convinced. He only locked his jaw like that when he was being particularly stubborn.

"Fine. But don't hold back now. Doesn't it make you wonder, even just a tiny bit, if nothing we've felt is real, if it's all from the magic?"

She reached up and held his chin, making him meet her gaze. She knew her Tristan. He wouldn't lie outright. He started to speak twice but stopped, reconsidering his words. Her hands trembled, so she wrapped her arms around her waist to hide them.

He finally said, "The tiniest bit of me, perhaps, is the slightest bit concerned, maybe, but it is far overshadowed by the rest of me. I trust you, Phoebe. You'd never take my free will."

Phoebe couldn't think past the first part of his statement. He *did* care that her magic was forcing him to be near her. She wanted to curl into a ball. The pull between them, powerful from the beginning, now turned out to be a magical welcome mat to any merfolk who came by, though no one had ever made her feel as he did. As much as she wanted to tell him how much she cared for him, dreamed about him, maybe it would be easier for him to think she just wanted to be friends. Far easier to lose a friend than a sweetheart. She'd been banished, after all.

It was too much to consider. They stared at each other without saying a word until her chest burned, reminding her to breathe. The tension rose, creating a magnetic pull between them. She wanted to lean against him—but couldn't. Not now.

Time to focus on the main problem here. Their tangled relationship would have to wait.

She cleared her throat, and the moment passed.

She said, "I understand it's complicated, to be sure. But let me help you and your people, no matter what the elders say. Maybe this magic I have that lures merfolk will attract the wraith. Or maybe I can sense where it's hiding."

"Phoebe..."

"Please. Tristan. I need to help you." The last words were barely spoken, but they reverberated. The water between them seemed to thicken like honey, swirling between them and connecting them.

His green eyes darkened, not with magic, but with emotion. "If something happened to you—"

"It won't. You'll be with me. I trust you."

He looked over her head for a long moment. Indecision twisted his face, but then the conflicted expression fell away, as if he'd made some kind of choice.

"We can't let the elders see you."

Hope rose in Phoebe. "It'll be like one of our games. Hide and seek. We hide from the elders and seek the water wraith. Mina would love it."

"I don't want her involved. She gets into too much trouble as it is. Getting caught with you again would be a lot worse for her than me. Okay. You can stay with me, but I'll take you back to land as soon as we find the lair, agreed? You can't let the merfolk know you stayed at all."

"Agreed."

"I hope we don't regret this."

She knew she never would.

CHAPTER FIFTEEN

"*W*here do we start?" Phoebe asked.

"Somewhere with a lot of magic, I imagine. The wraith would need to feed on it, even with the merfolk it's been stealing energy from."

"Let me guess," Phoebe groaned. "The ancient temple of Lyr? Wouldn't we have seen something while we were there?" She really did not want to return there, to the strange light that took over her body like that.

"Well, actually, the Abyss is the place with the most magic of anywhere in the ocean. Some believe our magic actually flows from there, in the depths of the midnight realm, but it's forbidden for many reasons. It's full of hidden dangers, even lethal ones. I think the ancient city will be powerful enough to start with. It could easily feed the wraith. Our civilization crumbled because of such power in the wrong hands."

"Well, if we don't do something, it looks like your civilization is going to crumble again, but this time, there's not much left to collapse."

Tristan flinched, and Phoebe offered an apologetic shrug. For a moment there, she'd sounded almost like Sierra. Maybe Sierra spoke like that because she was stressed and worried, too.

"Let's go, then," Phoebe urged. "Your family will be looking for you soon, no matter how many excuses Mina comes up with."

It didn't take long to return to Lyr, even being as stealthy as they could be. Phoebe and Tristan swam above the city, scanning it carefully. The darkened stone temple sat hulking across the open patch in the seaweed. A maze of buildings spread out beyond it, until the ground dropped steeply, disappearing into darkness.

Just beyond the drop, a narrow cliff of white rock rose up from the black depths like a fisted claw, with a cave entrance visible on one jagged side. The cliff sat between the edge of the fallen metropolis and the black waters of the midnight realm, a strange tower marking the change in the basin floor. Phoebe hadn't noticed it during her last, admittedly chaotic and unexpected, visit to this location.

"Do you sense the magic around us?" Tristan asked. "It lies over the city like a blanket."

Phoebe frowned while concentrating. She felt…

something. A stirring, a tingling along her skin. "Maybe. But it's not very strong."

"There's plenty of magic here, trust me. Let's explore."

They dove down into the city, past abandoned homes that still held woven baskets and the shells of sponge beds, through open squares that must have once held busy markets. The silence crawled along her nerves and hurried Tristan's fin.

But they found nothing. No sign of any living creature the size of a wraith, hibernating or otherwise. Tiny sea snails and fish, yes. Evil water wraith, no.

They rose back over the city for another panoramic view.

"I was sure it would be here," Tristan murmured. "It's really the only place with sufficient magic to feed such a powerful creature. Except the Abyss."

Phoebe thought for a long moment, her eyes continuing to be drawn to the lone cliff ahead, followed by sheer blackness beyond. It was like the land simply stopped. "What's that cliff? And why can't we see anything past it?"

Tristan looked where Phoebe was pointing. "That's the Last Stand. It's the cliff where our people lost their last hold on the city and retreated. Beyond that line is the midnight realm, and within it lies the Abyss. Even along the divide, the waters are nearly impossible to see through, and the trenches hide deadly creatures."

"Does this Last Stand have great amounts of magic, too?"

He sighed. "Yes."

They looked at each other and then back to the cliff. Its edges were craggy and rough-hewn. Long scratches were visible along the side facing them, gouges that looked made by giant claws.

In silent agreement, they linked hands and swam lower, dodging between the buildings as they slowly wound their way to the city's far edge. They gazed up at the cliff's striking white-rocked face, reluctant to move out into the open so close to the pitch darkness.

"And what else lives in the midnight realm?" Phoebe's voice was a mere whisper. This plan had sounded better before they faced the unlit waters.

"Sea dragons. Water horses. Giant squids. Things of legends, really. I think it would be unwise to enter there, with just the two of us."

Phoebe was relieved to hear it. Being eaten by a giant squid would help no one. "Maybe if we stay here, we'll see the wraith leaving or returning."

They waited in silence on the edge of the city for what felt like the change of several tides, though surely not even half a day had passed. Tristan doused his light, and the water was dark enough to make her tired. Phoebe's eyelids grew heavy, and Tristan's muscles relaxed as they leaned against the outer wall of a half-collapsed tavern. No one made her feel as safe like he did. His warmth where they touched kept half her awareness occupied, so she startled when he clamped his hand onto her arm.

"There," he said, pointing ahead.

A wraith swam from the cave entrance, moving toward them. The waters were so dark even along this slice of twilight realm that the frightening creature appeared as a shadow at first and bloomed into full color slowly, like a painting in process: an arm appearing, followed by its head, and a tail not far behind. It was much larger than Phoebe remembered.

Then another wraith exited the cave and joined the first, just as large, just as hideous.

She sucked in a long breath. One had been bad enough, but *two*? Did the creatures see or sense them? Her pulse picked up. Should she be concerned that the wraith they were hunting had found its way to where she was, along with another? Who was hunting whom?

However much a legend these creatures were, there was no denying that something had provided enough magic to awaken them. They had been feeding off merfolk, but something else had to wake them in the first place. Phoebe gazed at the swimming beasts with horror. Perhaps with the rise of magic on land, because of Sierra's efforts, there was a correlating rise under the sea, feeding sleeping beasts such as these. And others. Her stomach roiled.

"Don't move," Tristan said.

The wraiths floated near the city, practically lounging along the edge with lazy flicks of their tails, skirting the line of the buildings as if seeking something. Tristan and Phoebe followed them, slinking from one hiding place to another.

Either of the wraiths could have been the exact creature that grabbed Phoebe earlier; they were identical.

When the creatures reached what looked to be an open courtyard with a tall obelisk in the middle, they sped up and entered the city. No glowing light shot forth from the ground or through the water when the creatures crossed the city line, but the wraiths hissed and hunched their shoulders, as if remembering a time when they could have been rebuffed from entering. Faint glimpses of sunlight filtered through the shadowy kelp and seaweed, like ghosts sliding among a haunted forest.

"Shouldn't those things burn up from being in the ancient city or something?" Phoebe whispered, feeling cold not from the water around her but from the glowing red eyes visible even at this distance.

"Whatever magical shields the ancients once created are long gone. The magic remains, spread throughout the water, but not useful to us. We've lost the skill of gathering it and guiding it."

She shuddered as she stared at the wraiths, now

rubbing their backs against the buildings as if marking their territory.

"Ugh," she whispered.

"They are still part of our ocean, too, Phoebe, though they must feed on magic, unlike our people. In some ways, I pity them."

Clearly, he was a peace-seeking, soft-hearted merfolk. No wonder this big impressive city eventually fell. Merfolk weren't interested in conquest, even with magic on their side against an evil foe. If those wraiths weren't evil, Phoebe didn't know what was.

One water wraith reached out a clawed hand and snagged an electric eel swimming by. The eel sparked in the water as it tried to fight back, but it failed. The wraith gulped it down in one smooth swallow like a child might slurp up a noodle.

"Wow." Phoebe had no words for her revulsion. "Guess not even lightning would kill these things, huh?"

"Not much slays them," Tristan said, grimacing. "If the tales are to be trusted, they must be pierced through the heart. They can even live without their heads for a while."

She shuddered again. The two water wraiths twined around and around each other like snakes—if snakes had claws and shark-like teeth. If the creatures spotted the two of them hiding in the seaweed, no doubt those claws and giant mouths would be the last thing she saw.

Then she felt something that made the two wraiths look as charming and nonthreatening as goldfish.

The water grew even darker, a deep shadow looming over the sea floor as something oozed around the mouth of the cave that hugged the side of the city. Whatever it was didn't leave the cave, but somehow its presence sank through the water anyway, filling the chasm between the tower and Lyr's edge, reaching bony fingers to where they hid. The wraiths did a sort of dance and zipped toward the shadow.

Dread sank into Phoebe like sand spilling into an hourglass, filling her stomach, choking her.

"I've seen that shadow before." It was the one from her vision. That darkness was far too familiar to be anything else. She held tightly to Tristan's hand as her head buzzed, fear making his voice in her ear sound furlongs away.

"Don't. Move," he whispered.

She couldn't have if she needed to.

Red light shimmered around the dark shadow inside the cave's entrance. The sullen hue shone even through the seaweed, casting a sickening shade of blood red on her skin. The shadow rippled, and a low rumble flowed from the cave.

The rumble was like an earthquake, every agony she ever felt. It lodged in her heart like a sword. And twisted. Her vision of the shadow hadn't prepared her for this.

Piercing pain overwhelmed Phoebe as the noise reverberated down her spine, filling her with her worst memories and fears. It was being beaten by Donovan and believing her sister had died. It was being left behind time and time again through misguided good intentions. It was losing Tristan to the evil gaping maw of the creature before her. It was being trapped here forever to die without her sister ever knowing what had happened.

Phoebe wondered why she was here, in this dangerous place. She couldn't quite remember. Clearly, nothing in this world was worth fighting for.

She began to sink to the sandy bottom, ready to die, but something stopped her. What was holding onto her? She glared up to see a young merman, still not quite an adult, bent over at the waist. His glorious green fin was curled up like a beaten dog's. But he still gripped her hand. She stared at their clasped hands, at the way their fingers wove together. Something clicked.

Tristan.

Her best friend. Her secret sweetheart.

She forced herself to look up again at the menacing shadow stretching along the ground before them. She couldn't quite see. Her vision flickered. She thought the two wraiths carried the huge and shadowy thing from the cave farther into the waters, leaving the cliff, fading into the distance of the deeper midnight realm as if they had slipped through a hole in a wall.

Tristan and Phoebe stayed frozen in place until the giant shadow with its escort eventually withdrew so far into the midnight realm that even its red light disappeared. The roar faded, leaving her mind able to function, though it still spun with terror.

The merfolk are up against that? Phoebe thought. *They'll die. We'll all die.* The music that always hummed softly in the back of her mind had gone silent. There was no music in the world that could fight the darkness that creature brought with it.

She searched Tristan's face, which was drawn with fear. His hand gripped hers so tightly that her fingertips were beginning to tingle. She wiggled her fingers slightly, and he startled, dropping her hand and murmuring, "Sorry."

"Was that the beast? Baleros?"

He hesitated. "I want to say no. Baleros is just a children's story, but so were water wraiths. Maybe that *was* the ancient beast. Whatever it was is far worse than the wraiths. The stories of Baleros sound similar, the way he manipulated emotions, the way he stole the will of the merfolk in the ancient city, before taking their magic."

He gulped.

"Did it make you remember the worst things in your life?" she whispered.

He pursed his lips. "And see terrible things that haven't happened yet. And won't."

"But it's gone now. Let's go tell what we saw. The sooner they question you in the temple, the sooner they can take action."

"We need to look in that cave and see if we can find any proof to take back with us."

"They won't believe you? You told me the temple light would prove you told the truth."

"Water wraiths are one thing. Baleros is beyond the pale. But I didn't really see anything that was for sure Baleros, and the light will force me to say so. We only know we saw *something* monstrous. If I claim something as outrageous as Baleros, I'd better be certain, and it'd be best to have proof," he replied with a determined expression.

Shock dropped her jaw. Even after experiencing the most fear either of them ever had, he was ready to keep going, for his people's safety. Tristan was the bravest person she knew.

On impulse she leaned forward and pressed a light kiss against his cheek. Just a soft brush of lips, as she had kissed her friend Corbin a hundred times, a quick hello or goodbye, a mark of friendship to a boy who was like a brother to her.

This kiss wasn't anything like that.

It was awkward.

Shocking.

Delicious.

Somehow all at once.

Heat flashed across her face as she pulled back. He looked stunned.

He covered his cheek with his hand. "What was that for?"

"For being you." The words came out before she could stop them.

Tristan took her hands, wrapping them gently in both of his, a furrow between his brows. Was he upset? Or moved? She couldn't tell.

He gazed at her for a long moment, an odd look on his face she couldn't place.

"Phoebe, I hope you know by now how dear you are to me," he began, with his voice soft and earnest.

Her breath caught. Hope and dismay chased each other round and round. She didn't think she could bear to hear him confess true feelings for her now, not when she had to leave so soon. They had no future, three times over: she was human, her strange powers might be manufacturing their feelings, and his elders hated her. She shouldn't have kissed him—although she'd cherish that small moment always. Her hands trembled inside his grasp.

He glanced down, paused, and then tightened his grip, steadying her shaking hands.

"Forgive me," he murmured. "This must be a terrible time for you. This isn't the time or place for such discussions, after such terror. I know how the panic sometimes attacks you even now. We'll do what we

155

need to do and go. Together," he said. He squeezed her hands.

She smothered a slightly hysterical laugh and let him draw the wrong conclusion about why her hands were shaking within his.

Besides, maybe she was fooling herself. He'd never actually said he cared for her as a future bondmate, had he? Only her wistful mind had supplied that unspoken feeling. Maybe he had been preparing to say he could never love her that way, not with her humanity. Or with this alluring magic confusing their relationship. Or maybe he just thought of her as a sister. Better to move on, at least for now. She had her pride. And her heart could only take so much trauma.

"I'm fine," she announced. And she would be. Eventually. "Let's go."

Tristan smiled, the tension around his eyes softening. Phoebe called up her favorite tune and let it run through her mind for a moment. Even if it was only inside her, music was a reminder that life was not only made up of danger and misery but was full of hope and joy, too. Facing the frightening cave seemed less impossible now.

"Can I tell you something?" Tristan whispered as they set off toward the cave.

"Of course."

"I'm glad you insisted on coming. I feel much braver when I'm with you."

Oh.

Warmth chased away a bit of the chill that had settled over her like a cloak.

She squeezed his hand. "Me, too."

Saying it out loud made her feel even braver. It was just as well. They'd need every last drop of courage they could find.

CHAPTER SIXTEEN

Inside the entrance to the cave, the moonglow of Tristan's skin returned, allowing them to examine the space without having to enter far. They wanted to be able to escape immediately if the terrifying presence returned. Their eyes quickly adjusted to the darkness, but the cave was deep, swirling with skinny, tall grasses and glowing mushroom-like things.

Blinking eyes gleamed from pockets along one wall, and the two of them avoided those areas. The back of the cave was half-shrouded in darkness, even with Tristan's skin at its brightest. She wanted to run her fingers along his arm, to see what would happen to the light, but she resisted. If ever there wasn't a time for such a thing, it was now.

Phoebe peered into the darkness of the cave, trying

to concentrate on their goal. She noticed a strange shape in the far corner.

"Uh, Tristan, what's that lump over there?" she asked, voice barely audible.

It didn't take getting much closer before they realized the lump was a merman. Or what was left of him. Phoebe couldn't quite stifle a cry at the sad sight of the skeletal husk floating in the water, as if he had been starved for many weeks before arriving here. The skull was completely bone, not a tuft of hair or skin left. However, tattoos of starfish linked with swirling lines were still visible on the shriveled skin of the arms and chest. This skeleton wasn't as bone-bare as the one that had washed up on the shore, but the similarity of the destruction was too close to be missed.

"I know that tattoo pattern. That's Liam's father, Aedan, who's been missing since the last full moon." Tristan's voice wavered.

"Did he look… so shriveled when you last saw him?" Phoebe whispered.

Tristan's eyes were huge, his hands shaking. "No. No, he didn't."

Phoebe swam over to the back of the body and gasped. "Look at this! He has the same marks! The handprint that looks like a scorch mark, the holes in the skull. That must mean—"

"The wraiths or the shadowed creature stole his life energy. Both were in here. That must be what's been taking our people," Tristan muttered. "All those missing merfolk! This thing must be stopped!"

"Tristan, if this thing destroyed the ancient merfolk, I think stopping him might be beyond you and me," she said, eyes still straining toward the cave opening, into the distance where the red light had gone.

"It sucked him dry. The one you found at the coast, too. We have to do something."

"Like what?" she asked, as gently as she could.

"I have no idea, not if my people insist on playing the fools." He smacked his hand against the side of the cave. His light faltered, and her heart skipped a beat. Complete darkness in this cave would be more than she could bear. She grabbed him by the shoulders.

"We'll figure it out," she said. "Now, come on."

She pulled him to the cave entrance, hurrying. If she had been above water, her skin would be clammy with terror and sweat, but here, all that betrayed her was a galloping heart.

They almost made it.

A water wraith blocked the opening and smiled a slow, razor-sharp smile. Phoebe jerked to a stop so quickly that Tristan slammed into her back, sending them both spinning toward the wraith.

Dark green and blue blurs zoomed by as Phoebe careened out of control. She kicked her legs to stop her movement but instead kicked the wraith, sending it flying backward just far enough for her to turn and swim away toward the city.

"Phoebe! Go!" Tristan yelled, but she couldn't catch a breath to reply.

Something grabbed Phoebe's waist, squeezing so hard that her back arched, and her mouth opened in a silent scream. Claws raked along her sides. All she could see was her own hair, red as blood, obscuring her vision until the creature growled and the pressure suddenly released. Tristan must have done something to it. Thank goodness she wasn't alone.

A hoarse shout ricocheted around her, sending a fresh rush of panic through her. She knew the shout came from Tristan, sensed it like a zap of lighting along her skin. The water wraith was hurting him.

Rage shouldered aside panic, and she swung her head around, trying to get a good look at the snake-like creature so she could scratch out its eyes.

"*Stop,*" she yelled, not even thinking about what she was doing. She just knew that monster had to stop hurting Tristan. Her arms shot out, hands spread wide.

Phoebe locked gazes with the water wraith. It didn't have Tristan in its hands, but he was nearby and shouting at her to flee. She couldn't leave him. She had to fight through her fear. *Concentrate, Phoebe!* The sound of waves filled her ears, as it had once before when she first believed she could have power.

"Go. Away," Phoebe told it grimly. If she could draw

merfolk to her on accident, she should be able to drive the water wraith away on purpose.

The wraith's red eyes blinked, as if dazed. It paused, just for a second, as if it had forgotten what it was supposed to be doing. *Yes!* For a moment, victory filled her, but then the creature shook its head and reached toward her face, slowly, like a sleepwalker. Phoebe swam back, and terror burst through her brief moment of certainty. She didn't want to die, not yet.

The claws grazed her cheek, and a bright blue flash shot through the water. The wraith screeched—a horrendous sound—and darted off into the darkness of the cave, its black, pointed tail whipping back and forth.

Phoebe sunk to the sea floor, gasping, bubbles billowing up from her mouth. Tristan reached her and ran his hands along her arms. They had to go before the other wraith or the dark shadow returned, but she couldn't quite move yet.

"Did it bite you? Are you hurt?" he kept asking, eyes seeking some sign of a wound while blood floated in the water from his own neck.

She shook her head. "No, I'm not hurt, but you are. What did it do to you?"

He leaned his head sideways to show the deep puncture wounds along the curve of his neck. "I think it wanted to rip my head off," he snarled.

Phoebe touched the skin near the wound. It felt warm to the touch. Unusually warm. He flinched.

They swam quickly up and into the city, but it was obvious Tristan needed to rest. He'd never make it home at this rate. Looking down, Phoebe recognized the ancient temple. Without consulting Tristan, she dragged him down and into its sheltering arms. She didn't want to return to the place of her interrogation, but if any place here could be safe for him, it would surely be their ancient temple.

She carried Tristan to the floor and leaned him against one of the columns. He could no longer sit up by himself. She held him tightly while he took in great gulps of water, struggling for breath.

Tristan looked rather green now, the skin around his wound growing grey.

"It hurts still?" she asked, chewing her bottom lip. "Could it be poisoned?"

"Feels that way," he wheezed and turned paler than the underbelly of a fish.

"How did you send the blue light?" Phoebe asked, urgency making her voice sharp. "It saved us from the wraith. Maybe it would cleanse you, too! Use your magic to bring the light again!"

His voice was barely audible. "But I didn't do it. The light came from you."

Phoebe stared at him with wild eyes. "That's not possible! What do you mean?"

But his eyes drifted shut, and he passed out.

"Tristan! Wake up!" she shouted, shaking his shoulders, but he didn't respond.

No, not him! She couldn't lose Tristan.

What could she do? If she *had* created the blue light, she had no idea how. She was alone at the bottom of the sea, in an ancient merfolk temple, desperate to save the person she cared for more than anyone other than her sister. If he felt compelled to be with her, it certainly was no less than she felt toward him. She knew that wasn't magic. It was just Tristan. It had always been Tristan.

She cradled him in her arms, bending over him, searching for any signs of waking. The barest flickering glimmer remained along his skin. She knew intuitively that if the light went out, he would be lost to her. More blood seeped into the water. They were running out of time.

He couldn't fade away. That was all there was to it.

She wracked her mind, thinking of what she could do, and all at once, it came to her. It was a long shot but better than sitting here while Tristan died in her arms.

Gathering her strength and thankful for the buoyancy of the sea, Phoebe carried Tristan to the dais she had floated above before in the center of the temple. As she curled up on the raised platform with him, she tried to remember the ancient words the elders had spoken, but her mind was empty. She had no words and certainly none in the merfolk language. But she had emotions, and she let them pour out. If they were speech, they'd say something like:

Ocean, whatever you are who creates this magic, whoever is listening, hear me now. Save this merman. Take my energy, take my life, if you must, but, please, give me this one gift.

She thought about how Sierra described reaching the magic of the earth and tried to envision the magic of the sea. The light had come from her. She chose to believe it. What did it mean? She took a deep breath, closed her eyes, and imagined a shimmering deep light encircling them, filling Tristan, covering them both with its web of power. The familiar sound of the surf filled her mind, wiping away her fear.

A steady glow beat at her eyes and when she opened them, she was encased in a pale column of light, as she had been before, but this time, it was blue. The graceful sapphire glow pressed upon them both with the same easy warmth the silver offered before. Without even the sacred words, the ancient spot bathed them both in healing, magical light.

This time, truth was not pulled from her. Instead, she sensed something deep within, some kind of life energy, being pulled out and sent to Tristan, the power twisting and spinning freely, as if someone were pulling a long rope from a basket, or unraveling a knitted blanket. Further and further out it spun, until she feared she might pass out. Tristan's skin grew brighter and brighter until all at once, a bright blue flash rippled through the water again.

Razor sharp pain sliced through her body, and she shrieked in agony. Shocked, she grabbed frantically at her legs, which seemed to be almost *melting* into each other. Her pants ripped at the seams, floating away on the currents. Her feet were growing longer, extending, her toes unfurling long like lilies, waving slightly in the water, then spreading wider and joining into a single unit, until all that was left of her feet was a hint of foot bone beneath a tail fin as elegant as any merfolk's. Scales climbed up her body like tiny cat paws pacing along her skin until they stopped above her chest, leaving her shoulders bare. The worn tank top gave way under the pressure, leaving her dressed in shiny deep blue scales that began at her underarms and overlapped all the way down her legs, which were now, undeniably... a tail fin. Was this what Nell's words to Phoebe had meant?

The ocean had claimed her.

She was, impossibly, a mermaid.

The light faded. Her eyes fluttered shut, and she saw no more.

She awoke in a strange mesh basket made of sea fronds. She thrashed about, uncertain how to get out of the woven strands that surrounded her, but Tristan pulled back the top and smiled down at her, saying, "Good morning, sleepy little clam in your shell."

Was she dreaming? Didn't he almost… Wasn't she…

As the memory roared over her, Phoebe struggled to sit up.

"Tristan! You're okay!"

"I'm fine, just fine! And I see you're feeling better," he said, as she pulled herself free from the strange cylinder. "A good long sleep always heals. But I think you will find yourself much changed."

That was putting it mildly. She gazed down at her body.

"What on Aluvia happened?" Phoebe shook her head, confused. She ran her hands down her sides. Blue scales were cool and slick against her palms. The change was real, all right.

Mermaid.

Shock held her paralyzed for a long moment, fingers pressing against the scales. They felt pliable but resistant to pressure. She felt along her neck and confirmed that her scales and her fin were matched by gills like any mermaid. She blinked, able to see through the water as if it were crystal clear, like never before.

She didn't know how to move, how to swim with a tail, but she couldn't tear her eyes away from the unbelievable sight of her own body, so tremendously changed. What did this mean? Would she be trapped beneath the waves forever? If she were on legs, her knees would have given out. As it was, she sank to the sandy bottom of the small cave they were in, uncertain how to even catch herself.

Sierra. *Sierra*! What if Phoebe could never return to her sister? She may be bossy, but Phoebe loved her. Tristan's next words interrupted Phoebe's spiraling panic as he pulled her up, hands strong against her back and arms.

"After the attack and, well, what happened with the shadow and your, uh, *change*, I decided we needed more help. Maybe the elders would know what had happened to you. I came back home, with you, to Morgance. This is Mina's room." The words were stated simply, but she knew from his tone there was a lot more he wasn't saying. He guided her to a large sea sponge that looked much like a couch. She slid onto it with a bumbling thump but was too numb to care.

"I thought I wasn't permitted here."

"Well, obviously things have changed," a new voice rang through the little cave. A tall, elegant mermaid floated into the room, swishing her tail and moving with precision. Her eyes trailed up and down Phoebe's rumpled hair, even now swirling across her face. The regal mermaid sighed.

The black and white hair was familiar. This was an elder, one who had been at the temple when Phoebe was banished. This time she was near enough for Phoebe to see the detailed fish spears tattooed along her arms and neck. Unusual and intimidating. Her tail was a deep gold.

"Yes, Phoebe Quinn, I remember you well. I know who you are, what you are, and why you are here. As much as I hate to admit it, we need you. You witnessed the dark shadow from our past, and you somehow saved Tristan through your gifts. You used magic in a way no merfolk has done since the golden era of our people. Two hundred years ago! I believe you hold answers we seek, young human. No matter that you are shaped as a mermaid for the moment."

"For the moment?" Confusion battered at Phoebe's brain.

"There is no guarantee that you will remain a merfolk, my dear. That necklace of yours has been glowing nonstop since Tristan brought you here. The other elders think it is the reason you have been able to transform."

Phoebe caught her breath. Maybe she'd get to see her sister again after all! A second thought came right on the heels of her relief: an important merfolk leader admitted they needed her. Finally!

Of course, she had no idea what being a mermaid might mean, especially if it *was* permanent.

Then an even more exciting thought struck her. Maybe her magical hold over the merfolk wouldn't work if she were one of them. If Tristan had feelings for her, they'd be his own. She knew Tristan had always cared for her, but maybe, in *this* form, she could be something more to him. A human was clearly not a possible partner, but now? Thinking of the way his gaze often lingered on her, she blushed. Hope lifted her battered spirits.

"Thank you, but who are you? I remember you're an elder, but I'm afraid I don't know how to address you." Tristan used to call Phoebe *milady* when they first met. Maybe that was a word she should use with the elder?

"Oh, Tristan hasn't told you? I'm Elder Odessa. Yes, I'm one of the seven elders of the merfolk, married to one of the others. My family has led the merfolk in one way or the other since our earliest records."

Gulp. "Nice to meet you. Milady." *Definitely add the 'milady.'*

The mermaid smiled a chilly smile. "I'm also Tristan and Mina's mother."

Gulp indeed.

CHAPTER SEVENTEEN

*T*he three of them moved to Tristan's larger room, and he helped Phoebe onto another of the reclining sea sponge couches favored by the merfolk. It was much easier to stay on the ground under the water now than it had been as a human, which explained how gracefully all of the merfolk moved around near the ocean floor. A mysterious heavy weight balanced in her middle, keeping her from rising up accidentally, but she didn't understand how to use it to help her move properly. Phoebe flushed at her clumsy swimming; she was a better swimmer with legs than with a tail fin! But Tristan didn't seem to mind.

Mina arrived, carrying dinner in nets. Or lunch. Phoebe had lost track of time.

"The blue suits you," Mina said, for once without a flippant tone to her voice. Her eyes were sparkling as she whispered to Phoebe, "Maybe we can really be sisters now!"

A thrill coursed through Phoebe at the thought, overwhelmed only by the pain at the thought of losing Sierra in exchange.

Phoebe desperately wanted to know if she still had the magic the elders feared but was too afraid to ask. She didn't feel any different inside, though there was no denying she was a far cry from Ordinary Phoebe now.

Her stomach gurgled. Mina giggled, and even Odessa's lips gave a twitch.

"Eat, Phoebe Quinn. The magic that transformed you has also depleted you. You have slept long, but you need nourishment. Afterward, we must speak about the events of yesterday. It will be unpleasant."

That sounded ominous, but Phoebe was too ravenous to care. They ate oysters and seaweed salad. Phoebe found the raw food disgusting to look at, but it tasted divine, and her starving body acted as if it had decided to consume the entire contents of the ocean floor. She slurped another oyster off its shell and enjoyed the briny flavor.

As she ate, it dawned on her that Tristan and Mina were something like heirs-to-the-throne among their people, as close to royalty as the merfolk had. It was shocking to consider. When would they think it was important enough to mention that their parents were key leaders among the merfolk? That his mother and father were among those who said Phoebe had to go away? Would the lies ever end?

"Now that you have taken strength from our meal, tell me what you saw. Tristan has told us his version of what happened, while you slept deeply and long. He consented to be tested at the ancient temple, and his story remained the same even under the influence of the temple's blue light. His testimony in conjunction with your own magical transformation has convinced us. Our elders, save one, are in agreement that his report must be true. You must tell me your version, though. You surely have more to add," Odessa said.

With an uncertain glance at Tristan, who nodded at her, Phoebe took a deep breath and began her story. She left out nothing, telling of the wraiths, the red light and the shadowy form, the sense of dying, how Tristan's hand reminded her of who she was. The fight, the water wraith's attack, the plea she made. When she finished, she was trembling, and Odessa was frowning.

"This is serious business, young one. Beyond the amazing miracle of becoming a mermaid, if that is indeed what has happened, you witnessed Baleros stirring and felt his power. He is as powerful as I feared. Our people must prepare immediately. The wraiths which are known to be his servants, the glowing red light, the despair that overcame you, the half-consumed body of Aedan… these all align with the old texts about our ancient foe.

"This is dire news indeed. But even with this proof and agreement that our enemy is indeed rising, we must proceed very carefully."

"Milady?" Phoebe asked, uncertain what she meant.

Tristan spoke, voice low, "The elders do not like or trust you, Phoebe, as they made plain. Even though they must now reluctantly accept that our ancient enemy is rising, they still do not wish you to be here, not even Elder Maher. They fear your magic and believe you have charmed me. That you could charm all of us to your will."

"Charmed?"

"I suggested the word 'mer-charmer,'" Odessa pronounced with a wave of her hand toward Phoebe.

"I don't understand. What's a mer-charmer?"

Odessa stared at her with a raised eyebrow. "You, my dear."

Phoebe's confusion must have been plain because Tristan added, "Like a fairy keeper but different."

She clenched her fists, sealing her lips against a groan. "So you're... compelled to be around me right now? Even though I'm the same as you now? Mina? I'm... controlling you?" she asked the one she trusted most to be honest in this situation. *Please say no, please say no, please say no.*

"Whale manure," Mina said, moving to Phoebe and laying one arm around her. "You couldn't order around a minnow."

"They're grasping at straws, Phoebe. Pay them no mind," Tristan added, but his eyes didn't quite meet hers.

Neither one had answered the question, she noted.

Odessa sneered. "Denial serves only our enemy. Once I saw you, even before your change, I understood why my children were always sneaking away to be with you, a mere human. It's a strong pull. And Tristan has always been a bit impatient and impulsive with his emotions, haven't you, dear?"

She patted his cheek, chuckling a bit at the frown he sent her way before continuing. Impatient and impulsive really weren't words Phoebe would use to describe Tristan, but they suited Mina just fine. Phoebe cut her eyes over to her friend, who rolled her eyes in return. Phoebe steadied herself with her friend's so very normal reaction. Maybe Odessa and the elders were overstating the situation. Maybe her relationship with Tristan wasn't truly influenced by this magic, despite what the elders believed.

Their mother continued, "But now? In the form of a mermaid? You're even more powerful."

Phoebe's heart fell right through the sandy floor at the words. *More* powerful?

"A mer-charmer like you has never even been imagined. Elder Seamus was right that you were using magic, but I believe it's not on purpose. You can't help yourself. Yes, indeed, a mer-charmer would be hard to resist, even without the pretty red hair and big brown eyes. And now a tail fin, too." Her fierce smile brought to mind a cracking whip.

Phoebe actually flinched. No magical power seemed to connect Phoebe to this stern mermaid; that was for sure.

A mer-charmer? She rolled the word around in her mind. Her sister's calling as fairy keeper meant she served her fairies, helped them. Couldn't a mer-charmer maybe be someone good, too? A caretaker? A protector? All she ever wanted was to help! "Milady, please believe me, I didn't realize I was… am… doing anything. I don't know what I did with the blue light, why I changed like this, how I healed Tristan, and I don't know why I have some sort of… appeal… to some of your people."

So awkward. She couldn't even meet Tristan's eyes. Mina snickered. Phoebe loved her forever for that breath of lightheartedness. A solid thunk came from the foot of the reclining couch as Tristan thumped his sister with his tail. Phoebe didn't even look up. Best to just stare at her hands. A hot blush burned her cheeks.

Odessa toyed with her clamshell necklace. "You do seem to appeal to some of my favorite people the most. Perhaps the bond builds stronger with more time spent together."

Phoebe glanced up in time to see Odessa turn her powerful gaze to Tristan, who flushed a brilliant red and almost choked on an oyster. The mermaid elder resumed her intense focus on Phoebe.

"I don't like you, Phoebe. I still believe that you are a threat to our free wills, but you could unlock the secrets our people need to recover to keep our peaceful claim to this part of the ocean. As a historian, I am well aware that history tends to repeat itself, and unfortunately, our history is full of tragedy. That tragedy has continued already. The seawee Liam is missing. I believe he has been taken by the creatures you saw."

Mina gave a cry of dismay, and Tristan bit off a curse as his mother pinned him with a stern glare.

She continued, "The danger has grown past an acceptable level, far past it, but I have no wish to move. My studies show me it's a fruitless search—predators are everywhere. Baleros, if he successfully returns in full, will seek us out anywhere we go, as the ocean is all connected. He won't fade again if he can help it. I have studied the ancient shell carvings up through the golden era. Baleros nearly destroyed us when we had full use of our magic. We need to learn to use magic again, as you can, or we will surely perish. So we'll cooperate, Phoebe Quinn. I'll make sure all the Elders will, even if they must be dragged into the new era flailing their fins."

"What makes you think I can help?" Phoebe asked.

"Though I dwell beneath, I am not without information. Magical creatures on land have been swimming in a surplus of their earth magic since the fairies returned. They have grown strong, while we are still weak. Why has *our* magic not returned? How can we reach it once again? I believe you are the answer. You somehow have accessed the magic that has grown strong in the ocean over the years. We will learn from you."

"But I don't even know how to use this body properly."

Odessa's eyes slid to Tristan, and she tsked. "You'd better tell her everything else she needs to know, son. Our home depends on it. This isn't the time for being shy. Teach her how to be a mermaid."

"You know more than I—" he began.

"You know more than enough. While I feel her draw, I do not share the same bond with her you do. You are the best choice for this job. If you teach her to use the little powers we still have, perhaps the rest will come naturally to her. And then we will study alongside her and try to duplicate it. Surely if a mermaid who is really a human can do such miraculous things, we as true merfolk can all learn to do so. The magic is there. We just have to reach it. But Tristan, best be on your guard. Who knows how strong her charms may grow?"

With those words, her smile disappeared, and the bit of sparkle in her eyes shuttered closed. She turned to leave.

"Come, daughter. The fewer of us around her, the better. Let these two get to work." She beckoned Mina, who scowled.

Mina stuck her tongue out at her mother's back but blew a kiss to her brother and best friend.

"You have to tell me all about it later, you hear me? Make him work hard, Phoebe! I expect you to be able to keep up with us from now on!"

Phoebe said, "I'll do my best."

Tristan just waved in a shooing motion.

Watching the brother and sister dynamics made Phoebe miss Sierra more than ever. "Wait, milady—my sister! Does she know what's happened to me?"

Odessa paused on her way out of the cave. "We have sent word to your sister that you are with us and safe for the moment. But be aware: this is not her fight. She will not be permitted below the waves. She would be a distraction to you. She has nothing to offer us. But you, Phoebe Quinn? You do."

Odessa's green eyes turned black for a moment that spiraled into an eternity as their gazes held. Phoebe's breath sped up in fear. Then Odessa blinked and spun away, calling over her shoulder, "Gird thyself, Phoebe. The sea is generous, but she always demands payment for her gifts."

A pang of anxiety speared through Phoebe. Nell said the ocean would claim Phoebe if she accepted its gifts. Nell was never wrong when the voice came upon her.

Phoebe's hand drifted to the pearl. The sea itself couldn't give a gift. What gift had she accepted? And from whom?

CHAPTER EIGHTEEN

*O*nly Tristan and Phoebe remained in the cave, but the presence of Odessa was so strong it almost felt like she was still there. Phoebe wondered what Sierra or Nell would think of the elder mermaid.

Tristan met Phoebe's eyes. "Well, now you've met my mother. Maybe you can understand why I never introduced you before. Or mentioned her."

All at once, laughter burst from her. It reminded her of the night Sierra left for her long journey to find her fairy, how they both guffawed and snorted and giggled at the most inappropriate time. Sometimes, laughter was necessary in order not to cry.

"Okay. Now really, how can I help?"

"I knew you'd want to." He sighed. "Well, my mother knows a great deal about how magic was used by our forefathers. I'm expected to take over as historian one day, so I've studied alongside her. Your magic has many similarities to theirs. Her thought is that you could learn to duplicate all their skills. You've called me to you before, and we can assume you did so using your magic unintentionally. My mother thinks you could learn to sense the location of particular merfolk and even call them to you on purpose. And you've got to learn to control what you've done twice before with the light."

He ran his hand through his long green locks, woven through with braids. The gesture was full of frustration, but his voice was flat when he said, "You've only done it in moments of danger or panic. Maybe we can try to make it happen consciously. But first things first."

"What's that?"

"You've got to learn to use your fin, Phoebe."

He couldn't suppress a grin.

Before she could decide if she should laugh with him or feel offended, his expression changed from amused to awestruck. "You are the first human to ever become a mermaid, something we thought was impossible. Even if the pearl is causing it, you need to learn to use your body properly."

They both looked at the pearl for moment. It still glowed softly.

He continued, "It's natural that it'll feel awkward at first. But it's possible your legs will return if you go on land or remove the pearl. Mother is searching the oldest magic texts for solutions, but first she wants you to help us master this magic you have before she helps you regain your legs."

Phoebe narrowed her eyes. Who was being kept in servitude now? She was a hostage to the merfolk as surely as she had been to Bentwood. "She could help me but isn't?"

"She's searching for an answer she's confident she can find. She doesn't have it yet," he corrected.

"How is that different?"

"Mother is ruthless. Trust me, she won't change, but she is sincere about finding you an answer. So, let's get started. The sooner we get this part done, the sooner you can get your legs back."

She squelched a twist of disappointment at the thought of being human again and focused instead on Odessa's command. Anger at Odessa's presumption mixed with relief. As annoying as she was, Phoebe trusted that if anyone could help, Odessa could. Of course, she just wanted to get Phoebe out of her realm. Unlike Bentwood, the merfolk elder wasn't interested in keeping her.

"Okay, fine. I help her. She helps me. That sounds fair enough."

"It's not." He hung his head. "I'm quite shamed. You have already risked your life for us. You saved me from dying! I think she ought to help you return to your human form right away."

She touched the pearl. A new warmth radiated from

it now. "Well, at least I will have had this time with you here, even if it turns out I do revert to a human after I take off the necklace."

"I hope you do."

She flinched. He might as well have slapped her.

Tristan leaned forward, eyes wide, hands spread, voice cracking. "Don't you see, Phoebe? They're hunting us. If the wraiths took Liam, they could take *you* next."

"I want to be here, though." The words cost her to admit.

"Whatever your power is, little songbird, it's obviously grown exponentially to affect the elders, though I must confess *I* don't feel a difference. You have always drawn me this strongly."

She gulped, her heart kicking up to a speeding rhythm. Tristan wasn't finished, though.

"But what if your power calls the water wraiths to you? That's probably why one of them grabbed you in the first place. Or worse, Baleros? If he is seeking magic to return to his former glory, he will no doubt seek you out."

Phoebe shivered. Sierra would know what to do, but she wasn't here. Phoebe was. She'd have to be enough. "Hopefully not. But wait, what about the other elders? Surely they have a plan to rescue Liam and save the merfolk?"

Tristan cursed and threw up his hands in frustration. "They talk. And they talk. And they talk! By the time they decide what to do, we'll all be dead! It's always so with my people. If I had asked permission to help you and your sister, you'd still be trapped at Bentwood's!"

He didn't seem to notice when Phoebe shrank at the mention of her foe's name and continued, "So, since they will do nothing but sit on their fins all day, twisting their hands in useless concern, my mother has whispered to me that we must act. Because I have shown skill in teaching young seawees to master the little magics we have now, such as sending moonglow through our skin, she thinks I will be able to guide you into your own powers as a proper merfolk."

His voice stumbled a bit on the word 'merfolk.' Had he even winced? He hid his feelings well, but she'd known him a long time. He was definitely disturbed. Phoebe hoped that her new form was not too distressing to him. It wasn't every day that your close friend changed shape. It had been shocking to see Micah change from faun to human and back again, and that was when she'd known to expect it.

He was staring at his own clenched fists. If being with her was too difficult for him, she'd learn from someone else. "Are you willing to be my teacher? I don't wish to cause you any hardships." Her voice was softer than she'd intended.

Tristan looked up at her suddenly, face half-hidden by his hair. His eyelashes were a dark fringe shadowing those deep green eyes. He smiled, a charming lopsided grin that demanded a smile in response.

"Time spent with you, Phoebe Quinn, is never a hardship. Believe it."

His words—that voice—sent goosebumps along Phoebe's arms. His response vibrated with intensity, rich with deeper meaning. His serious tone didn't match the light-hearted, friendly smile. Which was the truth of his feelings?

She took a deep breath, focusing on their shared goal. Learn to control her magic. Right. "If learning to be better at what I can do will help, I'm all for it."

Tristan met her eyes, green to brown. He gripped her hands, and Phoebe was flooded with sudden warmth. "We will be in dangerous waters. I couldn't bear to lose you, Phoebe."

She pulled a hand free and touched his cheek. "You won't lose me. I promise. I come from pretty tough stock."

She smiled, and he reluctantly grinned back.

"Are you sure you're willing to stay?" he whispered.

"Absolutely."

"Then let's begin. First step: learning to be a mermaid."

CHAPTER NINETEEN

Tristan took Phoebe by the hand and pulled her along to an area of the ocean she'd never been in before, farther away from shore but closer to the surface than the mer-village. The trip was difficult for Phoebe; she kept feeling like someone had glued her legs together as a practical joke. Her movements were jerky and unnatural, not to mention slow. They finally reached a spot he declared acceptable for training.

"First of all, we must do something about your fin technique," he said with a small smile.

Phoebe flushed as red as her hair. "I'm swimming wrong?" She was moving through the water, wasn't she?

He laughed. "Not wrong. Just not efficient. It's the same as when you could swim before, but I taught you how to best move through the water with your human body, remember?"

How could she forget the hours spent in the water, laughing and pulling herself along until her muscles burned? The sea was the one place where the heavy sense of shame and grief from Bentwood's prison disappeared, washed away by the salty water. Any child living on the coast learned to survive in the water. Tristan had taught her how to thrive in it.

"So?"

"So." He shook his head at her. "You're being stubborn. This involves logic. Swimming with two legs is quite different than swimming with one tail. There are stories—myths—of merfolk who were land walkers, able to live in both worlds. I believe that once upon a time, magic was sufficient for such a feat. Their legs always returned to fins when in the water. If they could learn to walk on legs, you can learn to swim with a fin."

Phoebe's heart leapt at the thought of Tristan on land. He could see her home! He could see Sierra's fairy hatch and sit by the fire and have hot chocolate. She could barely imagine what that would be like, but if she was truly going to be a mermaid now, she supposed it no longer mattered.

She squared her shoulders. "Fine. Show me how."

"First, you should be able to sense the center of gravity inside you, can you not? It's a heavy place that keeps us from floating to the surface like humans do, and your new body will automatically shrink or expand this part to change your buoyancy, to help you rise and lower in the water without the effort of swimming. It's as automatic as breathing and happens in here." He pointed to his stomach, right where his scales met the flesh of his torso.

Phoebe nodded, relieved to have the strange sensation explained.

"Now, look at how I move my body. We don't move side to side like a fish. We are more like the dolphins, moving our bodies up and down in a wave pattern that allows us quite a lot of speed. Watch." He lifted one finger to indicate she should stay put. She twisted her swirling hair into a loose bun at the base of her neck so she wouldn't miss a thing.

He looked over his shoulder at her and then swam in exaggerated movements so she could see exactly what he was doing with his torso and tail. Up, down, up, down. She realized his body didn't roll from side to side at all the way hers did when she kicked her feet. The steady motion of his tail moving up and down pushed him quickly and efficiently through the water, and he didn't use his arms at all. She had still been trying to use the strokes he had taught her as a human. She realized now that her tail alone was so powerful that her upper body needed to stay straight to steer, like a rudder.

"I see!" she called out, a glimmer of eagerness sparking through her. How fast could she go once she mastered this?

He waved her onward, signaling her to swim to him. Properly.

Her tongue sticking out slightly from her intense concentration, Phoebe closed her eyes and allowed herself to focus on her body in the water. The salt levels added a different buoyancy in this form than in her human body, and when she flexed her tail, the swoosh of water against the fin sent her zooming in a fast jet. She squealed and stuck her hands out, as if she could stop herself, but of course, she cut through the currents easily.

"If you want to stop, point your tail toward the ground and flick your fin in the opposite direction, sort of like how rowers of boats drag their oars against the current to slow down."

She tried this and managed to flip herself upside down twice before mastering how to stop. They spent most of the afternoon practicing proper swim techniques, until she could swim, stop, and spin without flailing. She was getting much smoother.

"I'm really doing it!" Phoebe beamed.

Tristan looked pleased as well, and he tugged on her hair that had escaped once again from her attempt to contain it. "You're working very hard. Even my mother should have no complaints."

"I imagine she could find something." Phoebe rolled her eyes, and Tristan laughed, the deep rolling laugh she loved.

"Now, let's try to see if you can call me again on purpose. I can feel your presence. Do you feel mine?'

She stared at him, uncertainty replacing her small sense of victory.

He sighed. "I can handle it, Phoebe. Your worries are stamped on your face. You've called me twice, but both times were by accident. You've got to get this under conscious control."

"So I, what? Call you like a lost dog?" The words sounded harsher than she meant. It also evoked the wrong image.

He flinched, and she bit her lip. "I didn't mean—"

"I know, I know. Look, just try to close to your eyes and ask me to come to you. In your heart or with your words. I'll swim over there to the reef. If I feel compelled to come to you, you'll know you've done it."

Tristan swam far enough away that his expression was indiscernible even with her new, magically improved water vision. He was serious about this. She felt ridiculous. What if she called him and he didn't come? Worse, what if he did? She would hate for anyone to have that kind of control over her. If her call really was stronger now, he would most certainly fear her, then, like the mer-elders did. And maybe he'd be correct to.

"Your waiting does us no good, Phoebe," he called.

With a start and a flash of guilt, Phoebe closed her eyes. The thrumming of her heart distracted her, along with the slow swish of the currents over her skin. Concentrating, she pictured Tristan in her mind: tender smile, gentle eyes, tousled green hair, older now than when they had first met but still her friend. Still someone she cared for. She focused on that caring for a moment, allowing everything else to fade away, and whispered his name, so softly she knew not even his excellent hearing would catch it. He'd have to feel the magical call.

"Tristan." The name barely slid over her lips. "Tristan, come to me." She waited but heard nothing, felt nothing. She opened her eyes just a crack, enough to see him still over by the coral, several lengths away.

"Keep trying," he encouraged.

She squeezed her eyes shut again and flipped onto her back in the currents to help relax her whole body. She kept her eyes closed to concentrate better.

"Tristan," she said, a little stronger. She thought of the times they had played in the surf, of the gifts he had left, of his rescuing her from Bentwood and now Donovan, too. She would miss Tristan terribly. Calling her emotions a secret crush really didn't do them justice. She loved him, always as a friend, but also as so much more. She thought the words, "I love you, Tristan," but couldn't say the words out loud. She never could. Then a hand touched hers, and she gasped.

Her eyes flashed open, and Tristan's face was right in

front of hers. There was no twinkling smile now. His face was utterly serious.

"I heard you," he said.

He heard that she loved him? Panic surged through her until he said, "Not with my ears. Somehow I heard you call my name here."

He tapped his chest, just over his heart. They stared at each other for a timeless moment before he backed up. "You are more powerful than you realize, I think. This is good for our people."

But not for us, Phoebe thought.

He cleared his throat. "Soon, we will have to defend ourselves. The wraiths will not let us be, Baleros will surely come after us, and we cannot just swim away and abandon our city again. None of our people will pick up edged weapons. It goes against our ways. But the blue light you have called has worked like a weapon, sending the wraith away, twice, without true harm. This is part of what the ancient merfolk could do; my mother has shown me in the historians' records. They also knew how to build shields of magic around their city to keep it safe. We need to learn how you use the magic like they did."

"I don't know how!"

"We'll learn together." He took her hand and ran his thumb over and over against the back of her hand. Phoebe didn't even think he was aware he was doing it. It wasn't like Tristan to touch her so casually. It was not how mer-culture worked. Maybe she *had* charmed him. He'd never allowed them to be so close before.

Uncertain, she backed up, breaking their linked hands. She tried to keep her voice casual. They still had to work together, and she didn't want to allow them to begin something between them that could not last. If he were under her power, she'd have to keep her true feelings to herself. To do otherwise was unkindness. "So, how do I do this?"

"I have an idea, but it means moving to a more dangerous place. Come."

Phoebe raised her eyebrows and followed him. She might have charmed him, but he had thoroughly charmed her years before, even without a magical gift. Her own folly made Phoebe shake her head. The more time she spent with him, the harder it would be to say goodbye. But if this was the only time she could be alone with him for the rest of her life, she'd take it.

He took her to a deeper level of the ocean, where schools of bright fish scurried by and jellyfish hung in the water here and there like cobwebs.

"Some of our natural predators live here, but nothing I can't handle. I'm the fastest swimmer my age. We'll be fine. But you might find them frightening enough to cause your magic to flare. Learning to create moonglow in your skin requires steady, low-level power. Your energy has been too strong and sudden for that, so we're going to focus on the blast of light first."

"You brought me here to scare the power out of me?" Laughter burst from her.

"You can handle it."

Tristan wasn't looking at her like she was frail. Phoebe wasn't a little sister here. They were going to save Tristan's people. The old Phoebe would have been too afraid, but the new Phoebe could be strong and powerful.

"I'm ready." Excitement rose in her, just a little, just from knowing she had enough power to be a worthy foe for anything.

"Okay, then. See that octopus over there?"

She squinted in the direction Tristan pointed. "The little one the size of my hand?" Phoebe scoffed. "I think I can do better than scaring a kitten."

He laughed. "Look beyond that one."

Focusing where he pointed, Phoebe's eyes grew large. Concealed among the reef behind it, the bulbous head of a giant octopus was almost invisible, camouflaged to match the rocks behind it. Two tentacles swayed with the current swirling around the crevice where it hid—silent and watchful. The bulk of it was concealed, but she could imagine its size.

"Ugh," Phoebe said, averting her eyes from the sucker-cup lined arms. She tried to hide how the sight of the creature made shivers dance up and down her skin. Anything with that many arms was terrifying, and he knew all about her fear of squid and octopuses.

"Those arms have the strength to crush your tail before you can swim away. The beak at the center of its head is hard enough to break open anything that lives down here."

She shuddered. "Why are you telling me this?"

"You need to make it run away, using your light."

Maybe he'd lost his sanity. She laughed once in disbelief. "And how am I going to do that?"

He smiled, but it was grim. "You're going to get scared."

CHAPTER TWENTY

"Uh, I don't think so," Phoebe shook her head so hard that her hair spiraled loose all around.

"You must."

He pulled her forward toward the octopus. It shrunk slightly into the crevice, as if sensing their approach. Watching that bag of skin waver in the water made her skin crawl. What happened if she vomited? How mortifying would that be?

She imagined those cold, sticky arms wrapping around her legs, holding her down. Of course, she didn't have legs anymore, did she? She took a deep breath, almost a reminder of her new status. An octopus could kill her in a number of ways, but drowning at least was no longer an option. She shook off Tristan's arms. If she was going to do this, she'd do it on her own. She swallowed hard. *I will not throw up. I will not throw up.* She wouldn't get sick, not in front of *him*.

She swam forward a few lengths. The octopus tightened further into a ball, as if trying to disappear. Her hands grew cold and her lips numb. She was supposed to get *closer*? Sharks could kill just as fast or faster, but there was something singularly repulsive about the tentacles, the billowing amorphous skin of the head, sagging and bagging. Yet, she knew the lazy-looking blob could propel itself with surprising swiftness.

"Please?" she whispered. She wasn't even sure what she was asking for. But Tristan knew.

"My people need you to master this power. It's strong, but raw and unpredictable, which is not sufficient yet for what we need. I'm so sorry. I don't enjoy this, either." He remained right behind her.

She turned to him and knew he spoke the truth by the way his pale skin looked waxy in his silvery light, like he was ill at the thought of causing her fear. A few beams of sunlight shimmered through the coral, the beauty highlighting the hideous creature before her. Tristan's mouth twisted in a grimace, and he clasped her shoulders. "Phoebe, if I could do this for you, I would, but you must use your own strength. You can do this."

She could do this. She could do this. She tried chanting to herself, but the words sounded empty,

197

echoing in her mind. There was no song inside for her to draw upon. She was hollow.

Moving forward again, she stopped close enough that the tiny octopus she'd first seen dashed into a crevice of the rock by the bigger one. If she hadn't seen it go in, she wouldn't have known it was there. She shivered, wondering how many times she had swum by such a creature hidden in the rocks and reefs around her.

The big octopus only had to leave. She didn't have to hurt or kill it. Just scare it away with her light. She tried to call it forward, but the magic refused to burst forth. It was like a river covered with a thick layer of ice. Water passed swiftly below, bubbles slipping against the frozen slab. But the water remained unreachable through the blockade of ice. Likewise, her magic flowed inside her, but stayed trapped beneath her fear. Tristan was at her back, and she knew that at least he could take her and flee if necessary.

"Leave!" she called out, feeling foolish but hoping the verbal command would stir up some magic.

Nothing.

She swam a few more swishes forward. Now she could see the way the tentacles slid one over the other, seething like a nest of snakes.

"Go away!" she cried.

All at once, the octopus exploded out of the crevice, a wheel of arms spinning, aimed right at her.

She screamed, but before she could think to do anything else, Tristan grabbed her by the waist and dashed straight down, zig-zagging in evasive maneuvers that shook the angry octopus from their trail. Phoebe didn't even watch. The fear that so often choked her had sunk its teeth into her yet again.

Tristan sped away from where the sunlight reached its fingers into the ocean, going deeper and deeper. The water here was quieter, darker. Soothing. Sea horses floated by, along with puffy fish with spiny points and glowing tiny shrimp that hovered in clumps like lanterns nearby. Phoebe's ragged breathing slowed, and he held her hands.

"I'm sorry, I'm sorry," Tristan kept saying.

After a few minutes, he sighed, rubbing his forehead. "Obviously, this isn't working. We could be here all day and not get anywhere. We might have a little time but not that much."

"I think that even though it was scary for me, deep down I knew you wouldn't let that thing hurt me, so it didn't work. The blue light just wouldn't come. I was near death the other times, and this time I was terrified but not dying."

"I can't argue. It goes against everything in me to even let you near such a creature, knowing how you fear them. I don't think either one of us could risk your life to make this magic reappear. I do have another idea, but

I don't want you to think I'm being... how do you say... inappropriate?"

Baffled, Phoebe grabbed his arm. "What are you talking about? We've got to make some progress. We should try any and all possibilities."

"Well," he began slowly. "When we are seawees, we are taught several ways to silence our minds and relax. We are taught that we are all part of the whole, and through silence and meditation, we find this to be true. It's part of why merfolk do not fight, and it is through this unity that we are able to access our modest magics. Meditation is one excellent tool, but we do not have time for such a long, intense pathway. One is the path of pain, which I believe you have used to connect to the whole on those two occasions. Terror. Fear. These are deeply painful experiences and link us with the rest of the world as we intuitively seek connection in our moment of darkness."

"Riiight," Phoebe replied. "And we've been trying to duplicate it, but, so far, nothing is working. I know I'm safe right now with you, and I can't lie to my body."

He cleared his throat. "Exactly. So, there is another pathway we could try."

She raised an eyebrow. He was really, really uncomfortable. How interesting.

"What do you propose?" she asked, searching his face for clues as he swam closer.

"We are taught that close contact with others is

another way to feel united," he whispered, running his hands across her shoulders, and she shivered.

She wished she was as smooth with words as her father had been, but she had to ask a hard question. "Will it make the magic worse between us? Steal your will?"

He shook his head. "My mother has greatly overestimated that danger, Phoebe, even since you gained your scales. I promise. I've felt the pull from the start, and it hasn't changed or overwhelmed me. I'm not worried. And this is a necessary step for your magic."

Two bright red spots lit his cheeks. It was adorable.

He'd felt the pull from the start. Was that good or bad? Fireworks were exploding in Phoebe's mind at his choice of words, but she struggled to keep focused on the issue at hand. Magic. Saving his people. Helping the merfolk. Don't look at those green eyes. Don't hope that this relationship could actually work.

She lifted her chin. Right. On-task now.

"So what kind of… contact… do you have in mind?" She held her breath.

"A simple hug might suffice," he said gruffly, eyes roaming her face. He paused, clearly waiting for permission.

Her pulse galloped. She didn't think he meant the kind of hugs they had shared before. Something in his expression suggested this hug would be much different than the friendly, casual ones of their childhood. He may be only touching her to train her properly, but she'd dreamed of this moment for months now. This was a step beyond a peck on the cheek. Her handsome friend wanted to *hold* her. Instead of being little kid friend Phoebe, she could pretend they were something else to each other. Something more. Something with a future. He said he wasn't under her influence. He promised. So it wasn't selfish if it was just her who was heartbroken in the end, was it? And this was necessary. For her to learn magic.

She'd allow herself to enjoy it, as it would probably never happen again. He hovered perfectly still, the ultimate gentleman. The anticipation was killing her. It would be up to her to begin, then.

Heart hammering in her chest, she leaned forward, wrapping her arms around his shoulders, weaving her hands through his hair. Her fingers ran over the silky strands, and he closed his eyes. Water slid between and among them as he pulled her closer. He nestled his face against the top of her hair and took a deep breath. She pressed her cheek against his chest, closing her eyes against the soft illumination of his skin.

The strength of his body so close to hers was intoxicating. She fought to keep her breathing steady. No need to embarrass herself here. He wrapped his arms around her as if she were made of glass. Images flickered through her mind, of Tristan as a young seawee, Tristan as the young merman he was now. The two of them splashing in the waves together, the surf roaring, sea gulls twirling, her own voice singing...

She sighed, both relaxed and thrilled, and leaned against him. Their tail fins entwined slightly as they floated close together, and her heart fluttered like a trapped bird, waiting to fly.

She closed her eyes tight, forgetting all about magic until he said, "Do you feel anything?"

Did she *feel* anything? Only a tsunami of sensations. There were too many ways to answer that question. No magic light grew within, but so much emotion, too much, cascaded through her, leaving her wordless at the comfort and thrill of being held in Tristan's arms. He lifted his face away from hers.

"Talk to me, Phoebe," he whispered.

This was her one chance to show Tristan how she felt, perhaps before her power grew stronger. She could no longer bear the thought of leaving the sea without him ever knowing. He deserved the truth, even if he couldn't feel the same way, but no words could encompass what resided in her heart. So she reached her hands up to the back of his head and guided his face downward to hers, ignoring the nervousness making her hands shake.

"Are you sure?" he asked, though his expression was eager.

Phoebe just smiled.

He leaned down and pressed his lips to hers.

At his touch, everything else seemed to fade away. Tristan filled her mind, her senses, her heart. She never knew his lips would be soft, not when he was always rugged and strong. But his kiss was incredibly gentle; it felt like bubbles tickling her lips. Joy spilled up inside her, filling the emptiness that had echoed before, the music she had always loved swirling through her veins like a rushing current of blue flame.

The ocean—in fact, the universe—felt expansive and beautiful. Surely she must be glowing from these overwhelming feelings. She opened her eyes. She wasn't glowing, but Tristan was—brighter than usual. Incandescent.

He broke away, and Phoebe had to squint at the radiance shining from his skin. His light was like a beacon. A dark shape cruised above them. It had a sharply pointed dorsal fin.

Shark.

"Oh no," she whispered. The shark was unusually large, too.

Then the fins along its sides lifted and spread wide like wings, with translucent skin rippling in the water. The creature looked for all the world like a dragon soaring through the sky, down to the long tail with its pointed tip undulating back and forth.

Not a shark. A sea dragon.

"By the stars," she breathed.

Tristan muttered a curse and pulled her alongside

him as he began to move, gazing up at the huge outline on display against the light above. The dragon banked along in a turn downward, and the gaping mouth opened, showing several rows of glistening teeth.

"A sea dragon is more than I'd like to outrun right now. We're still learning how to best evade them," he whispered in her ear as they sped away.

She looked back over her shoulder, unable to resist staring at this magnificent creature of legend. The sudden staccato beat of her heart testified that the sea dragon was following them—and not just *one* dragon. A spiral of sea dragons spun above them, all drawn to the light, at least twenty of them together. Tristan's skin was still too brilliant.

"Stop glowing!" she hissed at him.

He grimaced. "I can't! I'm too full of energy." He gazed at her, eyes soft despite the danger above. "I've never felt this way in my life."

Joy, fear, and confusion tangled around each other inside Phoebe, a potent elixir that made her dizzy. The dragons were picking up the pace, vibrating her bones with their bass growls. They were coming up from behind, closing in. It was too late to run. The dragons were too close.

She stopped and spun in the water, closing her eyes and picturing the sharp, glistening teeth coming to kill her and her beloved Tristan. If he died, it would be because of her.

Shivering, Phoebe glared at the sea dragons as they lowered through the water like a cyclone touching down. The first dragon bared its razor teeth as it did its first pass-by, as though testing them to see what kind of fight they might give. Its eyes were flat black, cold and uncaring, like a shark's. Terror slid through her as easily as the creature slid past.

The water surged around them in the wake of the sea dragon's great hulking body. She rocked in the current of its movement. A second dragon prowled by. The flick of its tail slid against Phoebe's arm, and she cried out.

Tristan shouted, "Phoebe, go! They'll chase me. You can escape!"

Another sea dragon sped by Tristan, slicing him along the ribs with its sharp teeth. He gasped, and a red line floated into the water. At any moment now, the beasts would begin to frenzy, and escape would be impossible.

But Phoebe wouldn't leave Tristan. She couldn't. She reached deep down inside, to the place where the music sang while Tristan held her. She'd never felt anything like it. There was power there, in that emotion, she knew. She pulled on those blue flames and willed them forward, facing her palms outward toward the dragon.

A brilliant fan of blue fire billowed through the water and flashed over the nearest dragon. The light spread upward, into the spiraling tornado of fins, and the shape broke apart as if lightning had split it in half.

The sea dragon nearest to them wheeled around and fled into the darkness faster than an arrow from a bow. The rest followed suit. An entire hunting group of sea dragons—gone.

She'd done it! She'd used her power by choice. She sagged with relief.

Tristan crushed her into his arms and whispered her name against her hair over and over again. He pressed little kisses along the top of her head but didn't reach for her lips. Given all the messy complications, maybe that was just as well, though she rather wished he would.

The merfolk still needed help, and now Phoebe knew one way to control her power and call forth her magic. The blue light inside her still burned, ready to be called upon. It was time to tell the merfolk that magic like they'd never known could be within their reach.

CHAPTER TWENTY-ONE

Before Tristan and Phoebe reached the village, she began to worry. What if she told Odessa about their magical success, and Phoebe was sent on some mission before she could speak to her sister again? Odessa wasn't to be trusted. Her priority was the merfolk and nothing else.

Phoebe grabbed Tristan's hand. "Before we talk to your elders, I need to talk to Sierra. My whole life has changed and could change even more. I can call Sierra through Queenie, I think, like Micah called you that first time." The memories of Bentwood's fortress threatened to spill out from their dark lair in her heart, but she pressed forward. "I need to tell her what's happened to me."

And that I might not be back, ever.

"Of course. I'm a clownfish for not thinking of it

sooner. But Mother will be waiting for me and will ask what has happened if you aren't with me when we arrive. She might not understand your purpose. So let's go speak to Mother, and then I'll take you to see Sierra. Will that be okay?"

Phoebe didn't want to wait. "You promise I'll be able to visit Sierra?"

"My word of honor as a merfolk," he replied.

Odessa was tricky, but *Tristan*, Phoebe trusted. And she did owe it to the merfolk to return as soon as possible. Odessa needed to know that Phoebe could fight now.

They sped through the waters, but her mind wasn't on what to tell Odessa, but rather what to tell Sierra. For the first time, Phoebe was trying to pick out what words she'd use to explain that she had accidentally become a mermaid and might be stuck as one forever. There just weren't enough words in the world to make that an easy message to deliver to her big sister.

When they arrived back to Tristan's room, triumphant and proud, Mina hugged them both and squealed. "You did it, didn't you? Look at how you're practically glowing!"

Phoebe flushed, thinking of just how much glowing had been going on.

Odessa whisked into the room, her impatience as visible as her dark spear tattoos. "Is she ready?"

Tristan replied, "Ask her, Mother."

"Well?" The older mermaid crossed her arms and faced Phoebe.

Phoebe nodded. "I think I understand how to better control my magic. If you can study what I do, then I'm glad to work alongside you and help you rediscover your ancient magical abilities."

Odessa's smile was fierce and hard as they reported what all had happened. They left out the hug and kiss, though. Odessa studied them both, narrowing her eyes, and Phoebe had a sinking feeling the mermaid could see everything anyway. "Excellent work, Phoebe Quinn. I think it's time to convince the others of our case. The elders must agree to learn from you, along with the rest of the merfolk."

"Wait—I was going to tell my sister—"

"Later, Phoebe. Later."

"Mother, I told Phoebe she could speak to her sister before you asked more from her."

For one second, there was a glimmer of warmth in Odessa's face as Tristan stared directly at her, but the moment of fondness disappeared as quickly as it appeared.

"Of course. And I wouldn't want you to go back on your word, Tristan. But I must ask you to wait. I promise there will be time later, but we have an important meeting to attend."

"Phoebe, if you want to speak to your sister now, I'll

take you." Tristan gazed at her, ignoring his mother's stiffening back.

Phoebe's heart melted at his willingness to disobey—again—for her sake. But it was clear that leaving now would put Tristan in a difficult spot. "I can wait a while longer. Not much, but long enough for a meeting."

But she missed Sierra more than she thought she would. Sierra may be smothering sometimes, but there was no doubt in Phoebe's mind that Sierra's love for her was absolute and unshakeable. And Phoebe loved her back in equal measure.

"Of course," Odessa said, brushing past Tristan to Phoebe's side. "Now, Phoebe, not all the merfolk are willing to believe you can truly use magic like the old ones, much less that you could guide us into a new golden era. You'll need to be at your best. I'm assigning two of my assistants to you. They will help you appropriately attire yourself. Not because I want you to feel more at home here, but because I need you to be successful, and I know the other elders. They do not easily see what is beneath the surface. Luckily for all of us, I can. It's *my* gift, if you will. Let's not pretend we're on good terms, shall we? I believe you prefer honesty."

Odessa's piercing stare made Phoebe feel completely exposed, as if she were standing naked in front of them both. Talk about awkward. Odessa flipped her long braid over her shoulder and left to prepare for the meeting.

"Milady, we've been sent to tidy you." Two young seawees bobbed a greeting at the doorway. They looked to be about the age Phoebe had been when she first met Tristan. They swam over, shooed Tristan out of the cave, and set to work.

They used long spiny shells to comb out Phoebe's hair, which was knotted like a sailor's rope. The tugs on her scalp stung, but she held her peace. The girls' capable hands quickly wove several braids through Phoebe's hair.

"Such a lovely color hair," said one.

"Like a sunset," murmured the other.

Phoebe flushed. Among the merfolk, red hair didn't exist. Merfolk hair was intended to blend with seaweed, kelp, and dark waters. Her flashy bright hair would be a call to action no predator would resist. If she was indeed going to remain a mermaid, she'd need to look into dyeing it, perhaps with ink from squids.

"We will make you look like a princess, Miss Phoebe," whispered the one.

"But you don't have royalty," Phoebe replied.

The other winked. "Maybe not, but we have leaders whose families have led for eons. Same difference, if you ask me. And Tristan, well now, he's going to need a partner one day, won't he, to lead well? I think your blue scales match him very well."

Phoebe turned even redder than her hair, and the two seawees giggled.

"Will you sing us a song while we work, milady?"

Ah yes. They were from the crowd that used to come hear her sing along the shore, then. She chose a song from those long-ago days, a simple tune of hope and joy, and sang softly as the girls continued to braid. Their motions were gentle, and peace covered their faces. The seawees crooned along with her, giving happy sighs when the song was over. They brought her a mirror and said, "Now you're ready for those old barracudas on the council."

Phoebe took one look and nearly dropped the mirror.

They had braided and twisted her hair until it was safely contained in graceful coils. Her head felt wobbly, like a heavy crown sat on her scalp, and indeed, her braids crisscrossed and wove together in a way that brought a crown to mind. No doubt, done on purpose by the mischievous little seawees.

With her hair out of her face, Phoebe's eyes looked even larger than usual, deep brown and long-lashed. Her skin held a creamy richness she had never noticed before, with two spots of pink highlighting her cheeks where her flush still burned. Her neck looked long and swanlike, and her deep blue scales looked positively royal.

She hadn't really had a chance to examine herself yet as a mermaid. Things had been so hectic, so chaotic, and she had been concentrating so fiercely on the problem of the wraiths, she almost forgot at times how she had been changed. The pearl necklace still glowed against her skin, and the scales that began just under her arms left her shoulders bare with her hair pinned out of the way. She felt very grown up. She actually even had a bit of curve at the waist and hips that was discernible in this form, she realized to her delight. Her tail fin spread like a fan below her, tipped with indigo and purple. The scales and water deepened the sometimes carrot hue of her hair to a rich deep red, making her look older. For a long moment, she wondered, *Who is that girl?*

Tristan appeared behind her, and she spun to greet him. Her mouth dropped open, and his did the same. His green hair hung smoothly down his back, loose but for several thin intricate braids. A necklace of shells hugged his neck, and a thick band of gold gripped one bicep. His muscular arms and chest were impossible to miss, along with the red welts along his ribs from their sea dragon encounter and the faded marks on his neck. He was so handsome that her chest hurt.

His eyes were huge as his gaze traveled up and down Phoebe. The two seawees giggled and excused themselves, zipping out of the room, leaving her alone with Tristan.

"Phoebe," he whispered. He wasn't smiling now. He looked tremulous, almost shocked, nearly afraid. *Why?*

"You look… amazing," he said, swimming close and laying one hand against her cheek.

Her breath caught, and her eyes fluttered shut. When she opened her eyes a moment later, he was so close to her that she could see the tiny gold flecks in his green eyes. She had never felt so much like a young lady, ready to receive a suitor. And she had never wanted anything more than in that moment to have him be hers. From the way he was looking at her and the way he held her earlier and the kiss they shared, maybe a future wasn't impossible after all?

"You look worried," she whispered.

His eyes roved over her face, as if seeking answers to a question only he knew.

"Just trying to decide if your powers have grown, or if it's just how beautiful you are that makes me want to promise to be your servant always," he said with a wry smile.

Her heart stopped, and she recoiled from his touch.

"I'm joking, Phoebe. Not about your beauty. But I'm not your slave yet. Don't worry."

He reached forward and slid his hand under her palm. Lifting the back of her hand, he placed a soft kiss there, keeping his eyes on her. Their gazes locked. Phoebe was a statue, unable to move, afraid of shattering the moment.

"Well, yes, you look much more appropriate, don't you, dear?" Odessa's voice broke over them like a cold wave, and Phoebe shimmied back in the water, jerking her hand away and shifting it behind her back. Tristan stared after her, looking a bit dazed, hand raised as if he still held her palm.

Mina peeked out from behind her mother and gave a broad grin. She wiggled her eyebrows toward her brother, and Phoebe smothered a smile.

Odessa sighed and shook her head. "Phoebe, place this upon your finger." She held out a ring, one with a crystal that glowed deep green.

"What is it?" Phoebe managed to croak as she took it, avoiding Tristan's gaze.

"It's a symbol of my favor. It will allow you to speak among the elders as my representative. My champion, if you will."

Phoebe's eyebrows flew up to her hairline, as did Tristan's. That was a bit more than she had bargained for.

"What if I represent you poorly?"

Odessa quirked her lips. "Oh, I think you'll do just fine, as we share the same goals. The merfolk are in danger from the wraiths and Baleros. We aren't equipped to fight with force. But where there is a lack of force, we can use cleverness and stealth. When combined with our magical abilities of old, we will be victorious. There is no reason why we should not grow in strength as our brethren on land have. You will see. Let us go." Her eyes hardened as she straightened her shoulders and left without waiting to see if they would follow her.

They did, without question.

The four left Tristan's room behind and swam into the darker waters of the far corner of the mer-village. The lantern fish had been set free, so only the pearly light of the three glowing merfolk led the way.

"We've retreated to the most hidden part of our village," Odessa whispered.

Around the corner of a ledge, a different cliff wall appeared out of the darkness, smaller in stature than the main part of the village. No lights were visible, as thick curtains of sea fronds hung over all the openings. The four of them sank to the very bottom and swam through what turned out to be a tunnel that opened into a giant room, a cave so big that the top disappeared past the dim illumination offered within.

A collective of merfolk, maybe two hundred strong, sat reclining on giant sea sponges and clam shells. The crowd spread before a platform at the front of the cave, where six mer-elders already reclined. Odessa took the empty spot among them and gestured for Tristan and Phoebe to take their places at the center of the stage.

"Go get them, tigerfish!" Mina said and slid onto a clam shell in the front of the audience members, winking at Phoebe.

As soon as Phoebe and Tristan reached center stage, the merman who had shown such anger toward Phoebe leaned forward. Elder Seamus. He swam from his sponge-chair and addressed the assembly.

"We are here to discuss the likelihood of defending our home from the water wraiths that have already killed at least two merfolk, possibly more. For those who have not heard, young Liam is now presumed dead as well. May the ocean guard his soul."

"No!" exclaimed Mina, covering her face with both hands for a long moment.

The crowd members murmured to each other, a babble of noise that resulted in Seamus emitting a high pitched shriek in their language that settled everyone down quickly. He consulted a piece of coral with dark scratching on it that must have been some form of writing, because he furrowed his brow as he read it, then looked up, clearing his throat.

"Now," he continued forcefully, "Elder Odessa also brings forth a plan to build magical shields over our city to defend it from Baleros, as if this kind of magic is possible anymore." The tone of his voice clearly implied that the very idea was ludicrous.

Elder Maher called out, "Elder Seamus, we have gone over this. The human girl has shown evidence of such magic. Tristan has so testified in the temple. How can you doubt?"

Elder Seamus ignored this comment and went on, "Furthermore, Elder Odessa brings forth the motion that this human girl, this *Phoebe Quinn*, can teach us to use magic as the merfolk of old did. We will somehow learn to create this mythical city-shield. I doubt this. I think she is a fraud, using her black magic only to ensnare us, not to assist us. Therefore, *I* propose she prove that she is worthy to be the teacher of merfolk, even though she is a human. No matter what her appearance. She should have to defeat Baleros, if he is truly rising. If she's so strong, that shouldn't be a problem," he said with a sneer.

CHAPTER TWENTY-TWO

A shock ran through Phoebe. *She* was supposed to fight the rising evil sea beast? The dark shadow that stole her ability to even remember why she should live?

She thought she was going to *help the merfolk learn magic*. This was an entirely different proposition. Sierra would tear the village down around their heads if she knew what they were suggesting.

Tristan grabbed Phoebe's hand and turned to face his mother.

"What is the meaning of this?" he growled.

Mina darted forward onto the platform and grabbed Phoebe's free hand.

"Phoebe will do no such thing. It's ridiculous for the elder to even propose such a risk," Mina said, for once all trace of flirting and fun gone from her voice.

Elder Seamus said, "Mina, don't say another word. Hush, Tristan. Your mother has given her ring to Phoebe, who has accepted it. Your mother is not able to speak on the issue at this time, not while her chosen representative is here."

Odessa gave a small, triumphant smile. *What's her game?* Phoebe wondered. She knew Odessa wanted her people to be safe. Somehow, the mother mermaid believed that Phoebe was her best bet.

Phoebe pulled herself from her friends and turned to face the assembled crowd. Two hundred looked like a lot in a cave, but they were small in numbers compared to their history.

How did a species capable of building that sprawling ancient city dwindle to a mere couple hundred members? And how many more would be lost if they didn't learn to protect themselves with magic as they once could?

She cast about for a plan. What could she offer them? She wondered what Sierra would do. In fact, what *did* she do when she had to get Phoebe out of a dangerous location? Sierra used her magic to shake the very foundations of the earth. Maybe Phoebe could be as dramatic in a less violent way. As confident as she was in her magic now, she could never forget the horrific despair that clenched her when the red and black shadow slinked from the cave with the wraiths. That evil was more than a single girl could face alone, mermaid or human.

"I have seen the water wraiths," Phoebe said, projecting her voice to carry to the back of the cave. "Twice I have escaped them. I'm not sure how, but I do seem to be able to fight them. Tristan has helped me harness this power today, and I have better control now. I believe you could once again use magic like the ancient merfolk. As adults, you've all been to the original city. Do you recognize how much power they had? I want to help you use this power as they did. You could learn to protect yourself before it's too late."

"How do we know that we can learn this magic?" Elder Maher asked.

"I can show you the power you could have if you would attempt it."

She needed a volunteer. She glanced at Tristan, but no, she was better off without any potential distractions. "Mina, can you come here and hold my hand?"

Her friend swam over without hesitation and placed her small, slim hand in Phoebe's. How many times had they held hands as they swam? Too many to count. Now Phoebe was relying on that close connection to prove a point.

She closed her eyes and focused on Mina, sensing her presence, warm and bubbly.

"Focus on our friendship," Phoebe murmured to her friend, hoping this would work. "Think on how connected we've been over the years. Think of us being united as one." Well-trained as a seawee, Mina knew what to do and nodded.

Phoebe remembered the many times she and Mina laughed together, joked together. Remembered how Mina offered such comfort when Phoebe sobbed from nightmares of Bentwood's place. Focusing on their friendship, Phoebe imagined the blue light inside spreading to Mina, filling her, bursting forth from her. A glow simmered bright against Phoebe's closed eyelids, and when she opened them, her jaw dropped.

Mina was iridescent, as bright as Tristan had been after the kiss, but her light was blue, like the light Phoebe had called in her times of distress.

Laughing, Mina looked down at her skin. "I feel amazing!" she said. "So powerful! Is this how it feels for you, Phoebe?"

The merfolk looked at them like sunflowers yearning for the sun. They wanted that magic.

"Why would you hesitate, if you could regain what you've lost?" Phoebe demanded. Tiredness dragged at her, and she could no longer keep up the light.

The blue light faded from Mina, and she let out a sigh.

Phoebe spread her hands wide in appeal. "Imagine. Imagine every one of you learning how to access that kind of power. I'll teach you. I'll do everything I can to empower you. Come help me fight the wraiths, before

Baleros grows strong enough to come after you. Watch how I use the magic as a weapon and learn to use it yourself."

Tristan looked at her as if he had never seen her before. "Phoebe—" he began.

She cut him off, brutally aware of how alone she was at the moment. No one could make her point for her. She had to prove she was worthy of being followed. "I was able to frighten off a *flight* of sea dragons. I think if you all learn to do what I can do, we can fight water wraiths, and yes, even Baleros. Together!"

"And what if this 'evil presence,' as you say, is awake and ready to kill us all before we master this supposed skill?" said Elder Seamus. "Then what? Are you so afraid to fight the beast, little girl? You are eager for us to, but won't go yourself."

"She can fight, and she will," Tristan said, swimming forward. "But this danger requires all of us. Our numbers cannot keep shrinking as they have if we are to survive. And if this creature means to take the last of us as his meal, I say we give him a belly ache on the way down."

"That's not our way!" shouted a mermaid from the back.

"And has your way been working? *Really?*" Phoebe challenged.

No children were permitted at the meeting, but when she thought of all of those little seawees left to get picked off one by one, rage broke over her. "You're giving up. That's not peace! That's defeat!"

The pearl around her neck flashed with silver light.

"It's the pearl!" someone from the crowd cried. "Whoever has the pearl will have the power to fight! Give the pearl to an elder! See if *they* can control the magic!"

Phoebe startled. Was that true? She didn't have the pearl the first time the blue light came, but maybe… maybe she wasn't the cause of the light the first time. Who knew? Perhaps she was only a mermaid because the pearl channeled the temple's magic. She couldn't guess what other powers it contained. She wrapped her hand around the precious stone without conscious thought.

Tristan replied, "Phoebe has long had other powers, without the pearl. We don't even know where it came from."

Seamus shook his fist and darted back and forth furiously, sending small currents that brushed against Phoebe's skin. "And doesn't that concern anyone other than me? Who would violate our oath to never give that power to a *human*? A *dirt* walker?"

Quite a few gazes rested on Tristan, but Phoebe knew it hadn't been him. His shock had been too great. The other elders sat like statues, except Odessa. Her tail fin flicked back and forth, back and forth, her eyes never leaving Phoebe's face.

Phoebe couldn't stand it. "Look. I might not know how I did it, and I don't know who gave me the pearl, but I'm the one who fought off a water wraith and those sea dragons. I'm sorry if that bothers you. But it could help save your people. Doesn't that mean anything to you?"

"It means you can use a flashy light to scare off a few beasts of the deep, but you know nothing of survival for the long haul," Seamus said. "We survive by not stirring the waters. We hide. We do. Not. Fight."

A surge of frustration made Phoebe clench her teeth. For such a pacifist, the old merman was making *her* plenty ready to fight. But the merfolk were a slow-moving, peaceful people, despite this one merman's rage. Arguments made them uncomfortable. There was no way to win here with anger.

Her nails cut into her palms, but she took a deep breath. She closed her eyes for a moment and hummed a bar from her favorite peaceful tune. It balanced her. Anger wasn't her usual response anyway. From living with Sierra, Phoebe had learned that anger was usually a mask covering hurt or fear. Elder Seamus was just afraid.

She opened her eyes and gazed at him with compassion. "It's okay. I understand—"

"You can never understand! You will never be one of us. You will never, ever be a real mermaid." He reached out his gnarled hand. With a snap of his wrist, he yanked the pearl from her neck, breaking the necklace.

A flash of blue light blinded her. Power rushed through her like a riptide, a swirling whirlpool of magic, filling and filling her until she was sure she would burst. Her arms opened wide as if embracing the entire sea. Blue light flared all around her. The moment unfurled like a thousand days passing, the thunder of ocean surf echoing in her ears, the taste of salt strong in her mouth. Then it was over.

She shook her head. What was *that*?

When she was able to see again, Elder Seamus hovered in front of her, eyes dark with shock. She looked down, expecting to see human legs, and hopefully *not* naked human legs. Instead, the now-familiar sight of her blue tail fin greeted her. She reached to her neck, where smooth gills still remained. But her skin was the most shocking of all.

Dark tattoos of merfolk silhouettes wove along her arms and shoulders, made starkly visible by a new blue moonglow radiating from her skin. The light's blue cast set her apart from all the others around her. Even as a mermaid, she was different than the rest.

Inside her, something intangible had changed, too. A strange pressure grew in her mind, one that reminded her of the power of the temple. Magic was at work, and its steady force coursed through her. A chill shuddered down her spine.

She turned to face Tristan, whose mouth hung open once again. She whispered, "What happened to my skin? Where did these tattoos... Why am I still a mermaid?"

A triumphant laugh came from Odessa. "Because you accepted the gift of the sea, child! Now it's claimed you. Did we not all see the blue light surrounding her? Owning her? Filling her? Do you not see her tattoos, given by the magic of the ocean just as ours are during our initiation into adulthood? They symbolize our choice to serve as caretakers of the sea, so we must assume the ocean has vouched for her. And look at the tattoo pattern chosen for her! Ladies and gentlemers, meet your newest mermaid. Your champion. She isn't going anywhere."

"What gift? What are you talking about?" cried Phoebe.

"The magic of the ocean is a powerful thing, young girl. I warned you. And you obviously have an ability to channel it. You used it to save a life, did you not? In return, the ocean took yours as payment, your human one, at any rate. Magic is an honest but harsh mistress. The pearl might have allowed you to reach the depths of the ocean, but it was your own magic and your willingness to offer yourself for Tristan's life that allowed your transformation. Not that pearl."

Tristan looked at Phoebe with horror-filled eyes. "I would never ask you for such a fate," he said. "We're in danger here, and you have a life above these waters."

Phoebe touched the spot where the pearl had rested for days. *It wasn't the pearl. This magic is mine.* She felt dizzy.

"Is this… real? Or is it a dream?" She reached out a hand to steady herself, and Tristan placed his hand in hers without hesitation. His touch sent warmth spiraling through her, in a very real way, not only because of her feelings for him. He gasped, evidently feeling the same connection.

Phoebe had always been able to sense things about the merfolk now and then, but right now she could sense his presence right next to her, in her spirit, like a deeply rooted tree, steady in the face of any storm. Her power had never been this strong before.

On impulse, she dropped Tristan's hand, shut her eyes, and imagined the room, letting this new sense roam. One glowing merfolk after another brushed against her senses, like she was feeling their presence with her heart rather than her eyes. They glowed to her inner-mind like the billows of sea creatures with their moonglow in the deep, dark waters below. Phoebe found it hard to sense each individual, but maybe she could if she focused enough.

Thinking about this, Phoebe looked at Elder Seamus, looked deeply through him, and tried to push away her own shock. What was he thinking? Why was he so angry? A face swam into her mind's eye. A face of a little girl. She looked to be no more than six years old.

"You've lost someone, too. A little seawee girl. The one who died in the fishing nets. She was your grandchild," Phoebe whispered. If she could weep, she would have.

She understood his hostility now. He wasn't responding with logic but with a broken heart. She certainly understood a lot about hearts so shattered they cut a thousand slices inside.

The merman backed up with a snarl. Odessa sat up straight, and the others in the group leaned forward.

"*Get out of my mind!*" he roared, slamming his hand on the shell beside him. It cracked, and a fragment floated off into the current beside him.

He swam to Phoebe, eyes narrowed. "Just because you can know things about us, doesn't mean you understand us. You still aren't one of us. You aren't."

But she felt different than before. Tristan would never need to give her swimming lessons now; she knew she'd be able to easily keep up with him. Her tail fin felt natural. As natural as sensing all the merfolk in her mind. Unlike before, she had no doubt that this change was permanent.

It wasn't just the merfolk she felt, though. The energy of the ocean itself filled her even now, thrumming through her, filling the water all around her. Eyes opened wide in awe, she swept her hand through the magic she could practically *see* in the water, everywhere, fluttering against her like a thousand fairies. A rushing current of magic filled her, rising like a storm. Her breath caught at the sheer joy and power in it. Did the others not feel this? Looking at their worn, tired faces, it was clear they did not.

She could hold the world in her hand. She was stronger than she ever had been in her life. The fearful Phoebe who had once been beaten in a cell four years ago would never have to take such abuse again. This Phoebe had power. She smiled, a slow, victorious smile that Phoebe Quinn had never smiled before.

Tristan blinked. "Aren't you angry? Sad? If they are correct, you can never go home again. You have many years left in front of you. It's a long, long time in a prison you didn't mean to choose. You are trapped here, without your beloved sister."

Her heart twisted; her smile faltered. A world without Sierra was impossible to imagine, as impossible as a world without Tristan. And to never see Corbin, who was like a brother? Or Micah or Nell? Or the glowing fairies dancing in the trees? And to never get to feed another apple to dear sweet Sam the unicorn, with his dark, wise eyes?

But even such a tremendous loss would be worth this sense of belonging, of strength. The sea wasn't a prison—it was a home like she'd never known. "I'll miss her, true. But she can visit me like I used to swim with you, right? I'm full of magic now, and I'll have a tie to Sierra through Queenie. And I'll be here. With you."

She paused and hastily added, "With all the merfolk."

There were so many more things she wanted to say. If she could learn enough control over this power and curb any influence over the merfolk, perhaps she and Tristan could be together when they grew older. Now she could be a suitable bondmate for him as a full mermaid, a permanent inhabitant of the sea.

Unless he was afraid of this new, more powerful version of her gift.

She couldn't blame him if he were. She wanted to ask, but that wasn't the kind of discussion to have in front of an audience. Especially a stunned audience that included both his mother and his father.

Odessa approached and held out her hand without a word. Phoebe twisted off the jeweled ring and dropped it back in the mermaid's palm.

"Obviously, this requires some regrouping, some thinking," Tristan said. He took her hand again, and another surge of warmth, of power, rolled through Phoebe. He inhaled sharply as the magic surged inside him too.

"On the contrary, my son, this means our plan should go forward immediately, before the wraiths and Baleros can grow any stronger. Phoebe can undoubtedly call sea creatures with her magic, like merfolk of the golden age. Her magic can be sent forth as a weapon. Her completed transformation seems to have set free what was already there, buried deeply. It calls even to me at this moment, don't you feel it?"

A fissure of anxiety slid through Phoebe's triumph, making her joy stumble. She had a sinking feeling she didn't want to hear whatever Odessa was about to say.

But the elder mermaid ruthlessly continued, voice growing louder, "What was once a gentle nudge to trust her is now a clarion call to serve."

To *serve*?

Odessa—a powerful elder mermaid—felt compelled to serve her? That sounded even worse than before.

Much, much worse.

CHAPTER TWENTY-THREE

*P*hoebe looked at Tristan, who stared back at her, eyes huge. His breath heaved raggedly.

"Do you feel the compulsion, too? Is it worse?" she asked him. She had to know.

He was silent for a long moment, his grip tightening on her hand, and her heart sank.

"I'm not sure what I feel. It's all so... *much,*" he whispered back, short of breath.

Phoebe recoiled as if he'd struck her. Her hands flew to her mouth, covering the quivering of her lips. She wouldn't show weakness. Not here. Not now.

Based on watching fairy keepers with their charges, Phoebe had concluded that fairies didn't mind the compulsion to stay with their keepers these days. On the contrary, the wee ones now danced with delight when Sierra arrived to spend time with them. Then again, they weren't exactly fully thinking creatures, at least the little ones.

But how could she have a relationship as an equal with Tristan if she had power over him like *this*? As a master and a servant? Would they always be so close but so far from being true partners? She'd only been fooling herself to hope she could keep her power contained. She felt sure this was why he wouldn't meet her gaze after hearing the news of her increased magic. Even with all they had shared, surely he was second-guessing if their attachment was real enough to protect him from a life of servitude. To her, the mer-charmer.

The pain cut. She had to get away. Now.

Tristan tilted his head up enough to catch her eyes, and his confusion was evident. Shock, hurt, and bafflement paraded across his handsome face. She had wished to see excitement about her new status as a permanent part of his world. Hope. Instead, she saw pinched cheeks, upturned eyebrows. Fear for her? Or fear *of* her?

"Phoebe—" he began, hand out to her.

Holding his hand but knowing she'd never hold his heart hurt too much. She couldn't bear to feel that distance between them. She wasn't going to deal with fear and pain. Not anymore. She wasn't even human anymore. What else did she have to lose?

"Fine, milady. Just tell me what you want me to do,

and I'll do it. I'll even go fight water wraiths for you myself."

Odessa's smile was like a cat's with feathers plastered all over it. Tristan inhaled sharply, but Phoebe kept talking. "But first, you told me I could go see my sister when we were done here."

"We aren't done here, and we don't have time," Odessa said.

"Mother, you promised," Tristan protested, cheeks gaining twin spots of pink.

"Humans have broken many promises."

"Phoebe's not that kind of human." Tristan snapped, and then paled.

Odessa laughed. "That's right. She's not any kind of human anymore."

Tristan turned so he blocked his mother's view of Phoebe for a moment. *Go,* he mouthed.

Phoebe uttered a soft laugh that held no humor at all. How ironic that she could finally stand up to Tristan's mother, now that the power she had always wished for had destroyed the future Phoebe dreamed of with Tristan.

"Odessa, I'm going, and you can't stop me."

She then spoke directly to Tristan. "But I'll return. I give you my word of honor. As a merfolk."

His eyes were wider than sand dollars; his tail went completely still. A thousand words were in his eyes as he lifted his hand in farewell, but all he said was, "I am selfish enough to be glad of it."

Well, of course he wanted Phoebe's help for his people, even if her powers frightened him now. No one else could do for them what she could. That didn't make him selfish. It made him a loving leader for the merfolk, one the fools didn't appreciate.

Heart heavy, Phoebe swam off, leaving the merfolk behind her. Her magic whispered their hope and fear to her as she went. But she couldn't tell which they felt the strongest.

The moonglow of Phoebe's skin faded as she sped toward the shore. She tried to use the new part of herself that controlled the light to reach out her mind to Queenie, showing her images of where Sierra should go. Hopefully, the message would get across to them.

As Phoebe swam, she yanked down her coiled braids, never feeling less like a princess in her life. As confident and exhilarated as she had felt when all that magic blazed through her, stark reality was setting in. Even though they accepted her help now, she knew the merfolk weren't happy about her transformation and increased powers. And she still might not be enough to defeat their enemies.

When she surfaced, the small tent on the rocky shore

stunned her, along with the hundreds of tiny lights surrounding it. Fairies were everywhere. The tent looked like it had been there a while, coated with salt and sand. Someone burst out and ran toward to the water.

Sierra. It was Sierra. She was waiting for Phoebe.

Relief poured through Phoebe, and if she had still been human, her eyes would have overflowed with tears. Now all she could feel was a tightening of her throat and stinging at the back of her eyes. She waved at Sierra, who ran straight into the sea without stopping, sending droplets flying everywhere. Stark fear, anger, and relief flashed across Sierra's face as she rushed deeper into the water without any sign of discomfort from the cold. Phoebe swam until she was shoulder-deep, then stopped, waiting. Any farther and scales would show. Her hair plastered her neck and shoulders, covering her gills and the vivid tattoos. Good. She wanted to break this to her sister as gently as possible, but Sierra was about to get the shock of her life.

"Phoebe! By all the stars, where have you been? What were you thinking?" Anger was clearly pushing relief aside as Sierra reached Phoebe and grabbed her by the arms. "I've been out of my mind with worry! None of the merfolk would tell me anything except you were with them! Are you okay? Why aren't you saying anything?"

Phoebe moved her mouth, but of course nothing

came out. She patted her neck and shook her head, trying to communicate, but the water was too dark for Sierra to see below her shoulders without careful examination.

"Tell me what's going on!" Sierra's voice rose.

Phoebe did the one thing she could think of. She backed up slightly and then dove down, letting her tail rise about the water for a long moment. She even flicked it in her sister's direction. When she rose back out of the water, Sierra was paler than the white rocks along the shore.

"Is that... a *tail*?" she managed.

Phoebe motioned for Sierra to come under water. She simply knew her own magic would support Sierra the way Tristan's had so often supported Phoebe. Sierra didn't budge. Phoebe finally lost patience and pulled her sister under the surface.

To her credit, Sierra didn't panic, but she did look wild-eyed at Phoebe's fin. Who could blame her, really? The change was still shocking to Phoebe, no matter how natural it now felt. At least she finally could speak.

"I'm so sorry, Sierra. Tristan was dying from a water wraith attack. I saved him, but the magic of the sea took my human life and turned me into a mermaid in exchange for his healing."

One side of Sierra's lips curled up in a trembling smile, as if desperately awaiting the punchline. Her gaze moved to trace the many merfolk tattoos swirling over Phoebe's shoulders and arms. "This has to be a joke, right? People don't just... grow fins! It's not possible!"

"I know it sounds crazy, but I swear, it's true. I entered the water first with a merfolk tear—they do truly exist—but I didn't change until I told the magic of the sea to do whatever it took to save Tristan." The tale did sound outlandish, but her sister had to believe. Phoebe called out, "Queenie, tell her for me!"

The fairy queen flew over and floated just above the clear water. A wash of comfort slid through Phoebe. Queenie was telling her it was okay. Phoebe considered how to send images of her time under the water to the little creature, to share with Sierra. Focusing on the way she felt when she connected with Tristan, Phoebe followed the thin magical line connecting her to Queenie. Though the link was far, far fainter than hers with the merfolk, it was enough.

Frowning in concentration, Phoebe relayed an image of the water wraith. Queenie squealed and did a backflip.

Sierra cried out, "What? What is it?"

Quickly, Phoebe followed that image with others, more beautiful ones: the coral cliffs, the dancing seaweed, a smiling Mina, a serious Tristan.

Queenie hummed, trilled, and then glowed more brightly.

Sierra closed her eyes as she received the torrent of

images from her fairy queen. When she opened her eyes again, they were full of amazement—then blazing fire.

"Who gave you the right to throw away your life like that? Did you ever stop and think what it would do to me to have my sister stuck in the ocean forever or die at the hands of a sea monster? I would give up anything for you—" She cut off abruptly as her voice broke.

"That's just it, isn't it?" Phoebe said, compassion robbing her of any anger. "You've given up so much for me. And I'm grateful. But you have your life with Micah and your fairies. And now I have mine with the merfolk. It's not that I wanted to stay forever, but I do love the ocean and, Sierra, I have real magic now."

"Maybe you could still have your magic on land. With us!"

"No, Micah was right. I'm tied to the merfolk the way you're tied to your fairies."

"But I didn't turn *into* a fairy!"

"Look, I know you think I'm too young to handle a serious problem, but right now, the merfolk need me to help. I can use magic in ways they can't, and I'm willing to fight when they aren't. The creature Corbin talked about, Baleros? The merfolk finally believe he's waking up, and his wraith servants have been stealing their magic. I've got to stop him, or at least do my part. The merfolk think I'm charming them against their will, but I have to help them anyway."

The enormity of the situation struck, and Phoebe

hung her head. The passion and desperation that had been pushing her gave way to a cold gloom. She wanted to cry but couldn't. She looked down at the sandy ocean floor, struggling to compose herself.

Sierra started to scoff but then stopped. She lifted Phoebe's head and looked deeply into her eyes.

"They hurt your feelings." Sierra's voice was flat.

Phoebe couldn't force any words out.

"I'll kill them. Every last one of those ungrateful merfolk—"

"Stop it, no. It's not their fault. Don't you see? They were slaves for generations. They're afraid of what I can do to them. *I'm* afraid of what I can do to them. They think I'll turn into some sort of slave driver. You know how your fairies used to fight you? I think this is sort of like that, but worse. They don't want me around."

At least the merfolk didn't leave physical wounds like Sierra's fairies had. Just emotional ones.

"Even Tristan?" Sierra asked with a raised eyebrow, lightening the moment a bit, pushing her shoulder against Phoebe's

If only Phoebe could laugh at the situation.

"His response is the most confusing of all. He seems to sense magic from me more easily than others—so effortless, it's frightening—but I have no idea what he's really feeling. I'm not sure how we could ever be bondmates now, not with my power over him like this. It's not fair to either of us." She shook her head sadly.

Sierra sighed. "Do you remember the day we got home from Bentwood's? After I thought I would die in that earthquake?"

"How could I forget?"

"You asked me to me promise I'd never leave you. And I won't. I won't leave you behind anymore, Phoebe. Find a way to come home! You don't need those ungrateful merfolk. How can I live up to my promise if you do this? Surely we can find some way to reverse this spell or whatever it is!"

"You haven't broken your promise. You've never really left me, not where it counts. We can still visit, and I'll miss you terribly. But I've made another promise, Sierra. And I've got to keep it. I'm not a child anymore."

Sierra didn't reply while the current played with her hair like Phoebe used to do as a child. Phoebe willed her big sister to understand. This had to be done.

All at once, Sierra folded Phoebe in her arms and held on tightly. They floated in the water, silent, because there was no need for words to express the love they shared.

When Sierra finally spoke, her voice was husky. "I'm proud of you, Phoebe. I hate that you're risking yourself, but you're right you aren't a little girl anymore. You never really were a child again after Bentwood took you. You're the same age I was when I went searching for Queenie. I guess it's time I started treating you like that. I know you love magical creatures, and you've loved merfolk since the day you first laid eyes on one. And that particular merman seems to feel the same way about you. I hope they appreciate that you would do anything for them. You were always the better caretaker of the two of us."

Phoebe's eyes stung again. She summoned a weak smile. "Thank you." She sniffed and added, "Tell everyone I love them."

"Of course. Though Nell is going to kick my rear over this. Corbin, too."

Phoebe thought back to the moment when Nell spoke the prophecy. She remembered Corbin's sad, gentle smile.

"I think they'll understand."

"You could bring me with you. I'll help you fight!" Sierra's hands were like vises on her shoulder. Desperation edged her words.

Phoebe slowly shook her head. "Where I'm going, sweet sister, you cannot follow. Not this time. You have your role out there, on land, and with Donovan and others raising trouble, you and Queenie have to fight back. Don't let them make you lose ground. Queenie and I can communicate, so I'll call you through her when it's all done, okay?"

Sierra grumbled, Sierra argued, but eventually Sierra gave in. She backed out of the water, and Phoebe waved one final time. Sierra stood on the sand, teeth chattering slightly from the water that felt like a warm robe bundled around Phoebe now.

Saying goodbye to her sister was like a giant door shutting on one part of her life. Now Phoebe, not Sierra, was the protector. And it was time to get going.

Phoebe blew her sister a kiss and dove into the water, flipping her fin in a farewell salute. Then she headed back to the merfolk. She knew just where they were. They glowed like a city on a hill in her mind's eye, a beacon drawing her closer, closer, closer.

To home.

CHAPTER TWENTY-FOUR

*A*s Phoebe swam toward her new people, she pondered the situation. She wished she had used a little less bravado in the conclave meeting. What if she *couldn't* help the others use magic as she did? Maybe only her two best friends were close enough to connect to her that way. What if she wasn't really able to fight the wraiths herself? Her plan was full of holes.

As she approached the village, Tristan and Odessa were waiting. Before Phoebe could find a way to confess to him that she didn't really know what to do next, he sped over to her with anguish written on every line of his face. His pain slammed into her like a physical force.

She gasped. "What is it?"

"Mina's gone!"

"What? Mina's missing?"

"She went out searching for Liam, we think, but she's

not returned at all. Mother thinks the wraiths have taken her."

Odessa swam up next to Tristan, and took charge of the conversation. "Phoebe Quinn, this changes our plans. You must put your powers to work in a new way, sooner than I had hoped. You should both brace yourselves."

Phoebe glanced at Tristan, wishing he would reach over and take her hand. But he didn't.

"You must use your magic to find my daughter and to fight the beast that has her."

Dread filled Phoebe, leaving her heavy and exhausted.

Tristan snapped, "You don't know Baleros has her, or that the wraiths even took her. She was here during the convocation; she knew we had a plan."

"When does Mina ever wait for plans?" Odessa snapped right back.

He groaned, covering his ashen face with both hands.

"Yes, the wraiths took her, I'm sure of it. She went out looking for that foolish seawee who is most likely dead, and now she's gone, too," Odessa said. For the first time, agony pulsed through the older mermaid's voice.

"The wraiths took her? Did you see them?" Phoebe asked.

"I don't need to see them to smell their foul stench," Odessa said scornfully. "She went out, on her own, to the last place Liam was seen. And never came back. If

Tristan hadn't been so upset about you, moping about his room, he'd have known her plan and kept her from being so foolish."

Phoebe cut her eyes to him, but he was too busy glaring at his mother to notice.

"Phoebe's not a tool to use, Mother." Tristan's voice vibrated with warning.

Odessa lifted both eyebrows. "I believe she wants to help, don't you?"

They both turned to look at Phoebe at the same time. Now that she knew their relationship, she could easily see the mother's dark green eyes mirrored in Tristan's. Her hair was streaked with silver now but had stripes of sable as black as Mina's.

Tristan sighed. "That's what I'm afraid of."

"How can I help?" was all Phoebe said.

"Tell me about your experiences with magic. How did you sense Tristan? You need to find Mina, even though she might be far away."

"I can do one better than that," Phoebe said, thinking quickly. "The wraiths descended into the midnight realm. Maybe they took Mina there. Once I sense her, and we plan exactly where to go—if you'll help me—I'll draw them away with my magic. Then, you all could have a team sneak in and take back Mina."

"We'll have to convince the elders," Tristan said.

"No, not really," said Odessa slowly. "Phoebe just has to tell them. They'll come. They'll have to. I can feel her call so strongly now. She can force them to agree with her."

Phoebe was shocked. The very suggestion was abhorrent. "But I can't do that!"

"Even to save Mina's life?"

Tristan looked miserably at his mother then turned haunted eyes to Phoebe.

This was no kind of choice. If she forced them all to do her bidding, she was worse than Bentwood ever had been. Such an action would destroy any hope she had of showing Tristan she'd never abuse her power. Yet if Mina died because of Phoebe's inaction, she'd never be able to forgive herself.

"Let me talk to the elders. Let me show them there's a chance to save her."

"Tristan, go gather them. Tell them to assemble at the next tide, for the young mermaid to plead her case."

Now it was up to Phoebe to sway them—without unfairly using her magic. She'd better figure out what she was going to say. And fast.

Alone in Mina's room, Phoebe tried to focus. How would she find her friend before the tide changed? It was one thing to feel all the merfolk in the chamber with her. But if Mina were in the midnight realm, she was so far away. Maybe too far away to sense. Besides, there were many deep trenches along the ocean floor. Mina could be in any of them.

Right now, Phoebe sensed the merfolk as a giant group—like a pod of dolphins in dark waters. She couldn't distinguish one from another. Finding a single mermaid would be like trying to focus on one note out of a complicated song. She hoped that being in Mina's room and holding her belongings would somehow help distinguish her particular energy from the others.

Phoebe ran her hands over the knick-knacks Mina kept in her room. Baskets of woven sea grass held all her favorite things, hanging from the walls of the cave.

Next to Mina's bed, a knitted scarf Phoebe had made floated gently in the currents, held down by a heavy brass candlestick holder. Both were useless for a mermaid, but Mina had loved every item from land, saying they reminded her of their friendship.

Mina's comb lay on the rock by the bed, made of spiny sea shells. Phoebe picked it up and held it against her chest. *Mina, Mina*, she whispered in her mind. *Where are you?* Trying to find Mina's voice among the cacophony of merfolk was impossible.

Flopping into Mina's bed basket, Phoebe remembered the first time they'd met. Tristan had been at the shore the very next time she had gone to the beach after the rescue. She'd hobbled into the water, hoping the sea would ease the pain in her knee. She'd yelped when he popped above the surface, but his easy smile brought one to her face in return. Then Mina appeared, twinkling eyes peeking from behind Tristan. For all her light-hearted ways, Mina was the one who'd taken charge of Phoebe's healing.

Mina forced Phoebe to keep moving her knee even when it hurt. Tristan might have let it slide, hating to see her in pain, but Mina had no pity. She'd say, "Bend it again, Phoebe. You've got to use it, or you'll always limp."

And then Mina would goad Phoebe until she did it. Without Mina, she might never have fully healed.

Now it was Phoebe's turn to do the helping, but she was running out of time. Pulling herself from the bed, so defeated her skin didn't even glow, Phoebe ached in the general area where her knee should be, at the bend of her tail fin. As if the human parts of her were buried, not gone forever. Panic flared at even the phantom memory of the pain. Her hand spasmed around the comb, the spiny ridges pressing into her skin, reminding her of the present moment. She wasn't that girl anymore. She was here.

She tried to slow her breathing, still her panic, lock down all her bad memories that hissed and slithered from their dark corners when they scented fear rising. But her throat tightened despite herself.

She was here for Mina, she reminded herself. To find Mina. Failure was not an option. *Focus, Phoebe, Focus.*

Phoebe willed herself to relax. She needed to be fully

present to get this job done. Things were different now. *She* was different now. Maybe she could finally let go of those memories.

Settling into her mission, she squeezed the comb again, picturing Mina's dark locks and sweet smile. Phoebe held her breath and imagined sending her magic into the ocean, a magnet seeking Mina.

Nothing.

No spark of Mina's vivacity touched Phoebe. Despite the strong presence of the merfolk in her mind, Mina wasn't among them. And Phoebe had no idea where the mermaid was.

Phoebe bit off a yell of frustration and threw the comb across the room. It somersaulted lazily through the water, far less satisfying than a crash against her wall on land. She screamed again, tugging at her hair. Why couldn't she *find* Mina? The meeting would begin soon, and without a known destination and firm plan, no one could help with a rescue even if she convinced them to. What good was sensing all the merfolk if she couldn't use the power to help her friend?

But wait. Maybe, if she could get away from all the merfolk clogging up her newly awoken senses, she could locate Mina more effectively. It was easier to find a tiny flame amid darkness than in blinding sunlight.

She needed to swim away from the village. Not far. Just a little bit. As Odessa's "guest," Phoebe thought it would be prudent to let Odessa know. She didn't want any misunderstandings. As much as Phoebe hated to approach the mermaid, there was no time to waste.

Phoebe found the elder in her study room of the cliff apartment. Odessa looked up from shuffling through piles of shimmering opalescent shells with strange rune carvings on them, an expectant look upon her face. Phoebe didn't think this mermaid was used to accepting failure, on anyone's part.

"I'm sorry to intrude, milady." The honorific for Tristan's mother still tripped awkwardly over Phoebe's tongue. "I need to be alone to find where Mina is. I'll swim only as far as I need to in order to sense her."

"I can understand your need for space, but you cannot go alone."

"Milady, I promise you, I can handle a short swim away."

"And if you get taken, Mina would be lost to us forever. I won't risk my daughter because of your pride. Tristan will be your guard."

Phoebe's breath hitched.

Not Tristan!

CHAPTER TWENTY-FIVE

*J*ust hearing Tristan's name hurt. Phoebe couldn't forget his look of shock at their last touch, knowing he must finally fear her ability to control his emotions, his behavior. He'd said the sensations they shared were all 'so much'—she'd clearly been unable to contain her powers. And then he didn't reach for her, even when terribly upset. Now he might not even believe that he ever truly cared for her on his own, yet he had to keep working with her for the sake of his sister and family. The situation was just too painful.

"Milady, a guard is not necessary," she said, just as a much subdued Tristan approached them, fiddling with his clam knife. He'd obviously heard Phoebe's refusal of his company. His face was paler than usual, except for the flush along his cheekbones.

He glided to Phoebe's side, offering her a little shrug without a word.

"I just need to get a bit farther away from all the merfolk to listen for Mina. I won't be in any danger," she insisted. Anger bubbled up. She was trying her best, and they weren't helping.

Maybe if she just stayed focused on the immediate crisis, they could get through this. She couldn't even begin to think what she'd do when this was all over and done.

"Tristan has a special tie to Mina, too, as siblings, twins no less. Whatever has got your tail in a twist, I suggest you fix it. I think you will find his presence familiar enough to not distract you from seeking Mina. I believe, in fact, the link they share will most likely boost your power."

There was no arguing with Odessa. Her lips were smashed to a line. There was a darkness to her eyes that had nothing to do with magic and everything to do with grief.

"Fine," Phoebe said.

Phoebe and Tristan swam off in silence, leaving Odessa gazing after them with a face like stone.

The sun must have been setting above. Phoebe could detect subtle differences of light levels in the water. Her new, improved vision also allowed her to see far into the distance. Such magical clarity disconcerted her. How could the merfolk ever rest in this underwater world if their sharp vision rarely dimmed?

They swam to an old garden of some kind along the last edges of the village. Sea cucumbers and tubers trailed over a few half-hearted stakes. At the center was a boulder with a seat worn away like a cupped hand.

"Sit there," he said. "I'll be at the edge of the garden, close enough to keep watch, but hopefully not close enough to bother you."

The words stung. "Tristan, you don't *bother* me." She hadn't meant to hurt his feelings.

"That's not what I meant."

The two stared for a long moment. Then Tristan backed away and took up his post, little clam knife at the ready.

Phoebe tried to focus, but all she could sense was Tristan. He wove through her mind, images flickering, nerves jangling.

"This isn't going to work," she said. She slapped the rock beside her. "Why can't I feel her?"

Tristan sighed and floated over. They sat in silence for a long moment.

"What am I going to do?" she whispered.

Looking down and tracing patterns on the rock, he said, "You need to reach unity with the ocean."

He was so close, his presence warm like the sun against her skin, but so far away in all the ways that mattered. How ironic to have so many of her dreams realized only to lose the one that had become most important to her. His refusal to even look at her snapped her patience.

"I don't suppose it would involve *connecting through a hug and a kiss?*" she said sharply.

He flinched. "Phoebe, I should never have—"

"Well you did, didn't you? And now what? I'm truly stuck as a mermaid and not acceptable to you? Or are you really afraid I'm manipulating you, like everyone else?" Anguish cut off her tirade. She could feel more from the others than she could from him. His presence was clear, but his emotions were guarded as if behind locked doors. Why? Was he fighting harder to keep her out of his heart and mind?

He looked stricken.

"No! No, of course that's not it. I... I just don't want you to think I kissed you because of your powers," he stammered, flushing pink. His glow faded to a dim light.

She stared at him. His eyes remained trained on the sea floor, and his green hair floated over his shoulders like a cloak.

"You mean you don't regret kissing me?" Phoebe couldn't keep herself from asking.

He swallowed hard. His gaze finally met hers, and he touched her hair. "I've never regretted anything less—or more."

She pushed herself away from him with a cry, but he rushed after her.

257

"You must understand, Phoebe. My mother would never allow me to court you, even if you remain here. She'd be too afraid of you; she doesn't like to share her power. You deserve better anyway. We need to find you a way back to being human. It would be selfish of me to seek you as a bondmate and keep you here forever."

Now she knew: even a broken heart was not enough to produce a mer-tear.

"Why do I have to go home?" she said. "Even if I could, which I don't think I can, it's never called to me like the sea does. Sierra understands. She told me so. Here I can at least help."

"Here, you could die!"

"I almost died there, too. Or don't you remember?"

The memories pierced her, and this time she let them. The swollen knee that kept her from running. The bruises along her arms, the whip marks on her back. Worse, the feeling that her life would never be hers again. All her hopes had been destroyed in one fell swoop. No magic, not for her. Her sister hadn't come in time, was maybe even dead. Stunned, Phoebe hadn't even put up a fight when they took her. For those few dark days, she believed she would be a slave, apart from her sister forever.

But here, for the first time, those memories didn't reach so deep. Phoebe studied the delicate merfolk tattoos that danced along her skin. Miraculous. She was no longer that scared girl. Those men could never reach her. Here, she belonged to the first thing she ever loved besides her sister: the sea.

"Don't you see?" Phoebe whispered, placing her hand on his chest. She let everything she felt for him shine from her eyes, no holding back. "This is where my heart really is."

She looked up, and her jaw dropped at the wild intensity on his face. He looked almost wounded, torn between the most outstanding grief and the most ecstatic joy.

With a small gasp, he pulled her in his arms and held her. He buried his face in her hair. The new warmth she felt twice before spiraled through them both, connecting them closer than ever.

"*You* are my heart, Phoebe Quinn. Always," he murmured in her ear.

At last. Relief and happiness sketched a song in her mind. Blue lightning flowed between them and filled the water with its power. In her mind's eye, the light of her magic coiled into the currents in the ocean, its powerful light spiraling out, seeking like reaching fingers.

Then Phoebe froze as her vision exploded in blue light, followed by a series of images. Mina's hands tied. Mina in a pen shrinking away from a taunting wraith. And Mina looking out from far inside a deep trench, in a stone building with an intricate carving of a dragon-headed beast with tentacles.

Then, in her vision, darkness came, something

slithering inside a thick soupy lake on the bottom of the ocean floor lined with clams opening and closing like hundreds of eyes staring... and the dark, dark shadow belonging to a many-armed beast, stirring like a waking giant.

Phoebe reeled back with a gasp. "Did you see that?"

Tristan shook his head.

"I saw Mina! She was in a ravine or a trench of some kind, and I think it was a temple to Baleros because there was a carving of a giant sea beast I've never seen. I think it's the evil shadow from before. There's a colossal amount of magic down there, and the strangest thing was there was a lake inside the ocean floor. How is that even possible?"

Tristan groaned and dropped his head into his hands. "She's deep in the forbidden midnight realm. They took Mina to the Abyss, the most feared place in the sea."

"Why is the Abyss so terrible?" Phoebe asked, shocked at how pale Tristan became.

"It's the source of the worst legends of our people, stories of dark magic and certain death. My mother believes all the stories are true. Most merfolk don't, but superstition has always been enough to keep everyone far away. Add in the very real, deadly creatures already known to live there, and no sane merfolk would venture near."

"But what was that lake I saw? How could that be?"

"That had to be the Lake of Dragons. It continually separates itself from the rest of the ocean, sinking below it, and is deadly to most sea creatures. Our histories say that's where the water wraiths and sea dragons hid during the golden age of the merfolk, drinking in the sulfur and brine, surrounded by boiling water vents."

"That's pretty bad." Phoebe gulped.

"The legends also say that Baleros demanded sacrifices at his altar in the Abyss. Mina must be a planned sacrifice to Baleros, who must be rising very soon, as we feared."

"We have to get her out of there!"

He shook his head, "You don't understand. No merfolk in living memory has ever gone in there and come out alive. The merfolk do not fight."

Resolve firmed inside Phoebe. "They will today. Take me to the elders."

In the great hall once again, two hundred pairs of eyes had locked onto Phoebe and weren't letting go. Her stomach quivered, full of flitting sea horses, but she kept her head high. Giving her testimony was intimidating, but the vision had come on so suddenly, the image so clear. She had to trust herself, or at least the magic inside her.

"So, let me see if I understand you, Phoebe Quinn,"

Odessa's voice rang out. "You had a vision of my daughter, trapped in a domed temple with a carving of Baleros in it, near a sulphurous lake beneath the ocean?"

Tristan said, "She saw the Abyss. Do you not believe her?" He looked mutinously at his mother, who glared back.

"I do. We must go there to rescue Mina."

"The Abyss is forbidden for a reason! We'll die! We will all die!" said someone from the gathered tribe in the great hall.

"Not if I lure the wraiths far away from there first." Phoebe called up her magic and let it flow through her veins. Blue light shimmered from her scales, from her skin, even from her hair.

The crowd exclaimed and surged backward.

"They won't be able to resist me when I call," she said. She had to prove it to them. They were as stubborn as old tortoises, every one of them. Fine. So be it. She remembered what Odessa had said, about telling them, compelling them to do her bidding. It would certainly be convincing.

No. No matter what, she couldn't force everyone to do her bidding. It would be hideously wrong, even if she could manage it. But she could force *one* of them if it meant proving that she had enough power to lead this mission safely. Even if Tristan never looked at her the same again. She squared her shoulders.

"You. Elder Seamus," Phoebe said, beckoning to the angry merman.

His glower matched his aggressive shark tattoos. He'd certainly make her point best. If anyone here wanted to harm her as much as the wraiths, it'd be him.

"Come here." She spoke simply, softly.

He shook his head, paling.

Phoebe pictured the blue lines she had seen swirling through the currents and pulled on one that ran alongside the merman. He wasn't tied to it, but she could use its strength to force his movement. She imagined hauling it hand over hand, pulling the merman to her. She hummed a little tune to calm herself and then broke out in song, imagining him coming closer and closer. She used the power of her singing—something she had always felt inside—to boost the power of the magic, and it worked. His fin began to move—jerky and stiff at first—and he swam to her side, cursing all the way.

The crowd remained still and silent. Phoebe glanced at Tristan, who looked… Was that horror on his face? Shock? She almost cried out, "I take it back!" but it was too late now. And she had a job to do.

Phoebe shook her head. "While I would never call you somewhere you didn't want to go, I believe I can and will call those water wraiths away from their guard duty. I can defend myself from them in a way that you cannot. If we can get to Mina before the dark shadow stirs again, we can figure out what to do about the beast later. Right now, we must save Mina!"

Tristan swam to her side and clasped her hand. "She has my trust." His voice carried through the water, deep and sure, but his hand shook in hers. Whether or not he really did trust her after seeing such a display of power, he acted confident. Mina needed the merfolk to take action. He squeezed Phoebe's hand, and she held on for dear life.

"Who will go with us?" she called out. Her voice echoed in the chamber like a bell. She let the magic release Seamus, pulling it back into herself so it wouldn't charm the crowd. Yet hands rose, and a crowd of merfolk came to them, came to help, came to her. Came to Phoebe, because she had called. Whether they came because they respected her, feared her, or were compelled by her, she didn't know. Maybe she'd never know.

CHAPTER TWENTY-SIX

The plan was simple, almost too simple. Phoebe would swim into the rift ahead of the merfolk and use her magic to charm the wraiths to her side and send them away like she did the sea dragons. In the meantime, the merfolk would descend into the Abyss to find Mina.

Odessa and other scholars poured over the ancient maps in her study before agreeing on the exact location and path to take. It would be easy to get lost once they entered the midnight realm, but they were as prepared as they could be.

The journey was a stilted, silent one. Phoebe led the merfolk, along with Odessa and Tristan. Phoebe barely noticed the kelp, the fish, or the colorful shellfish. Each flick of her fin brought her closer to when the ocean might very well claim her for the last time. Her pulse thundered in her ears like the surf she might never hear again. She said nothing and kept swimming. Mina needed her.

As the crowd of silent merfolk soared over the old city, their fins swished stronger, jerking up and down without their usual smooth flow. Some pointed at parts of the city below, in low conversation with each other. Did they long for the old ways, or was it just Odessa who wanted the old power back? Maybe they were just worried about the upcoming mission.

They moved quickly, their natural luminescence doused. Dread rose in Phoebe as they reached the far edge of the city, along the drop into the midnight realm where she and Tristan had seen the dark shadow slipping into the Abyss.

"That's the place we saw it." She pointed to the towering rock, trying to keep her finger from trembling. These merfolk needed to see a show of strength to follow her into such darkness.

"It went that way."

The merfolk swam into forbidden territory.

Entering the waters of the midnight realm was like swimming into an ink-spill. Phoebe had to use her moonglow to even see where the trench might start. Those two wraiths couldn't have dragged the beast far. The ground below her contained only grey powder, barren of any signs of life.

Despite how it felt to Phoebe, it wasn't long until

even the deep floor of the midnight realm opened like a gaping mouth. The trench was below them.

The waters near the trench faded to a black darker than a night sky devoid of stars. A clammy chill sifted through the currents. The Abyss had come by its name honestly. The water looked empty, but she knew it wasn't.

Tristan kept his eyes roving, squinting into the cloak of blackness. "The creatures here hide from the few predators that lurk. There might not be many of them, but they're worth hiding from."

Gathering her courage and humming a quick tune beneath her breath, Phoebe swam to the fissure's entrance. The crack was narrow at the top but opened wide along the way down to the depths. A temple below would easily fit. Phoebe shivered.

Tristan and their small crowd of merfolk hid among the strange orange coral that lined the opposite side of the fissure, but Phoebe swam openly. She called every bit of light she could. Her blue light flickered across the faces of the nearest merfolk still within her vision, their eyes wide with awe. They were too well-disciplined to murmur, but their unwavering attention weighed against her very skin.

"Come to me, water wraiths!" she called and began to sing without holding back. She sang a song of hope, of light, of dawn, of love. She imagined the blue light filling her and pulling the wraiths to her.

Things hissed, deep inside the channel, but Phoebe kept singing despite the darkness she felt drawing closer. The magic was amazingly rich here, a feast for her senses. It sang through her veins, intoxicating with its power. She gorged herself, fear making her take more than she might have otherwise.

"Come here, come forth, come to me!" she sang, louder and louder.

And they came.

Four water wraiths, perfect in face except for those red eyes, slithered forth from the trench. She had been expecting two. Her heart stuttered in her chest. She couldn't fight four. But she couldn't admit that. If she did, the others might not risk their lives to fight with her.

The wraiths blinked in Phoebe's blue light, their forked tongues flickering. She backed away and taunted them. "Surely you would like another prisoner for your sea beast?"

The creatures exchanged a glance and then burst toward her, faster than she could escape. That wasn't the plan at all!

In a panic, she spun around, dodging a claw. Which way was up? Which way to go? She had to move. She chose a direction and swam furiously, hoping she was going the right way. Everything was dark except her own glow. Confused, she sped past another swiping claw, and a strange building came into focus in the distance below her. A temple, the one from her vision. It was actually in the fissure, on the bottom of the trench.

The bottom of the trench… her light pulsed brighter in response to her panic. She was supposed to lead the wraiths up and out, not down. They were too close. Beyond the temple, the impossible lake shimmered, its darkness easily discernible and somehow separate from the water in the trench.

She shook her head in amazement. To the side stood the temple, its clamshell roof an otherworldly blue in her light. Mina was in there, if the vision was correct. The plan would never work if Phoebe stayed this far down. She had to get the wraiths away so the others could reach Mina. A single water wraith nearly killed Tristan once. Four of them could kill all the merfolk without Phoebe to distract them. She darted upward with a hard kick of her tail.

Before she traveled more than a tail length, though, a fifth wraith slid out of the temple like an evil shadow, its pale skin gleaming like marble that should never be so alive. It sped toward her, looming suddenly, unnaturally fast. Phoebe screamed, and the creature slammed her into the wall of the fissure, rattling her ribs. Her face mashed against the rough stones. Grit pressed into her cheekbone. The wraith grappled with her arms, and she fought to keep it from getting a grip on her. Talons tore along her skin, raking along her new tattoos. Blood was black ink in the dim water. Her cries were muffled, but the screeches of the wraith were as loud as ever, right behind her, reverberating through the water.

Come on light, come on light, Phoebe chanted, pulling it from deep within. Her concentration disintegrated as something heavy leaned against her shoulders, and a giant hand gripped the back of her skull, pressing sharp points from five claws against her scalp.

At the base of her neck, she felt a sharp prick. The bleached skeleton from the beach flashed before her eyes. The half-destroyed skeleton in the cave. The skeletons! Both had died like this. Five crushed holes in the back of the head. Sucked dry.

Coldness drenched her, radiating from the wraith's touch as it drew her magic from her. She gasped. The magic spun from her slowly, resentfully, long blue tendrils that resisted leaving Phoebe's center. It was nothing like sending her magic to Tristan. That had been a gift. This was a theft.

No! She would die before giving up her power to a monster like this. She fought the increasing pressure on her skull. The wraith growled, irritated by the insufficient droplets of energy it was receiving. Phoebe kicked her tail backward, but the wraith blocked her. She squirmed, but the claws tightened. Whimpering, she froze.

The tiny river of magic trickled from her into the wraith and then streamed through it to somewhere else, a deep pit of need that wanted everything Phoebe had.

The greed from that shadowed presence just beyond the wraith oozed toward her, as if tentacles wrapped around her. Her magic had definitely attracted something seeking power. A lot of it.

Well, whatever was lurking couldn't have it. Wouldn't. Scowling, she stopped trying to free herself. Instead, she leaned into the wraith, sending her consciousness through the blue magic tendrils linking them. When she reached its mind, an explosion of blue light lit up the waters like fireworks.

Eyelids flickering, Phoebe shook as images burst into her, pouring into her mind from the wraith as the path of the energy reversed. Her magic rushed backed to her, like waves drawn back into the sea.

Visions rife with emotions—one right after another—sped through her. She looked out of the eyes of the wraith, and for this one moment, they shared a mind: she was the wraith.

Never-ending darkness in the cave, so alone, so hungry... so empty.

A screaming merman with face in agony, delicious, but not enough, not for all of us.

Sisters arising... together again after so many years, dark glee.

Master waking... but weak. So weak. Rumbling. Reaching. Calling me.

We dance around a shadowed body of our master, hungry for magic, we will serve.

Master needs energy, energy we can feed him. It is our ancient function.

A red, seething haze filling the darkness, finally healing, but so slowly...

A new, strange mermaid—human but not—is filled with light, far away... we feel her—so strong, so rich, so... powerful. Yes...

Get her.

Burning hatred swamped the thoughts, and Phoebe cried out. She might burn up from the rage. She fought to sense the claws on her skull, anything to remind herself where she was.

I'm right here. I'm in the fissure. These aren't my memories... The torrent of images slowed.

The blue light grew around them, refracting through the water, making her squeeze her eyes against the brightness.

The wraith shrieked, a sound of agony and rage, and the pressure on her skull eased. Phoebe shook her head and spun around, fighting to orient herself. The wraith floated in front of her, stunned, mouth still curled in violence but unmoving.

No time to lose! She darted toward the opening of the fissure, her vision clearing. This one wouldn't be stunned long, and there were all the others to contend with still. The walls of the fissure sped by, jagged cracks and crevices full of deeper shadows.

Phoebe's mind raced. What was waking? Was that

Baleros? The last memory was a sense of ownership from whatever was watching her. Though no words were spoken, the greedy hunger clearly pronounced: *Mine.*

Not if Phoebe had anything to say about it. She was nobody's prize. She wasn't a little girl, and she wasn't a victim. Not anymore. She had a chance to prove it today.

CHAPTER TWENTY-SEVEN

Screams met Phoebe's ears as she sped out of the fissure. Tristan and a mass of merfolk were swirling through the water in dizzying acrobatics, just out of reach of four very angry wraiths. By keeping the wraiths distracted, they had probably saved Phoebe's life, but they couldn't last long. Her heart jumped at the sight of Tristan brandishing his little clam knife at one of the wraiths.

She only stood a chance against them because of the magic that made her unique among the merfolk. She had to get the monsters away from the others. Phoebe raced past the wraiths at the edge of the fissure, catching them by surprise. The fifth flew up from the crevice, rage on its face.

She focused as hard as she could, and her blue light came again, billowing out around her like a shield.

"Mina's down there! Go!" she cried and fled.

The wraiths cawed like crows in the forest back home and then took up the chase.

She led them throughout the orange coral before dodging behind a sharp outcropping, dousing her light, and hiding as best she could. She'd never be able to outswim the hulking beasts. The sea might claim her, but the wraiths would not. She would not end up as a corpse with five holes in her head.

She needed to concentrate enough to create a stronger burst of the blue light. This time, though, she'd need to be able to direct it at one of them on purpose. It was too dangerous to hope that her body would produce a bolt of magic at just the right time. And while shining with blue light appeared to draw them to her, it didn't seem to hurt the creatures. Only the powerful flash of light did that.

Phoebe waited, the coral rough against her back as her chest heaved. The wraiths, swimming above and below her little section of coral, were black shadows undulating through the water. Looking for her.

She'd taken on too big a job. She couldn't defend herself against all five. At least they were still searching for her, instead of guarding the temple like they should have been. The tie between the wraith and her... the thought made her shudder, but at least she knew her magic attracted even evil sea creatures, not just the merfolk. She'd read the wraith's mind like she'd read

Elder Seamus's. But she never wanted to experience that vileness again.

The wraiths started to drift away, and Phoebe slid to a different location, curling up in the coral. Sending off another pulse of light, she quickly doused it and pressed back into the rock.

Thanks to her gills, there were few bubbles to give her away, but she held her breath just in case. The chill of the nearby wraiths crawled along her skin. Her muscles cramped from holding so still, and she cautiously flexed her fin. All she needed to do was keep them occupied long enough for the rescue team to grab Mina from her prison, which shouldn't take long. Tristan was the fastest swimmer she'd ever seen.

Had they found Mina? Phoebe tried to picture the merfolk in her mind's eye but was far too distracted by the wraiths. Tiny shrimp-like creatures crawled along next to her, testing her skin with their pinchers. They acted like little fairies, curious about their surroundings. She smiled at the comparison. Then one pinched her with shocking strength, and she let out a yelp.

A dark silhouette with a whipping, slinky tail moved in the coral beside her, and she ducked. A claw plowed into the space where her head had just been.

With a gasp, Phoebe darted along the edge of the reef, scraping her shoulder as she went, leaving a trail of blood in the water. A long shark passing by backtracked and swam closer to investigate. A tiger shark was almost as dangerous for her as the wraiths. Could this rescue attempt get any worse?

One of the water wraiths screeched at the tiger shark, swiping at it with its claws. The shark charged, beginning a fierce battle above Phoebe. She snuck away, eyes fixed on the five wraiths and the shark as they dodged each other in a massive underwater dog fight. Snapping teeth and ferocious howls echoed through the water.

She reached the fissure in time to see Tristan and Odessa hauling an exhausted Mina past the edge of the trench. Phoebe sped toward her friend.

"Mina! Are you okay?" Phoebe cried, wishing she could pull the girl into her arms, but Odessa and Tristan held Mina wrapped between them. She was thrashing in her family's arms but wasn't even crying. Phoebe hadn't realized just how terrible something had to be in order to produce mer-tears. She once again touched the empty spot where the pearl had rested. Who had sent her that gift?

Mina shouted, "They have Liam. He's down there! You've got to go to him!"

Odessa disregarded her daughter's protests, checking her over for any wounds. Other merfolk were already dashing away now that Mina had been found.

Phoebe turned her senses to the space below,

searching past the brilliance of her friends beside her. Phoebe sensed him now, along with some other strange presence she didn't understand.

"She's right," Phoebe said. "There's someone else down there. Definitely another mer."

Odessa's lips thinned, and she wrapped Mina up in a sea frond blanket, ignoring Mina's struggles to get away.

"But, Mother, Liam needs us. He's in the temple. That hideous temple with its bloodstained altar! He's going to die. We have to go to him!"

Odessa didn't blink. "We'll come back soon, after we regroup. We can't risk any more lives."

She whisked Mina away, calling the others. The remaining crowd of merfolk followed, and Phoebe was too stunned to even consider using her powers to make them stay and fight.

Tristan remained beside Phoebe. Odessa's attention was so focused on her daughter that the venerable mermaid didn't notice her son had not immediately obeyed. The group of merfolk swam with such speed that they would be too far away to reach within moments.

"Should I make them stop? Or try to?" Phoebe spun around, unsure what to do. She tried to imagine controlling that many merfolk, but couldn't fathom it. Impossible.

His eyes were dark when they met hers. "They'd never forgive you overriding their free will."

"I don't care!"

"But I do. It matters a great deal to me that you're accepted by my people after this is done, Phoebe."

The sweetness of his words took her breath away, but she realized in a moment of clarity that if she loved him, she needed to let him go. Even if he would accept her as she was, being involved with a mer-charmer wasn't safe for him, not with power she might unconsciously use on him.

He'd never abandon her, not now that he'd confessed his affection, but she loved him too much to accept anything but his total freedom. He didn't know what he felt for her, not really. How could he, with a mer-charmer like her around? He needed freedom to decide what he really wanted. And his heart wanted to help his people stand strong. She'd seen it time and time again.

Thinking only of his happiness, she restrained her power as closely as she could, careful not to leak a drop of suggestion, and said, "Go convince them to stay! I know you want to! Tell your mother that you won't stand by her decision!"

How could anyone leave a child behind? What kind of leaders were these elders? They needed lessons on how to lead.

He bit his lip, glancing over his shoulder at the departing elders. She winced at the indecision and worry on Tristan's face. He wouldn't just be defying his elders but his own mother, his own family. Beyond unthinkable for a merfolk.

He squared his shoulders.

"I'll be right back! Don't do anything!" he said, tracing one hand along her cheek.

A blush stole across her face as she watched him speed away, strong tail fin almost a blur. That was the Tristan who led her to safety. That was the Tristan who could lead his people to a truly safe and peaceful life one day, though it might mean changing the rules they lived by.

The others were moving so quickly they had faded into the murky waters. If anyone could catch up and talk sense into them, it was Tristan.

In the heavy silence, the presence of the merfolk in her mind grew fainter. Except for one, invisible below, which flickered like a candle about to go out. If Liam was indeed down there, he might not have enough time for her to wait for Tristan to return. Dread swamped her. If she was going to judge Odessa for leaving the little child behind, how could Phoebe pretend she didn't know the child was dying now?

Simple. She couldn't.

Phoebe chewed her bottom lip, looking back at the entrance to the fissure. The seawee's fear bit at her, goading her into action. She had to save Liam. She just hoped her power was enough.

Extending her senses as far as they could reach, she

carefully maneuvered her way back to the entrance of the fissure. At least Tristan would not be in any danger.

The swishing of the sea currents was the only sound other than the very faint call of a whale many furlongs away. Where were the wraiths? She was tempted to mentally look for their location. But no, extending her senses would draw their attention to her.

As Phoebe stared down into the dark hole of the canyon, the blackness wavered, bringing to mind another darkness, one she tried hard to forget: the darkness of a jail cell, with the acrid stink of sweat, urine, and blood.

She shook her head. The terror of being locked up by Bentwood couldn't touch the loathing she felt now at the possibility that her hesitation could cost a seawee his life.

She squinted, trying to discern any shapes in the shadowy depths. The temple was there, the wraiths were gone, and she had to swim down. But her fin did not move.

"Liam?" she called out. Her voice quavered, and she tried again. "Liam, are you down there?" *Please don't be down there. Please don't be down there.*

A high, piteous scream shattered the silence: the shriek of a terrified child. The magic in her vibrated in response.

Phoebe swallowed her fear and dove. With her light doused for safety, the darkness closed around her like a fist. She swam past where she had reached before, her terror a cold ache in the pit of her stomach.

Things brushed against her arms, unseen things that left rasping scratches behind on her skin. Fish shone like translucent ghosts, their beating hearts and stomachs like ink spots inside their clear skin. Almost all of them had sharp teeth. She held her arms closely to her side, hoping they wouldn't attack.

A ripple of pain scored her back. She bit back a cry and flailed away. Dangling ribbons of a pale pink jellyfish floated beside her, ready to tangle prey in lengths even longer than her body. She took several calming breaths and proceeded even more cautiously than before. The water was hotter here, even against her mermaid flesh, and she remembered the boiling water vents Tristan had mentioned.

Finally, the roof of the temple loomed before her, cracked clamshell tiles coated with dark red plants and moss. Unlike the temple in the ancient city, this one was closed all around except for a single entrance. Phoebe floated, paralyzed with fear as she stared at the opening. *Go in. Go in. Just do it.* But she couldn't.

Then a shock zinged through her like a lightning bolt. She arched her back, biting back a cry. The child she had sensed was gone. It was like a candle blown out in her mind, leaving just a smoking wick. Was she too late? Grief pulled her apart, ripping through her gut, stealing her breath.

She'd been too afraid. She'd caused the death of an innocent child because of her brokenness. Phoebe's mermaid body didn't know how to handle the overload of pain that burned inside her, unable to be released. The merfolk were not built for such tragedy.

She had to check to see what happened to the little seawee. If nothing else, she would take his body home. It was the least she could do.

She'd never dreaded anything so much in her life, but she swam forward, trembling fingers reaching out toward the open stone door of the temple. She couldn't enter such darkness, not here. She needed light.

Then a hiss slid through the water.

Phoebe spun around, and two water wraiths converged on her at once. She screamed as they grabbed her arms. Their hands were like ice as they pulled her into the gloom of the temple. Thrashing, she kicked with her fin as hard as she could, trying to escape.

Blue light flashed, but it now slid along them and disappeared without a trace, as if they were funneling her energy through themselves into something else. One even smiled at her, a long slow smile that promised a great deal of pain. They dragged her deeper.

"Stop!" Phoebe glowed brilliantly, but the wraiths continued forward. Her biceps felt like they would snap in half from the pressure of their grip. Her blue light dimmed and went out completely.

The water wraiths growled, their glowing red eyes turning the walls the color of blood.

"I command you to let me go!" Phoebe said, shaking. She tried to summon her blue light again, but her emotions were out of control, and with them, so, too, was her magic.

A low booming laugh filled the temple.

CHAPTER TWENTY-EIGHT

"So, little girl, you think you can command my servants to do anything? Not now, with my consciousness awakened." The voice was gravelly, the grind of a dungeon door swinging closed.

The hairs on Phoebe's neck rose. "Who are you?"

More red light flared. With her new vision, Phoebe could easily make out the laughing figure. It took a long moment for her brain to make sense of what she saw.

A young seawee glided toward her with a smirk on his face.

"Liam?" Phoebe shook her head and blinked her eyes hard, but her vision didn't change. It was the boy who had told the elders about the water wraiths, the boy who had been full of terror and utter belief that evil had returned. He wasn't dead after all. But she had sensed him disappear. Liam's presence remained shadowed

285

even now, like a banked fire. Yet there he was, grinning at her.

Grinning? "Liam, what are you doing here?"

"Liam? What are you doing here?" mocked the seawee in a hideous parody. The deep voice didn't belong there. This voice was ancient, laced with hatred. He eyed her with derision, lips quirked in a cruel smile.

"I see you aren't wearing my necklace anymore. Did those mean merfolk take it away from you? Too bad for them it was too late. Good for me, though. Yes, definitely good for me."

"And, uh, why is that good?" Phoebe asked, desperately trying to grasp what was happening.

"I need a rich meal to embody my true form again. You are by far the most powerful creature in the sea. Aside, that is, from me." Liam tapped his chest with his finger and giggled.

The little child's sound was like an off-key note. The evil eyes, the red glow, the menacing words... all delivered from a sweet child's body.

Phoebe shuddered. "And what did you do with Liam?"

Again, the booming laugh. "Very good, little mermaid. Oh, Liam's in here, too, crying in the back of my mind. Because it's mine now. He's a whiner, just like his feeble drunk of a father. Like father, like son. That was his father's mer-tear I gifted you with, you know. He gave it up in an attempt to bargain with me, to spare his life when my wraiths came for him. Didn't want to die, though of course, he did when we squeezed every last drop of magic out of him. But even his tear didn't have enough power for what I needed."

At a nod from the boy, the wraiths released her. Phoebe eased backward, trying to make space between them without being too obvious. "So that's why the wraith tried to take my magic?"

"Tried and failed, unfortunately."

"Why not take my energy yourself if you're so powerful?"

"I've been trapped in a dream for quite some time, leaving me weak. Fortunately, my consciousness escaped it. Freeing my mind from my dream prison required several sacrifices."

"Like Liam's father? And the merman I found on the coast?"

"My water wraith servants killed them and sent their magic to me, yes. We are deeply connected, my servants and I. Yet I could barely whisper in my servants' minds to wake them enough to seek sustenance for me." He scowled.

Phoebe gulped. Maybe if she kept the monster talking—for monster he assuredly was, no matter what body he wore—she could figure out an escape plan. "So, what did you do once you had... replenished your energy enough?"

"You really must keep up. I took over this boy's body,

since he had the poor judgment to come looking for proof of my wraiths. He made it so easy. A physical body makes any feeding more solid. I planned to use him to funnel a great deal of magic into my physical form here, but it turns out something is wrong with this body. With all of these merfolk. Somehow, none of them can use magic properly anymore." The seawee swam closer, back and forth, back and forth, and Phoebe retreated farther.

"They *are* magic," Phoebe said, automatically. Everyone knew that.

"Wrong. They have magic in them, yes, but they can't channel it like they used to, and I don't know why. They can't direct it, fight with it, heal with it. Except you."

Phoebe tried to hide her shiver but failed.

"Oh yes, I know what you are. None of the foolish merfolk knew what they were dealing with, letting their son and daughter sport around with a human with sea magic in her blood like you. You call all of us, even me, little girl, and I'm a merfolk simply because of the body I chose to borrow. Once I'm finished with this one, you'll lose that advantage, I assure you. For you know who I am. Tell me."

"You're Baleros, the ancient sea beast," Phoebe managed to whisper. The darkness weighed on her heavier than it had since her days at Bentwood's. At least the paralyzing horror she'd felt from the oozing red shadow was vastly diminished, perhaps contained by the seawee's body.

"That *was* me. My own true body is slowly waking in the Lake of Dragons where it can heal best. My children moved my body to this deepest, safest place for this final moment. "

So somewhere in this trench, deep in the black pits of that impossible lake within the ocean, the giant shadow was grumbling in its sleep, perhaps tossing and turning its many tentacles, full of poison and power. She knew if she had to face *that*, she'd die. Ice ran through her veins.

"Soon I will arise in full. My consciousness is here, borrowing this merchild's body until I can wake my physical shape. It's close now. My body will be awakened once you open the door for me with your magic."

"*My* magic?" Phoebe said, startled. She braced herself for what the creature might do, but he only laughed.

"Well, I could take over your body like this one, but it's a tedious process and one I doubt would go smoothly with someone like you. I sensed you before, when my servant first tried to bring you to me as food."

Baleros continued, "I felt your magic fight back and knew you were more powerful than any of the others. That was the whole point of luring you into the sea with the mer-tear, silly girl. I'm not all evil, you see. I won't kill you. You'll probably even revert to human form once the last drop of magic is drained from your little body. I am quite sure your mermaid form, completely transformed as you are, should be able to unlock the boundless magic all around us."

All Phoebe's breath left her. By feeding this sea beast, she was actually putting the merfolk in more danger than they ever would have been without her. What a complete failure.

An image of Sierra sprang to mind, face set with grim determination. And Nell. Neither of them would be scared, Phoebe thought. They would fight. Nell would certainly be able to use her sword to escape, and Sierra would stop at nothing to reach her goal. But if Phoebe attacked Baleros now, what would happen to the young seawee himself, his consciousness trapped in his own mind? Phoebe couldn't pass up the chance, even a small one, to save him if he could be set free from the control of the evil sea beast.

This wasn't a fight she could win with sword and steel, anyway. Those were never her weapons and never had been. She'd spent her life singing, helping others, caring for others. And while Sierra was mastering the use of a bow, Phoebe was cowering in a prison cell. She hadn't even tried to fight back. It just wasn't in her nature. She was no Sierra.

Phoebe alone stood between this evil creature and all the power he used to have. She remembered Tristan's stories, the dark times that brought about the destruction of the golden era of the merfolk. Baleros had done that. He could do it again. She had never wished so deeply for the power to change something.

"Well, what will it be? You *will* help me. The question is: will it be the easy way or the hard way?"

"Why should I help you? You'll kill the merfolk anyway if I give you my power. And you've already proven you can't take it from me without my consent."

Baleros tsked and shook his head. "You shouldn't make assumptions. No, I wouldn't kill the merfolk. Remember, I am part of the sea, too, though of course I'm a killer whale compared to a merfolk's minnow."

He chuckled, but then his eyes darkened, glistening with power and madness. "I don't need to kill them, not anymore. No, no, no. What a waste of manpower. I would simply enslave them. I hear they allowed themselves to be enslaved for years already. And by *humans*, of all the disgusting things. You'd enslave them yourself if you stayed, what with that charming magic of yours. Just another reason why you can't remain here. There can only be one master."

Phoebe flinched. It didn't matter that she herself had never used a merfolk as a slave. Entire cities of humans had for years. Now that she knew she could actually force the merfolk to do as she chose, the guilt hit too close to home.

The beast in the boy's body smirked. "Hmm. Yes. At any rate, this way, their service would be to their own king. Because I am the rightful king of the ocean, which includes the merfolk. I'll take care of them, the way an adult must care for wayward, disobedient children. The merfolk would flourish with some strong leadership for a change."

They might need stronger leadership, but someone like Tristan, not like this thing. "You are nothing here, Baleros. I'll never help you!"

It was the wrong thing to say.

The child-beast snickered, a low, rippling sound that was powerful and evil and completely wrong coming out of a child's mouth. The soul-crushing edge of the shadow thrummed through it. The sound disappeared, and there was such a deep silence for a long moment that only the roaring of Phoebe's heartbeat filled her ears.

The waves above were just long-lost memories. She had surely been in this dark cavernous temple forever, trapped with a madman. Fear battered at her, but she pushed it away.

Baleros said, "You think you're brave now. I respect that. But know this, girl—my body is not like yours or even my wraiths'. Mine is beyond your imagination, and once you see it, your mind will break. So help yourself and work with me in this form. My servants and I aren't evil, no more than is the shark and the giant squid. Just different than your happy little merfolk, always dancing about. Wasting time. Wasting their talents."

"I won't help you. The merfolk deserve a peaceful life."

"I thought you might react that way. Luckily, I'm always prepared."

The three other water wraiths erupted out of the darkness, spiraling around Phoebe, a whirling cyclone of red eyes and sharp teeth. All coming at her.

CHAPTER TWENTY-NINE

*P*hoebe tried to summon the blue light, but panic rose instead. Nothing happened.

Two wraiths grabbed her wrists while another held her tail.

"What are you doing?" she screamed. Suddenly, she was ten years old again. Phoebe stifled a sob. She had sworn she would never be powerless again.

Baleros rifled through her memories like a stack of cards. He didn't even need to use the wraiths to reach her now. Being full of sea magic came with its own ties to this creature. She tried to block him, tried to reverse the line of magic to him as she had with the wraith, but met a wall of seamless steel. The beast smirked, acknowledging her attempt and labeling it unimportant in one devastating second.

"I see Bentwood tied you to a stake, little girl.

Whipped and beaten. Hmm. You cried a great deal, didn't you? You probably didn't even need breaking, weak little human that you were." Baleros all but hissed the words, any pretense at cheerful camaraderie gone.

"You will do as I say," the sea beast continued. "If you refuse, I will simply hurt you until you obey. I'll do a better job at it than his men did, too. What do you say to that?"

Phoebe couldn't think. She couldn't move. *Couldn't. Move.* Somehow a wooden mast from a sunken ship had speared up from the darkness, put into place by one of the wraiths, and during their dizzying turmoil they had tied her wrists behind the mast, stretching her arms back so far that her shoulders ached. Her tail fin was tied to it as well, right at the most narrow spot where her ankles used to be. She jerked against her bindings, mindlessly yanking until the ropes cut into her wrists, pulling the knots tighter. Despair swamped her. Baleros loomed closer, his innocent little seawee face with malevolent red eyes grotesque to behold.

The wraiths surrounded her, their faces alight with an evil joy. One held a switch of sea grasses. Another held some sort of scourge. A basket full of jelly fish floated beside one. Gaping, toothy angler fish were on a leash with another.

"My servants will enjoy your terror, little fishy." And then the first claw sliced down her arm, leaving a wispy trail of blood rising like smoke into the water. Her blood.

Time flowed in jerks and stops. Lashes across her shoulders stung, and a harsh buzzing filled her ears. Confusing sets of sensations and images flashed and disappeared, one after another. Cuts along her tail burned. Disorienting fragments of the present stuck with her briefly but then shook loose. A shocking close up view of sharp teeth was followed by darkness.

Phoebe embraced the chance to retreat. Ignoring her body's pain, she hid away in a corner of her mind, refusing to awaken. Only more torment would be waiting. But somewhere in the depths of her misery, she remembered: Tristan was coming back for her. He couldn't come here. They would take him, and he would suffer, perhaps worse than this. They weren't killing her. They needed her, but they wouldn't need him.

She came to with a scream. The world snapped into focus. The light was brighter now, and she squinted to see that Baleros was lounging nearby, looking bored. The wraiths swam around her in a steady circle.

"Oh, good, you're back. My wraiths were getting tired of waiting for the fun to begin again. I've held off the sharks for a bit, because we aren't done here. They know a bigger predator when they meet one. But maybe if you don't cooperate, they can have you when I'm done."

She could barely stifle a plea to stop.

"Or you could just send me your magic, and we'd be all finished here. So easy, so quick. So painless."

As much as Phoebe hated herself for it, in that moment, she was tempted. The power she thought would keep her safe couldn't save her from this. But she couldn't give in. She loved Tristan and the merfolk too much. They were worth any price.

And when that thought floated into her mind, a deep peace came with it, sinking into her like an anchor. She lifted her head and met the eyes of Baleros, packaged in the body of an innocent seawee.

His eyes widened in response, as if sensing a change.

Panic receded. This was reality. This was her now. She could wish she had never come here, but that would mean wishing she had never seen Tristan's home, never met his family, never kissed him. She couldn't wish for that. Instead, she wished for the strength to not give in. She managed to whisper, "I won't help you. Not even if you kill me."

"If you won't give me your magic, then you will call all the others. Maybe all of their pathetic amounts of magic combined will be enough to wake my body."

"No."

"You will call them," the beast within the little seawee demanded, "and I will consume them all."

"I can't call them," Phoebe said with a gasp, hoping Baleros couldn't sense the lie. She focused on how impossible it would be for her to betray the trust of the merfolk, so any emotion he might pick up from her would match her words. She'd never turn her friends over to this beast.

Baleros narrowed his eyes. Then, nodding, the sea beast pressed its fingers into Phoebe's chest, his nails pricking her skin and sinking *through* her, with no more effort than reaching through sea foam. Phoebe shrieked in agony.

The sea creature muttered an ancient word and then clapped his hands *inside of her.* A burst of blinding red light shot from them both, sending Phoebe into merciful blackness as the pain grew too huge to hold.

When she opened her eyes, she was on the floor of the temple, unbound, but so disoriented that escape would be impossible even if an opportunity arose. Baleros looked down with a smirk.

The pain from his evil touch had eased. Instead, inside Phoebe's heart, she suddenly sensed each and every single merfolk in their village, one by one, vibrant and clear. No longer were they distant or muddled; instead, it was as if a great multitude of singing voices rang through her mind, each one in its own distinctive key.

"Now," Baleros said, pointing at her. "You're a liar. You can call the merfolk, because even this body I've borrowed wants to serve you, though of course I won't let it. And you have called them here now, without a doubt. All of them will have felt that delicious pain and panic bursting out of you. There's a reason the sea gifted you with tattoos of the merfolk. They'll come to your distress call, your charming self. Then I'll make them watch as you hand over all that beautiful power to me. They'll know which way the current really flows around here."

She glared at him and focused just enough to send blue light rocketing from her body, striking the monster right in the chest. He yelled, and light splintered all around him.

Maybe she *could* actually defeat him. Exhilaration replaced exhaustion, until Baleros laughed.

He smacked his lips. "Do that again, little girl. That magic tasted delicious. Can you feel my true form stirring?"

Dismayed, Phoebe stared at the monster, her nails digging half-moons into her palms. She could indeed feel the darkness reaching out to her from the hideous impossible lake outside the temple. His ancient body was so close to waking, but it couldn't quite reach her yet. Though its mind roamed freely in Liam, the body of the beast remained trapped. For now.

She felt again the curious calmness that had touched her briefly, bringing her back to the moment. *Don't come, don't come*, she tried to tell the merfolk through the link that connected them. Their fear for her screamed through her senses, jangling her nerves, but she tried again: *Don't! Turn back! It's a trap.*

Their terror for her overrode every warning.

Tristan burst into the temple, glowing bright silver. "Phoebe! Phoebe!"

Mina was right behind him, Mina who had just been trapped in this dark nightmare. She had come back for her friend. Phoebe's heart swelled with love. Their presence was a shining beacon. She felt the magical connection between them, and it was strong and complete.

"Go away!" she cried out. *He'll hurt you! Escape!* She tried one final time to tell Tristan and Mina, specifically, focusing on their smiles, their laughter, all the years that united them, but their own panic blocked their communication.

The wraiths scurried up to the two young merfolk and grabbed them. Phoebe screamed in frustration.

The beast laughed.

"Leave her alone!" Tristan struggled in their arms. "Phoebe, are you okay?"

She met his eyes across the room. He had to live.

Baleros laughed and said, "I think it's time for you to do what I asked. Don't you?"

It was time to do something—that was for sure. Anger rose in Phoebe, anger at her inability to save her friends. They had suffered too much.

An idea came to her, simple and direct. It would mean giving up everything she'd ever wanted, but it could save Tristan and Mina and the others. She didn't think twice.

"Okay," she told Baleros.

Tristan moaned.

"Don't do anything the lying monster says!" Mina called.

"I'll help you, but you must promise not to hurt them." She pointed to her friends.

The beast inside the seawee licked his lips, eyes still red with power. "They will remain unharmed, if you do as you have said."

Tristan shouted, "Phoebe! Don't do anything you'll regret."

And she looked back to him. "You're worth everything. Trust me."

He looked stricken. Mina's body wracked with sobs that produced no tears.

Phoebe knelt on the sand, splaying her hands against the grittiness. She closed her eyes and felt the power flowing out from the center of this deep fissure, like sap seeping from the trees back home. She still sensed each and every merfolk, like they were on a map in her head, and this time she knew their emotions, too. They were a chaotic surge of fear, hope, and fury. They would fight for her, this peaceful group of beings who should never have to go against their nature in such a way. The rest of the merfolk were almost here, racing to rescue her, but they'd be drained dry by the beast. Even if they managed to fight back, they'd never forgive themselves once the turmoil was past and they could think clearly. She had stolen their free will, or Baleros had, just as Elder Seamus warned she would. Phoebe couldn't let them fight. Not like this.

She understood they were all connected through the very pulse of the ocean, the same magic she held. Here at the heart of the sea, a great reservoir of that magic had swelled over the last two hundred years, straining to be released. And Phoebe could reach it.

Lifting her cracked voice in song, she imagined weaving together the loose threads of magic in the water, building one strong rope. She sang of peace, of compassion, of unity. All anger, rage, and doubt disappeared as she let the music guide her. She used the song to pull the magic from the waters where it had been sleeping. No fairies had ever been able to come below the waves to draw the sea's magic forth like they had on land, bringing healing to the magical creatures there, but now Phoebe could do that for the merfolk. The music boosted her magical strength until she knew she could release the source of power feeding into them all. She was more than a key to unlock the magic—she was the door itself. All she had to do was open up and let the magic through.

A fast current of magic sprang up, coiling all around her. As she linked herself to it, a shock raced through her like a bolt of lightning. Magic poured through her fingers, leaving trails of itself wherever she touched. She felt the wounds along her tail and shoulders heal closed as the power danced along them.

For a moment, she was tempted to keep it all. Such richness, such wealth, such glory. But she made her choice. It was a kind of surrender, she supposed, but it was the kind of surrender she could live with. She pulled the power up through herself in a snap, glowing a brilliant blue. The light flickered all around her, pulsing in time to her heartbeat.

Tristan and Mina's eyes grew huge, shadows of her light playing over their faces.

Baleros whispered, "Yes, now touch my hands, Phoebe. Send me that power."

Phoebe smiled sadly at the sea beast. "This magic belongs to everyone."

With a clear, wordless shout, she lifted her arms and sent the magic back down and out through every single connection she had to all the merfolk, a sudden flood of energy that ripped through the magical world around her like a tsunami.

CHAPTER THIRTY

$\mathcal{P}$hoebe sensed the shock as magic filled one merfolk after another. Each of them lit up like a bonfire in her mind's eye. Tristan and Mina cried out, stunned, blue light shooting from their skin, mixing with their silver luminescence. What was once a flickering candle now became a roaring fire. A new star being born, each time. One after another burst into life, drawing from Phoebe more of her magical strength, unraveling her, unspinning her, draining her. And still she kept giving.

Baleros roared, an impossibly loud sound, and tried to grab her, but the power pushed him back. The wraiths spun around like leaves in the wind.

The magic of the sea fed into her as her own magic depleted. She started to sing again, a song of hope and joy and love. Her voice trembled through the water, roughened from screaming, but the notes still rang true. Magic soaked into her from the water and refilled her, and she channeled shockwaves of energy into the merfolk over and over. The connections between her and the merfolk were incandescent, overflowing.

It wasn't enough. The beast was getting some of this magic, as he was tied to Phoebe through Liam's merfolk body, and Baleros was strong to start with. She needed to make sure that the merfolk could fight back.

So Phoebe smiled grimly and forced more power into them, until the links connecting her to each merfolk burned up like fuses, destroyed by the raw power rushing through, cutting her off from them, one by one. They were too strong to be held by her charms now. Each link sizzled out of her awareness with a small pop, leaving her emptier and emptier. Less and less light filled her.

Her magical charges. Her bonds. Her specialness. She was going to lose it all, give it all up, because if she didn't, the merfolk would be enslaved, and that would kill them. And that would kill her.

It wasn't just her connections to the merfolk that were disappearing like sea foam on the beach. Her mermaid body was disappearing, reverting to human. Baleros had foretold it. A burning sensation slid along her tail fin. She had given up too much magic, but it was too late now to try to stop. It belonged to the merfolk anyway. It was only fair. Besides, what was there left for her down here?

As empty as she felt, still magic poured from her, like blood flowing from a fatal wound. Her ankles throbbed like someone had snapped them in half. She gasped, and the light faltered.

But she wasn't done yet. *More, more, more,* she sang to herself, seeking to rouse the last of her magic to share with every merfolk. Not many were still connected to her. Only three, in fact. Baleros. Mina. And Tristan.

Phoebe focused on Liam, the sweet boy trapped inside with the poisonous sea monster.

"Liam, come to me," she beckoned with every ounce of persuasion a mer-charmer could ever have. "Don't hide in the dark of your mind. You have the power now. This power is yours, not his."

Baleros's eyes flared bright red for one second. "No," he shrieked, and then a flash of blue shuttered the red from his eyes. Liam's sweet expression looked out of the young face.

He blinked, baffled. "What happened?" he whispered.

And just like that, the link between them broke. The wraiths shrieked and sped from the blue light, slithering off into the darkness.

"Phoebe, what are you doing?" Tristan called. "You've got to stop!"

Mina was crying, "Your legs! Phoebe, your legs!"

More power left her.

Suddenly, the link to Mina was gone, too.

Phoebe felt her legs now, water swirling between separated limbs. Her eyes snapped open, but all she could see was her wild hair in tangled knots against the brightness of the bonfire of light. Her skin ached with the sudden coldness of the water, the crushing pressure of the depths. A blistering fire filled her lungs before Tristan caught her hand. His magic flowed through her, soothing, giving her breath.

"You'll be okay, Phoebe. You can stop now. Stop. We're all okay."

At the sound of Tristan's voice, the bond that linked him to her snapped. She couldn't feel him inside her mind anymore. It was a dark and lonely moment. But she had the tired satisfaction of knowing that with as much power as she had given the merfolk, Baleros could never terrorize them again. Even if he found another host, they could resist him.

Through Tristan's magic, she still breathed, though she wasn't quite sure why she'd want to. She'd given up everything she loved. The merfolk had no reason to love her, a human, now that their magical link was destroyed. *By herself*, of all people. She shook her head. Sierra would laugh at the irony here, if she ever got over being furious. Phoebe was so tired, though. She needed to sleep. Sleep.

Someone was caressing her hair, holding her hand. A familiar voice said, "My silly little songbird! I told you I

307

wanted to hear you sing again one day, but I didn't mean for you to nearly kill yourself doing it!"

"Tristan?" His voice roused her from her exhausted stupor. She was just aware enough to be thankful someone had covered her with a sea frond blanket.

"Right here, Phoebe. I'm at your side. And that's where I'll stay."

She opened her eyes and stared right into Tristan's. They were black once again, as he supported her underwater with his magic. That meant her power was truly gone, and he was freed from her charms. But he said he was going to stay right here...

"You mean you still want me around? After everything?" she whispered. Hope sang its first soft notes, hesitant but beautiful.

He traced the tattoos that still lined her arms and shoulders and smiled at her. "I think you'll always be a part of the merfolk in some way, Phoebe Quinn. Nothing will change that." He blushed, his eyes drifting shyly back to hers. "And nothing could make me happier."

Suddenly, she felt like she was glowing incandescent blue again, but this time from pure joy.

"Though I have a feeling that many things *are* about to change." He let out a deep sigh of satisfaction. "I can feel the magic at work inside me, churning like a flood. I don't know what will happen, but I know something is about to."

She couldn't wait to find out what.

"So, have you gotten used to standing on dry land yet? What's it like?" Phoebe asked in hushed tones one month after her return home, astonished still at the sight of Tristan with long, muscular legs. The hollows under his eyes were gone, and his ribs no longer could be counted beneath his skin. The influx of magic had returned the merfolk to a full state of health.

His trousers clung to his wet skin, with a small bag for carrying his clam shucking tools at his waist. His chest remained bare. Habit, she supposed. He didn't even wobble like she thought he would. The magic that had given him the ability to be a land walker appeared to take care of muscle memory, too.

"Like… magic," he hesitantly replied. Beneath the wet ends of his trousers, his toes curled into the sand.

"I know what you mean." She traced the new tattoos lining his arms and chest, images of songbirds in trees. His were the first tattoos to represent land among the merfolk, because, as he put it, the sea knew half of his heart dwelled among the humans, with his own little songbird. His eyes sparkled as he gazed at her. She leaned into his shoulder.

"What did Mina say about the birds?"

He laughed. "What do you think?"

"That it was about time?"

"You know my sister well."

"Her sea flower tattoos are very beautiful."

"Not as beautiful as you," he murmured against her hair.

"Okay, break it up, you two," a voice called out across the shore. They both turned to see Sierra picking her away across the slick rocks.

"I hate to interrupt, but I wanted to tell you, Tristan, that my friends and I would be honored if you'd travel with us to the next port. I'd like you to share with everyone there what has happened among your people, the way you built that shield to keep magic out of Baleros's resting place, to prevent him from awakening. We could use your counsel as we discuss the new challenges we're facing on land." Her eyes moved to Phoebe. "Both of you, I mean."

Pride swelled in Phoebe, but she smothered a grin.

Tristan replied, "Of course. We're investing much time rebuilding below, but I'll explain to our people the importance of assisting your mission. Everyone should support such a thing, and work with you on land if they are capable. I'll need to inform my mother, in particular. She is quite happy in her chosen home in the old city now that we can live there again, but she's still coming to terms with some of us becoming land walkers and some of us not."

'Coming to terms with' was a generous way of

putting it. Odessa was beyond incensed that her own fin refused to turn to legs. Phoebe was secretly relieved.

She noticed that Tristan intended to inform Odessa, not ask permission. Yes, Odessa was finding life after Baleros to be quite different indeed. Maybe she'd grow to like it one day. If she hadn't wanted to bring about change, she shouldn't have involved Phoebe.

"We'll leave tomorrow if you can join us. Besides, it would be good for certain humans to be reminded that our treaty with the merfolk is alive and well. I think it will quickly curtail the problems you've been having with humans breaching the treaty, now that you can talk to the fishermen on their turf. Hard to ignore your existence when you can walk right up to them." She laughed, delighted, and Tristan joined in.

Sierra continued. "Can you come right back tonight and let us know? This message is urgent. Your new magic might well impact us all."

Tristan nodded. He might not ask permission from the elders, but Phoebe knew the answer would be yes if he did. The other merfolk finally understood it was his decision that had led to their freedom, from the very beginning. They looked to him as their leader now, him and Phoebe both. They would never forget that she had given up her power for their lives. Their trust in her was unshakeable now.

The two sisters sat on Phoebe's favorite rock and watched while Tristan strode out into the water and transformed into the mer-form she knew so well. He'd settled on tucking his pants into a little bag attached to his work belt, his clever way to deal with the practicalities of all the transforming he planned on doing. He gave a quick flip of his tail and dove with a showy splash that made Phoebe laugh.

The girls sat and waited. Phoebe watched the surf, exhilaration tumbling through her. The sun sank closer to the water, and she shivered. Tristan could be speaking to the merfolk right at this very moment, asking them to join in the fight to protect magic on Aluvia—all of Aluvia, land and sea. It could change everything for them. Not everyone would be happy about more change, but for Phoebe, this was the best gift of the sea she could have imagined. It was more than she deserved. She sighed, and it was a happy sound.

"Are you ever going to tell me everything that happened down there?" Sierra broke the silence with an unexpected question.

"It doesn't matter now." Did it? Could Phoebe stand to relive it?

"Like it didn't matter what Bentwood's people did to you?"

Fear slithered out of that dark cave in her mind. This time, Phoebe stared right at it. She'd already fought the scariest thing she could imagine and beat it. She wouldn't let her own memories continue to terrorize her when she had stopped the most powerful sea beast from doing it.

"Would you like to know about the time at Bentwood's, then?" Phoebe asked.

"I would."

So Phoebe told her sister everything. The sun dropped below the horizon, and still Phoebe talked. It wasn't as hard as she thought it would be. Sharing about that dark experience was like letting out a breath she'd been holding for far, far too long. The relief was sweet, like the cool of the ocean on a hot summer day.

After a long moment of silence, Sierra stroked Phoebe's hair and said, "I wish you would've told me sooner. Maybe it would have helped. I hate that you ran away in part because I didn't understand."

Phoebe took a deep breath as memories flickered by, but they didn't hurt her heart. Her fear was still there, but it no longer had teeth to bite with. "I couldn't. That's all. Just couldn't. But I guess now I can. Thank you for listening."

"Do you regret coming back?" Sierra's voice was so soft it was nearly impossible to hear.

Phoebe squeezed Sierra's hand and whispered, "Of course not. I love you. You are tied to the land, and I'm tied to the sea, but we'll always be tied to each other."

Sierra sniffed and cleared her throat. "Does the sea still call to you, then? Now that you've given everything up?"

Phoebe tilted her head. "It doesn't compel me, but my love for the sea is still there."

"Just for the sea?" Sierra teased.

Phoebe flushed as Tristan broke the surface of the water. The birds tattooed on his body seemed to fly as his arms swung by his sides. She would never get tired of seeing him walk out of the water, walking to her.

"Maybe more than just the water."

The sisters laughed. Phoebe leaned her head on her sister's shoulder. All that remained of the day was a pink glow where the ocean kissed the sky. A few gulls still wheeled around and around, giving their melancholy cries. The waves whispered their melodies. Tristan smiled at her as he drew nearer. It was a perfect moment.

Phoebe let out her breath. For the first time in four years, she could smile at the future.

Sierra had her magic and her fairies. That was okay.

Phoebe might not have magic anymore, but she had something much more important.

Love was its own magic.

The End

Nellwyn Brennan's tremendous skill with a sword was matched only by her love for it. The sword never lied. Its justice was clear and sharp. Simple, though not always easy. It cleaved through tangled knots of conflict until the only thing left was the swing, the slice, the shine of steel. The sword could most often solve any problem. But not these days, which really got under Nell's skin.

The late afternoon sun slanted across her as she hacked and swung her blade in the empty glade, glaring at her invisible opponent. In years past, she envisioned Jack when she trained, sometimes Donovan, and often Jasper, all members of the old Flight crew she worked with. But now, in this new life, she didn't know who was there, waiting to exchange blows. There seemed to be no fight left—only politics and persuasion, never Nell's strong suit.

She spun, ducked and twirled. A stranger watching would see a dance, a lethal dance, but one beautiful in its stark strength. People might not describe Nell as *pretty*, with her white blond hair pulled back in a plain braid and her intimidating blue-eyed stare, but when she moved, she was *arresting*.

Her sides heaving, Nell finally lowered her longsword as the sun dropped below the treetops, as vanquished as her imaginary foes. There were no *real* fights these days, only skirmishes, hardly worthy of a weapon. She kept training because it calmed her. Soothed her. Her beloved Corbin didn't understand, so Nell practiced alone, just her and the lilting birdsong among the towering trees.

By all the stars, she missed a good sword fight.

But life went on.

As if to remind her of that fact, her mother called out, "Time for dinner!"

With one last look at the sunset, Nell sheathed her sword and went to clean up, thankful it hadn't been her turn to cook. She might be nineteen now, but running a household wasn't one of her strengths. After a quiet dinner with her family, Nell kissed her sisters in their beds—though they were almost too old for such things—and then curled up on the cot in the living room where she stayed these days, sword within easy reach on the floor. Old habits died hard. She traced the dagger under her pillow with her fingertips, before resolutely flipping onto her back and closing her eyes. Her hands twitched to hold her dagger. It always brought comfort, like a worn baby blanket, but she took some deep breaths to calm herself instead. Despite the late afternoon training session, sleep came slowly. Eventually, though, slumber carried her away.

Sometime in the blackness of the night, the front door creaked. Nell's eyes flashed open. The noise made the barest whisper of sound, but that was all she needed. A sliver of moonlight fell on the floor, and a tall shadow, a man's, stretched across it. An invader, in her home. She hadn't even heard the person pick the lock, which suggested someone had a lot of skill—and practice. It had been a while since the last late-night visitor.

This time, though, the shadow of a knife extended from the intruder's hand. That was new.

She slid her own dagger out from under her pillow. She didn't need to test the blade to know it was sharp.

Nell might not be an enforcer anymore, but that didn't mean she could relax her guard. Jack's death hadn't destroyed the dark alchemist's crew entirely. It only meant a new ringleader had moved to the top, like fat rising in a broth. The first year had meant repeated night time intruders trying to threaten her back into the crew. She thought they'd finally gotten smart, but she figured you just couldn't cure stupid.

Too bad for them. If she had to knock sense into every one of her former colleagues, so be it, though she'd tried hard to avoid violence since her... change. Still, the hilt felt comfortable in her hand, an old friend. No sweat slicked the surface of her palm. The door inched open another crack, and Nell tensed her muscles, ready to move.

The toes of a pair of dark green boots poked through the shadows. She knew those boots. Fury burst through her. Jasper. He was the worst, always skulking around Nell when she was working for the crew, like a creepy rat sniffing for its next meal.

Nell focused that anger into a fine point, the intensity that gave her such skill with a blade for one so young, as good as any mercenary. One of Jasper's boot strings had unwrapped and coiled along the floor. Always sloppy. Her lips curled with disgust. He took one step further, crossing firmly into the home. That was enough.

Training kicked in hard. Nell whirled out of bed as silent as an owl swooping on its prey and snatched up the long blade on the floor. By the time her spin ended half a heartbeat later, she held her sword tip pressed to his throat and her other hand had knocked his weapon to the floor with a clatter before aiming her own dagger toward his chest. His speeding pulse throbbed in the hollow of his neck, right next to the steel aimed directly at it.

"Nell!" he gasped, voice strangled. Trembling, he threw his hands up in surrender.

She didn't care that she stood in her nightclothes, loose linen pants and a baggy shirt, with her hair down around her shoulders. She might look like a young, vulnerable girl, but appearances could be deceiving. She took a moment to pray that the prophetic voice wouldn't take over her body now. Whenever the mysterious voice issued another warning for Aluvia, it spoke through Nell without any apparent concern over what she was doing at the moment. It had led to some awkward situations, but this time, it could be deadly. "Come to kill me this time, Jasper? You couldn't take me then; you can't beat me now."

"I came with a message. That's all, I swear. There's a new boss in town, Nell. He either wants you on his side or out of the way, you with your devoted followers." His voice grew whiney and wheedling. "If you come with me, I'll convince him to assign you to my crew. You're too good to waste."

She snorted.

His expression darkened. "You never knew a good thing when you saw it, Nell." He lowered his arms, and Nell let him, though her own weapons remained ready.

"My life is full of good things now."

"You mean your little fairy keeper? I reckoned there had to be a reason you weren't even hand-fasted yet. He's not enough for someone like you."

"Like me?"

"Someone born with a sword in her hand."

The hands in question suddenly felt icy. Her reasons for not formally committing to Corbin were tangled and confusing and nothing she would discuss with this scum. He was eyeing the exit, coward that he was. She moved slightly to block him. "You're just jealous."

He glared. "Don't flatter yourself. Just saying it's a waste, you running around like some messenger of peace. Come back to us, one last chance. The new boss is gonna tame the dragons, stop 'em from setting the mountains afire. He's promised they'll carry us into battle for Aluvia. Can you imagine anything better? You're a fighter, not some fairy fanatic."

"Your new boss is clearly a madman, and I haven't been with Jack's crew in a long, long time." She kept her voice low in hopes of not waking her family.

"You mean *my* crew."

She paused. "I thought Maddox took over."

"Maddox recently mistook poison for a healing drought. Shame."

So, Jasper got rid of his competition the same way Jack had. Jasper had learned ruthlessness from the best.

"You said your new leader wants me gone."

"Or a part of the action. Our crew's joined up with something bigger now, Nell. You could, too."

"There's nothing bigger than saving Aluvia's future. Just leave me alone. I've got a new life now," she said.

"That new life's about to come crashing down around your shoulders." He licked his lips as they turned up in a ghost of a smile.

"Is that so?" She tilted her head and scanned Jasper more closely, alarms going off in her mind. He looked older than his thirty years—life in a crew aged a body faster than most—but his eyes had a new brightness to them. His shoulders were low and relaxed, his hands no longer trembling. His pose hinted at *something*. Something he thought would win him this fight. Dread shifted her feet.

He laughed, low, making the hair on the back of Nell's neck stand on end. "Things are about to get real exciting around these parts, girl. You don't want to come? Fine, but at least hand over some nectar. Then we can keep everything peaceful, all between friends. I'll tell the Dragon you're on our side after all. I'm in tight with him."

"The Dragon?"

"That's the name he's taken. Down in the ice-locked lands. You've never seen someone with such power."

"Are you threatening me?"

"I'm warning you. You'll regret leaving your crew when you're not seen as a savior anymore. The people won't love you forever. The Dragon will be ruler and you'll have nothing," he snickered.

She pressed the sword harder against his skin, until a single drop of blood welled up, looking black in the dim light. "Who are you kidding? The people don't want a ruler. We have no kings."

"We might not have a king—yet—but you're practically a queen, ain't you? Always so above everyone, so high and mighty is our little Nellwyn, with people chanting your name. Not good enough for the likes of us, eh? But we'll have our day. You'll see. We'll have magic like you can't imagine, and we'll use it as *we* see fit."

She scowled and delivered a swift kick to his shin without lowering her weapons. Being barefoot reduced the impact, though, and she gritted her teeth when he laughed. She snarled, "Without the fairies, without Flight, you're nothing. Haven't you gotten the message?"

"There's always poisons to sell, lovie. And there's bigger things than that yet to come, much bigger. But oh yes…" Jasper hissed, leaning harder into the sword point and blood welled up thicker, dripping down his neck. He used a falsetto voice and fluttered his stubby eyelashes at her. "The fancy prophetess gets to tell us what's we can do and not do, touch and not touch, take and not take. No taking nectar! Save the world!"

Nell's hands didn't waver, despite the flush burning across her cheeks. Luckily, it was too dark for him to see the crimson stain. She kept the sword steady, but pushed the dagger harder against his chest.

"I'm not the one saying it," she said. She still didn't

know who was using her body as a messenger, but she sure wished they'd let her in on the secret—or get out.

"That's not what I hear. I hear you have all sorts of things to say, things about your former employer, about dark alchemists, about anyone using Flight. Never saw you for a fairy fanatic, Nell, and now you're being courted by one and are best friends with another."

Jasper snapped his teeth. "Don't you miss enforcing? I bet you do. The power. The fear. The rush."

"No." Her voice was flat.

"Liar. You can take the girl out of the fight, but you can't take the fight out of the girl."

"The job was just a means to an end."

"What end, little girl?"

Her lips tightened. "Survival."

"The Dragon is coming. You want to survive, you'd better prepare to bow. It'll be too late to fight."

"It's never too late to fight."

Nell reversed her hold on the sword and knocked Jasper hard on the head with its pommel. He went down like a sack of grain. She sighed, staring at the unconscious slob of a man at her feet.

Her unwanted gift of prophecy might have brought her instant fame as well as gifts of food and supplies from fervent believers, but it still couldn't deliver her from her past. She'd do it all again, but it had been a long road to keep the peace, to walk this new path. Especially since she did really miss the fight. And now someone named The Dragon was drawing rats like Jasper?

She'd heard nothing of this man, though. Jasper could be lying. She discounted the bit about dragons immediately. Those weren't the kind of beasts that submitted to being ridden like donkeys. Either Jasper was trying to intimidate her, or the so-called Dragon was making impossible promises to sound more impressive. But even so, some kind of battle could be coming. Sounded like it.

A battle. One she'd have every right to fight, in self-defense.

She fought to suppress the thrill of longing. Oh, she didn't miss the pain or the fear. But the sheer physical beauty of battle, the competitive nature of the beast, oh yes. The singing slice of a sword was like nothing else. A thing of perfection. And hand-to-hand combat meant the best person won, fair and clear.

And the best was usually her.

There was none of that for her now. There were few honorable ways to earn coin as a sword swinger in Aluvia, almost none for a woman. And for someone touched by magic? Exactly zero. The voice that spoke through her needed to be heard—the people wanted a prophetess, not a warrior. Besides, if she let herself go down that path, she might lose herself to the darkness all over again. Jasper was probably just trying to scare her. He'd never accepted her refusal of him. As if she'd ever marry such a scavenger.

She wasn't sure she could marry anyone, much to Corbin's dismay. But they both understood the situation and were in agreement to wait for a more peaceful time to make a formal commitment. What kind of life could she offer a family now? She'd hoped for things to settle down, for the voice to move on, for a chance at... normal. It obviously wasn't starting tonight. Normal young women didn't have unconscious dark alchemists in their living room in the middle of the night.

She shook her head, tucked her dagger in the waistband of her pants, and got to work dragging Jasper out of the house by his heels. His head bumped along the worn wooden floor and clunked over the threshold of the door to the ground outside. She didn't try to be gentle. The grass of the yard made pulling him easier, but even with muscles kept strong from her workouts, she grunted with the effort of maneuvering his heavy weight. The wind blew chillier than usual, cooling her brow.

Killing him would be smarter, more expedient. Stronger message, too. But she shook her head. She could hardly redeem a life of violence by killing all who opposed her.

Even if it would feel incredibly satisfying.

Nell tied Jasper to the fence post along the edge of their land, making sure the knots of the thick rope were extra tight. Considering his rise to leadership, she added a chain around him and secured it with a padlock, the key kept on her belt loop. Then she tossed a sign around his neck that read: "This man thought he could threaten Nell Brennan. He was wrong. Payment of forty gold coins required for the release of Jasper Gallagher from his penalty."

Smirking, she backed up to admire her work. His cronies would find him in the morning. Just like the others over the years. By all of Aluvia, would they never learn?

The wind blew hard for a moment, whipping her loose hair across her face. She shivered, and her smirk faded. It had been a mild summer, but tonight felt different. Colder than it should be. The soaring sky held a deep darkness, despite the moonlight dusting the ground like sugar and the tiny pinpricks of stars glittering as if chipped from ice. Trees moaned in the wind, shaking their arms full of green leaves that looked black in the shadows.

Nell curled her bare toes against the chill of the damp grass. She took a step back and a thin branch cracked beneath her foot. A loud flapping among the trees had her reaching for the dagger in her waistband. Wings flashed briefly, silhouetted against the glow of the moon, but then were lost in the blackness above.

Just a bird. She shook her head at her own fancies.

She'd let the rat play with her mind. He was just trying to scare her. She'd never admit it had worked. A little.

Nell cast one more look at the unconscious man in her yard and went inside, rubbing her arms. Goosebumps crawled down her legs. She told herself it was just the chill of the air. But inside, a small part of her, a part she ruthlessly ignored, screamed... *Change is coming.*

ACKNOWLEDGMENTS

Writing a second book has been even more fun than the first! A special thank you goes to Carol Pavliska, Lara Barrett, Jeannine Johnson Maia, Christina Nelson, and Stacy Webb, who all shared valuable insights as I wrote.

A heart-felt thank you goes to my editor, author Krystal Wade, Amalia Chitulescu for another gorgeous cover, and Ricky Gunawan who made such a beautiful map. Thank you to everyone at CQ. The second edition was made possible by Snowy Wings Publishing and the support of several wonderful people, but especially Matthew Cox and Clare Dugmore.

Of course, none of this would be possible without my family, both immediate and extended! I love you!

And last but not least, a giant thank you goes to everyone who has read and shared my books. It's an honor to share my stories with you.

This second edition would definitely not be possible without all of you who have read and left lovely reviews over the years. Thank you so much for reading and sharing my books!

ABOUT THE AUTHOR

Amy writes fantasy and light science fiction for young readers and the young at heart. She is the author of the World of Aluvia series and SHORTCUTS (CBAY Books, 2019), for grades 4 and up. She is also a former reading teacher and school librarian.

As an Army kid, she moved eight times before she was eighteen, so she feels especially fortunate to be married to her high school sweetheart. Together they're raising two daughters in Texas.

A perfect day for Amy involves rain pattering on the windows, popcorn, and every member of her family curled up in one cozy room reading a good book.

You can find Amy online at www.amybearce.com.

FAIRY KEEPER: World of Aluvia Book 1

Sierra hates being a fairy keeper, but unfortunately, it's her destiny. In the world of Aluvia, little fairies aren't cute or friendly—more like irritable and dangerous. But when the fairy queens mysteriously vanish, the consequences threaten everything Sierra loves. She will stop at nothing to find the missing fairies, but the journey will risk even more than she thought possible.

DRAGON REDEEMER: World of Aluvia Book 3

The voice calls. A sword will answer.

To win their fight to protect their world's magic, Nell and her friends must find the fiery sword of Aluvia before their new enemy does. Nell up against the toughest foe she's ever faced---and this one has ice-breathing dragons on his side.

SHORTCUTS (CBAY BOOKS, April 2019)

When psychic powers and secrets collide, no one is safe. Parker Mills is a fun-loving girl with a secret supernatural gift of psychic empathy who tries to turn heartbreak to happiness when a new student arrives with a mysterious, tragic past. But when her psychic power goes haywire, dangerous secrets begin to unravel… starting with her own.

Snowy Wings
PUBLISHING

Wayward Stars, by Mary Fan (Book Two of the Starswept Series)

High school senior Ember Goodwin never had a sister, but after her mom's remarriage, she now has two. The eldest is no stranger to her—Ivy is a witty girl in her grade who's almost never spoken to the shy bookworm before —but she's surprised to find the popular girl quite amiable. Their burgeoning friendship is tested, however, when Dean Horne, a pale, besuited charmer, shows interest in them both and plans to reveal his appetite for blood to the one who'll stand by his side.

Seventeen-year-old Ivy Sheppard is tired of splitting

her time between her dad's and her mom's, particularly when her dad uproots their lives to move them in with his new wife and step-daughter. Used to rolling with her parents' whims, she tries to make the best of it and befriend her nerdy new step-sister. Her hectic life grows more unwieldy when she catches the eye of junior Calder Poole, whom she swears she sees swap well-toned legs for a pair of fins during a dip in a lake. Now she's fending off suitors left and right, all while trying to get to the bottom of the strange happenings in her town.

Available now!

Braid of Sand, by Alicia Gaile

In the shade of a tower hidden in the Realm of the Gods grows a sacred tree tied to all life in Phalyra. Entrusted with its protection, Raziela—the last surviving priestess of the Great Mother, Naiara— spends her days honing herself into a weapon worthy to serve the goddess.Meanwhile, mankind is turning from the old ways. Now the tree is dying and time is running out. Hoping to save it by rekindling the people's faith, a desperate Raziela commits an act of sacrilege to perform a miracle.But when the disillusioned Phalyrians receive a gift from the gods, they send their most ruthless mercenary to hunt down its source. His arrival forces Raziela to question everything she knows. As the two execute a careful dance of secrets and hard truths, they pit the fate of humanity against the wrath of the goddess. Available now!

www.snowywingspublishing.com

Lightning Source UK Ltd.
Milton Keynes UK
UKHW011846021219
354632UK00001B/39/P